TRUDI'S
TRICKS

...WESTMINSTER WOBBLES

TRUDI'S TRICKS

TRICKS

...WESTMINSTER WOBBLES

PETER SPENCER

Matador
Unit E2 Airfield Business Park,
Harrison Road, Market Harborough,
Leicestershire. LE16 7UL
Tel: 0116 2792299
Email: books@troubador.co.uk
Web: www.troubador.co.uk/matador
Twitter: @matadorbooks

ISBN 978 1 80313 486 4

British Library Cataloguing in Publication Data.
A catalogue record for this book is available from the British Library.

Printed and bound in Great Britain by 4edge Limited
Typeset in 11pt Minion Pro by Troubador Publishing Ltd, Leicester, UK

Matador is an imprint of Troubador Publishing Ltd

For my granddaughters Binky, Pinky, Molly and Boo.
And Trudi doppelgängers Sophie and Hayley.
Not to be messed with… any of them.

PROLOGUE

It's not every day a girl gets to be five, she'll have you know.

A candle at each corner of the cake? So last year, dear. It's the one in the middle that counts.

Trudi steps gingerly forward, as you do in high-heeled shoes several sizes too large, grips the flowery hat which also might belong to someone considerably bigger than herself, and leans forward.

The lavish if irregularly applied eyeliner glitters and four carefully chosen necklaces jingle as she wobbles her head vehemently, one could say theatrically, from side to side. One false eyelash falls off, but the hat and the dangly clip-on earrings stay on, amazingly, as she blows out all five candles in one go.

Her secret wish, appropriate for one who's just turned this sort of corner, is for everyone to kindly show due deference to age and maturity. Not so much a wish as a preference, bordering on instruction, though she might have to wait a little longer for it to be carried out.

Loads of love, mind. Plus a healthy dose of respect, for such a small person with such a large ability to make the impossible possible. Not that she ever set out to please all of the people all of the time. Florence Nightingale certainly ruffled feathers, so did Emily Pankhurst.

The party's in full swing… balloons, bunting, blaring music and blancmange. Oddly, no other five-year-olds, as Trudi requested an intimate gathering of just her nearest and dearest.

And what Trudi requests, Trudi tends to get. It's a way she has.

Her adoptive Chinese sister, Yu Yan, gives her the kind of cuddle you'd expect from one who has no one else to thank for an unquestionably improved change of circumstances. Some would prefer to be a semi-enslaved member of an oppressed minority than a post-doctoral research student. But they'd be a very small minority.

Suddenly Trudi switches off the music, grabs several cushions and makes herself relatively comfortable at the ancient Bösendorfer piano. Almost everyone present gawps as she teases out with three fingers: '*Happy birthday to you, happy birthday to you, happy birthday dear good heavens, where are these twiddly-widdly Trudi variations going now? Happy birthday to you.*'

Next, she clambers down and announces boldly, though tailing off a little at the end, 'Of course, I don't play accurately, anyone can play accurately, but I play with wonderful express… er… expresso… er… express trains…?'

Only Isla and Ella aren't gobsmacked. They've been giving her secret lessons in playing, and plays, and are dead impressed she's got those lines right. Well, almost. They're also fascinated by her improvisation technique. Rock? Baroque? Girl's got talent.

Like Yu Yan, they have good reason to adore the little girl. Rather, as of today, big girl. Important to get these details right. Having spent years struggling to raise enough money to finish their studies, they've teamed up with Trudi's daddy, to everyone's benefit. They know all the right words for the definitive history of Ireland; he knows how to put them in the right order. Sorted!

Then there's Fang, whose feelings are nuanced. Mostly, he almost worships Trudi but hated her for a while because of a new addition to the inner circle, Lady Casement. How could the feckless little hussy and her fellow female have so much to say to one another?

Nanny too can find Trudi frustrating, for reasons of her own. Though, as with one or two other things in the little lady's life, the dots don't join up.

She's got the measure of Monty and Bakyt, mind. A young lady of her calibre couldn't miss an ace marksman with a soft spot for opera and dangerously fast cars. Or a Kazakhstani expert in obscure nuclear weapons and lassos, who's also a horse whisperer and witch.

Her parents complete the ensemble. They gaze round the small but elegant living room in the small but elegant Georgian mansion that they laughingly think of as theirs, when anyone with any sense knows it's Trudi's. Viv, under the mistaken impression that stuff in her wardrobe, make-up bag and jewellery box was hers too, wonders if she'll ever get any of it back. But, as any mummy will testify, the answer to such a question is generally no.

The ample and colourful rugs over the worn flagstones

are useful insurance against serious injury caused by anyone falling flat on their face. Particularly anyone who's only just turned five. Though it's thanks to someone who in an earlier incarnation was only four and a half that Daddy did once knock himself out on that very unforgiving floor. His friend, who happened at the time to be prime minister of the United Kingdom, as someone has to be, suffered the same fate. For the same reason.

Trudi certainly has her moments. Fang will testify to that, in spite of the limitations to his vocabulary. He can't help being short in the words department, because he's a cat. Lady Casement has a lot more to say for herself, as is often the case with parrots.

Percy Penislow, aka Daddy, once had the same job as his friend who once had a bad headache at the same time thanks to the same playful little person. And Percy has at times helped out the poor man tasked with running the country after he butted out.

It can be devilishly tricky, keeping Downing Street strutting along. As Percy found out to his cost. But the rescue operation of a few months back had a remarkable twist to it.

He couldn't have done without Trudi.

CHAPTER ONE

Percy's sitting in his rickety garden chair at his rickety garden desk thinking back to where, and when, it all started, a few months prior to that fifth birthday party. A lovely day, flowers in full bloom, cheery chirruping in the trees and the sun shimmering on a gently undulating Atlantic swell. In his post-prime ministerial world, all was well.

Was, unfortunately, being the operative word.

One minute loving the birds and the bees, and the thought that even educated fleas do it, the next he was glancing at an email from his old head of communications at Number Ten. Biff McNasty made sure everyone knew how brilliant the Penislow government was, while it lasted. Which wasn't long. At least, now he was making his own mark as an MP, he might have happy news of how well he's doing these days.

Or might not.

Percy adapted the old John Lewis slogan... never knowingly undersold... to fit Biff. Never knowingly understated.

1

'Mental Orientals. They're out to kill you, fecking eejit.'

Fang chose this moment to viciously claw Percy's naked toes. He's a shoelace kind of cat, so sandals never did cut it, though tiny crimson spurts indicated cutting had come into it. Quite deep into the flesh. This didn't do a lot for Percy's mood, though he grudgingly accepted they were kindred spirits, thanks to Fang's feral side. Walking on the wild side always appealed, even if at times like this it was more a matter of hobbling.

Cat claws man, it occurred to the journalist in him, is not news. Man claws cat is. He reached for the pointy nail file then told himself not to be so ridiculous. According to Biff, he was about to die, and he could hardly leave a legacy of cruelty to cats, much as he'd like to sometimes.

He was cheered, at least for a second, by little Trudi's sudden appearance, armed with a rolled-up newspaper, hard on Fang's heels. Now she'd turned four and a half, and a bit, she'd got really good at language. Bad language especially. 'Leave my bludi daddi alone!' That's my daughter, Percy thought, such a gift for the well-chosen word.

Her dear little blonde pigtails, huge blue eyes, immaculate dress sense and dainty way of skipping about masked a sinister reality. Perhaps not that bad; she was ever a kindly little soul. Though her weakness for sparkly pink bling only emphasised her strength of character. Same as her habit sometimes of swopping skipping for marching, and stamping.

Anyone crossing her should cross themselves first, if they know what's good for them. Beyond an old head on young shoulders, she knows everything almost before she's had a chance to learn anything. Not spot-on at all times, but who

2

cares? If she's right in her own mind, she is right. A woman thing, she'll decide in a few years. Meantime, if she's wrong, all's always forgiven anyway.

A great asset in life being cute, Percy thought, with a smile, as he called out to her a few well-chosen words of his own. Well, not quite his own, actually.

'Trudi Penislow has lived nearly five years in the world with very little to distress or vex her.'

Not having reached the Jane Austen stage, Trudi didn't spot the reference to *Emma* but gave him a cheery wave of encouragement, as grown-ups need all the help they can get. And, from time to time, cats need to be taught their manners. She'd always adored Fang, and they'd always got up to all manner of mischief together. But he could go too far. And, at such moments, he must pay.

'I was firm, but you can't say I wasn't fair,' she shouted as he scrambled up a tree. To give emphasis, she stamped extra hard, wrinkled her nose and stuck her tongue out at him in a really scary way.

In years to come, she might look back on such moments and compare herself to a nineteenth-century sea captain, whose great respect for his men wouldn't stop him dishing out the odd lashing. The cat o' nine tails would, after all, seem appropriate in Fang's case. She turned back to Daddy and studied his face carefully. He looked worried, she knew not why, but felt like finding out.

'What's the trouble, Daddi? Spit it out, you know you want to.'

Percy smiled at his daughter's way of using her mother's turns of phrase, and tone of voice, even though half the time she didn't really understand either. But he was of two minds,

3

a Gemini thing, he'd always thought, about how much to share with the young. He'd learned too much, at too early an age. Then too little, when he really could have done with the info.

For a start, he accidentally stumbled on a couple he'd always had down as his own mum and dad, ahem, at it. In far too adventurous and explicit a way for a kid not much older than Trudi. Percy shuddered at the thought of what his dear little daughter would have made of that. In his case, it drilled in the impression that he was a friend of Dorothy's, manner of speaking, until he was much, much older.

Staring out to sea, he considered how the sight, sound and scent of it used to be so comforting. Perfect antidote to London, where the fun and frolics went so swimmingly they nearly drowned him.

The return to Cornwall, where he spent his childhood, gave him the chance to take a deep breath. And to get to know his adored wife, Viv, in all senses, which was nice. Their relationship up until then had been pleasantly platonic, fine as far as it went, but definitely more bread and dripping than cakes and ale.

Still, you can't beat a good nervous breakdown to get yourself straight, so to speak. The shrink's hypnotherapy worked wonders. Good news from Trudi's point of view, as she would otherwise have been just another unborn infant sitting up in heaven waiting for a mummy and daddy to do the honours, so to speak.

She knew all about such things from the age of three, because she had the good sense to consult an expert.

'Mummi, where do babies come from?'

'Well, you see, dear,' Mummy took a deep breath and

thought quite hard before going on, 'God looks after them until Mummy and Daddy are ready for them. Then he pops them into Mummy's tummy and the baby pops out again when Daddy's grown up enough to help look after the new tiny person.'

'And was Daddy grown up enough when I came to say hello?'

Dearly though she loved her husband, and enormously though she lusted after his body, Mummy wasn't sure Daddy would ever be quite grown up enough for anything, least of all child-rearing. But she decided she'd already told quite enough fibs for one day. Not that Trudi's insatiable curiosity was sated, yet.

'But how do babies come out of mummies, Mummi? There aren't any gaps big enough. Unless little babies are very, very little.'

At this point, Viv uttered a little prayer of thanks to the god she didn't actually believe in, because Fang chose that moment to play a little game with the dainty little coffee cup on the dainty little inlaid French empire-style coffee table. One dab and it was shattered on the flagstones, its contents miraculously not indelibly staining any of the rugs.

'Oh dear, just look what naughty Fang's done now!'

'Straight to bed with no tea, naughty pussy,' was Trudi's take.

Viv tried to hide her smiles at her daughter's choice of words. It'd be a few years before she felt Trudi would be ready to associate childbirth with that part of a lady's anatomy.

*

Percy's problem with how much a small child should be told stemmed from his father's not telling him anything, even who he was, until he was on his deathbed. And it took the old rogue finally coming clean for Percy to realise what a misfit he'd always been. His simple upbringing among simple people didn't fit with who he was to become.

Pater penned Percy a note explaining that bringing him into the world had been too much for Mater. Whereafter, bringing baby up alone was too much for him too. Only one thing for it then: shunt him off to a manservant. Plenty of them kicking around, and easy to sort a council house for the fellow, begad. One of the perks of being the lord lieutenant, what?

Not that Pater didn't have redeeming features. Didn't drown Percy at birth in the water butt for a start. And got a military decoration for conspicuous gallantry. A coded way of saying, in this case, suicidal lunacy. Somehow or other, he survived, handily for his parental prospects.

But, later, one bad thing led to another. After a fall-out with the Inland Revenue, he let the family seat fall to bits as well. Tax exiles often have that problem.

In short, he was half crazy and utterly irresponsible.

Like father, like son? Maybe better mater genes? No way of finding out, annoyingly, though not for want of trying on Percy's part. But, after drawing a blank everywhere, he can but hope his mother was a much nicer person. Though, stuck as he is with his nature, he can at least give nurture a go. Telling the truth, for example, as often as he dares.

Hence, his reply when she asked him to, to use her phrase, "spit it out".

'Well, you see, my dear, there are some not very nice men who aren't very happy about me trying to persuade my friend who's the prime minister not to buy some trains that go extra fast from some people who might not be very friendly.'

'But, Thomas the Tank Engine's lovely, what's wrong with that? Chuffing away, making everybody happy.'

Like his wife when trying to explain the miracle of childbirth to a three-year-old, Percy was finding the conversation, even with a four-year-old who was actually four-and-a-half-and-a-bit, a tad tricky.

The feud with the Chinese started during his spell as prime minister. Those two guys with the ridiculous names planning to sneak in masses of hand-me-down uranium. Cost him his marbles for a while, and sunk a stonking great nail in his administration's coffin.

They asked permission to export their country's surplus radioactive material to a nuclear reprocessing plant in Britain. Polite. But when the answer was no, they tried to smuggle it in instead. Rude.

At that point, Anglo-Sino relations hit an all-time low, in Percy's mind. And stayed that way. Bad news for them, he liked to think, in his new incarnation as a political armchair general. Especially as he was a lot younger, friskier and sexier than most.

They had been warned. Or so he reckoned.

Anyway, after Beijing blotted its copybook with the coronavirus pandemic, public opinion was on his side about the bargain basement trains they were trying to flog us for the High Speed Two project. Which was something, but not really enough. Percy looked at his daughter intently and cleared his throat, uncomfortably aware that what he was about to say might be a little complicated for her.

'Well, you see, my dear, it's been a while since jolly little Thomas started putting a smile on little kiddies' faces. Gone now are the dear little puffers, harmlessly deafening anyone in range, half crippling their drivers and firemen and polluting the planet to death.

'In their place are giant computers snaking through the countryside spitting sparks and, like as not, coded messages, all over the place. Probably as far as the Pentagon.'

'Oh, I see,' Trudi answered in a tone of voice that clearly indicated she did not see.

CHAPTER TWO

One of Trudi's many characteristics that Percy and Viv greatly respect but could often really do without is her determination to get to the bottom of things. If there's something she doesn't understand, she's all over it like a dog at a bone. Or, as she once patiently explained to Fang in language he would understand, a cat at a mousehole.

Fang licked his lips happily at her words, though the slug of brandy Percy had carelessly but obligingly spilt into a saucer might have had something to do with it. Anyway, as far as Trudi was concerned, the subject of the wrong sort of trains was anything but closed. What Daddy had started, Daddy was going to have to finish. And she wasn't going to take *I wonder what we're going to have for supper* for an answer.

'It's sad that Thomas does nasty things to train drivers,' she announced, 'but the penta-pointy-thingy should protect them. It saves witches, says so in my special book about magic.'

Percy thought about this and felt more out of his depth than ever. He looked up at the tree, hoping Fang might come to the rescue, but the cunning little monster had slunk off. Instead, he thought back to his email exchange with Biff.

My honourable friend was ever idiosyncratic, he'd begun, tentatively. *Would he care to elaborate? When you say kill me, do you mean damage my career or destroy my body? Forgive me if I seem inquisitive.*

Then, after pressing send and having paused, he'd started again. This time, throwing caution to the winds.

For God's sake, Biff, spit it out. Call me old-fashioned, if I'm to be killed, I might as well who by and why.

This dragged an admission out of Biff.

Bejasus, Percy, wish I had a fecking clue. But me fellers in Falls Road say it's connected to the Chinese train scam. Someone in the food chain wants you for breakfast.

Search me what anyone's playing at. Maybe someone not right up the apples and pears. But you better Adam and Eve it. They want you brown bread.

Reading this, Percy scratched his mass of wavy hair. It was thick and lustrous, and the occasional streaks of grey could be by Vidal Sassoon. Be a shame, he thought, to smear it with gore. But that's what comes of a bullet through the brain, which felt like it was already tickling his temple now that Biff had started talking in code. His theory that rhyming slang would beat the Bletchley circle never did do it for Percy.

Yes, it would be funny hearing a sleepy street vendor in Marseille saying he wanted to head up the apples and pears. Hearing one's about to have one's head blown off is not.

With that depressing thought in his for the moment still-intact head, Percy tried to seem perfectly at ease, as he didn't want to worry Trudi by looking scared out of his wits. The trick worked, judging by her demand for more information about the penta-pointy-thingy. The crossed arms showed how cross she might get any minute now.

Amazing how quickly, and randomly, thoughts flash through heads. Same as bullets, come to think of it. Percy's mind strayed to how a prime minister of yesteryear used to puff at his pipe during live television interviews to give himself time to figure out how the hell to answer a devilishly tricky question.

Not having ever smoked a pipe, he did the next best thing. Reached for his engraved Edwardian silver cigarette box, appeared to give due consideration to which untipped dark tobacco Gauloise would be most appropriate to the occasion, carefully slipped it into his ebony cigarette holder, and lit it.

At this, Trudi's big blue eyes also lit up. Triumphantly. Because at that very moment, Mummy stepped into view. And, like mother like daughter, she strongly disapproved of what they both termed Percy's weedy weed habit.

His counter-claim, that it was his redeeming vice, for God's sake, didn't help. A lightning executive decision was called for. Into the back pocket went the ciggie. Only partially, unfortunately, stubbed out.

*

Though only a few paces from the bijou little manor house with its Cornish stone walls, slate roof and gothic windows she and Percy have styled "Penislow Palace", Viv has travelled a very long way since they first met nearly thirty years ago.

11

Back then, he was the dashing, dazzling PhD student, she the naïve little fresher. Also, he was as bent as a nine-bob note. Since then, he's turned fifty, been prime minister, ballsed everything up, come out as definitely more Arthur than Martha and become a father.

Not that he's any less hungry for life, or she any less lustful for his body. Though these days, it's more girls on top. He doesn't mind, mind. Not a bit. But he does tread more warily, especially when he's got a funny feeling about how she's likely to react.

Worse, this was a three-way conversation, which took a moment or so to get going, given the rush Percy was in to sort his ciggie problem. A puff of smoke from the Vatican's a handy way of announcing a new pope, but billowing out of Percy's pocket a pain in the bottom.

Viv read the sign correctly. So did Percy when his rear end started smarting alarmingly. Trudi, who'd clocked that Fang had done a runner, found another use for her rolled-up newspaper.

Several good whacks and the fire was out. Hard to tell if she was trying to help Percy or punish him. Viv winked at her thoroughly grown-up child and doubted the thoroughly childish grown-up she was married to would ever catch up. At this moment, all he really wanted was another fag, which wouldn't have been a good start.

Instead, he sat down. Then stood up abruptly, for obvious reasons, then sat down once more, cautiously this time, and started again, hoping his coded language would soon have Trudi skipping off in pursuit of Fang, or to find her dollies, or anything else that might grab her mercurial attention. Fat chance, but always worth a try.

'Er, Viv, you know something? An AK-47 pointed at your temple can quite spoil your social life.'

Her delicate, petite features don't do puckering. She doesn't do putting hand on hip either. In fact, time's treated her so kindly that a girl in the offie recently asked if she'd got proof of her age. She said no but told the kid she could have a kiss instead. The kid looked puzzled, which made a happy moment even happier.

Nonetheless, Percy's known his wife long enough to clock her hovering between Viv the giver and Vivienne in vehement mode. She fell in love with the fire in his belly, and, ahem, adjacent parts of his body, but long wished he'd save more of his energy for the bedroom, where satisfaction was guaranteed, and waste less of it on his campaigns, where it often wasn't.

Trudi studied the look Mummy was giving Daddy. She'd seen it plenty of times before and knew exactly what it meant. So did Percy.

'I know, I know, I've got a bee in my bonnet about those wretched Chinese chuffers. Banging on about them in my newspaper column and the House of Lords is bound to raise a few hackles. Goes with the job. But getting murdered for it does seem a bit strong.'

His woebegone expression softened Viv/Vivienne's mood. All in the eyes, she decided. Beyond hangdog. Looks like he hasn't been given anything to eat since he was a tiny ball of fluff. Trudi, who enjoys books on a surprisingly wide range of topics, wondered if he was a Labrador in a past life.

'Look, this is none of my doing, darling,' Percy went on, unhappily, 'but Biff says there may be trouble ahead.'

Listening intently, while pretending to be frightfully busy trying to teach her Barbie dolls to stand up straight, which was never going to happen, Trudi let them all fall over. She'd never met this Biff character but got the distinct impression Mummy wished she hadn't either.

'What's wrong with Biff, Mummi? You don't like him very much, do you?'

'Well, he just gets out of bed the wrong side sometimes. And we know how horrid that can make people sometimes, don't we, dear?'

At this point, Trudi had another distinct impression. That Mummy was having a dig at someone. Nanny, perhaps. Or Daddy. She sincerely hoped she was not included in the list of people who weren't at their best if they'd got out of bed the wrong side.

Even at the relatively tender age of four-and-a-half-and-a-bit, Trudi was savvy enough to recognise that getting out of bed could be a problem. Not so much a matter of which side as what time, though she always cheered up after a while. To the great relief, she sometimes suspected, of every living creature in earshot, including Fang.

Given that during the period when Percy and Biff worked together in Downing Street, Trudi wasn't even a twinkle in Mummy's eyes, let alone a stirring in her loins, Viv was hard put to explain to the child what she found objectionable about Biff. His personality would do for a start, she thought. He was born and would probably die the type of Irishman who would never, ever, forgive the English for the way they'd always treated his countrymen.

Viv would be the first to agree it'd mostly been pretty appalling, and efforts in recent years to make amends had been lamentably slow in coming. She'd also freely concede that Oliver Cromwell was guilty of appalling massacres in Ireland. But she always thought Biff's habit of throwing things at the statue of the man outside the Palace of Westminster when the police weren't looking was taking things a bit far.

Not that he could help it. Sometimes he curled his lip and snarled at the mirror, which even he found a bit frightening. And he felt he made Judas look like the good guy when he took the job in Downing Street. Only agreed to it because he was fond of Percy. Not that he liked to admit it, or to stop being dour. Ever. Not fair the Scots should have all the fun.

How to explain all that to a four-and-a-half-year-old? The and-a-bit bit would hardly tip the balance. Though it was probably the and-a-bit bit that was making it impossible to just let the matter rest. Faced with the kind of look really grumpy judges use to make defendants squirm in the dock, Viv tried again.

'Well, you see, dear, he gets cross about bad things that bad men did a long time ago. Even though good men, like your daddy, have done their best to put them right.'

Knowing how much Viv had resented his spending so much more of his time in Downing Street with his chief spin doctor than with her, Percy was pleased to learn he was still a good man. Especially as it was only after he left that he realised how much better off he'd have been listening to her sensible advice than Biff's crazy notions. It's all in his memoirs, which, the reader will not be surprised to learn, Trudi hadn't yet got round to reading. Though she thought the look Daddy was giving Mummy at that moment was ever so sweet.

Percy could but hope Viv wouldn't notice the burn mark behind the back pocket of the rather nice white linen trousers she'd bought him for his birthday.

CHAPTER THREE

Percy took the sensible precaution of not getting up.

Instead, he beckoned Viv over to read Biff's emails, and his replies. Sitting on his lap, she frowned but shared his pain and, hoping to perk him up a little, edged forward slightly and discreetly slipped her hand somewhere he normally liked.

His response, or lack of it, was not hard to fathom. Even though, in spite of himself, he was admiring for the millionth time her svelte form and elegant profile. A little firm in the jaw, short in the nose and high in the forehead. A total turn-on, he'd always found. Likewise her dress code, ever figure-flattering – not that it needed any help – and neat bobbed hairstyle almost always set off by a jaunty little beret, or, in more formal settings, a cloche hat. A nattily nineteen twenties look, which made her attitude to ciggies all the sadder, Percy always thought. She'd have looked so cool with an Audrey Hepburn-style holder.

'Hmm.' Viv is a quick thinker, same as him. Though, as long experience has taught them both, a lot better at thinking things through.

'I'll put out feelers, my dear. Maybe there's a whisper in high places. And if not, maybe there should be.'

This left Percy even less minded to rise to the occasion than before. He couldn't quite figure out what Viv had in mind, but had a horrible feeling she might be right. As was her way.

'Behind every great man there stands,' he paused, 'an astonished woman.'

'Who's a clever lover then?' Viv's smile is mysterious. Gets to him as much now as the night they first met, all those years ago. A bit late, his face turned a telltale shade of pink.

Trudi recognised that special glance and wondered, for the trillionth time, why grown-ups were so weird. Scratchy one minute and sloppy the next. She raised her eyes skywards and set off in search of Fang, her fave bestie beasty, happy with the thought her behaviour towards him was utterly consistent at all times.

'Come to Mummi, dear ickle moggy woggy,' she cooed lovingly, and loudly, in the hope the silly grown-ups were paying attention to the fine example she was setting.

Not that Fang saw it that way. He asked himself, for the zillion zillionth time, why little girls were so unpredictable. Not that he'd had much experience of them, apart from Trudi, though one's probably quite enough, he decided, as he'd only got nine lives to play with.

But while he was off risking them with this dangerous commodity, Percy and Viv could get on with the business in hand without interruption, for the moment. The friend in high places she had in mind was Fanny Tiddledick, wife to Ponsomby Tiddledick, Percy's one-time sparring partner across the despatch boxes in the Commons, who took over as prime minister in a blaze of Tory glory when the Labour administration went kaput.

They'd subsequently devised an updated version of the two sword-lengths between the front benches, designed to prevent opposing MPs from skewering one another. Percy and Ponsomby would, from time to time, fire up the barbie and share kebabs.

Even in the Commons, the sound and fury of their up-and-downers generally signified nothing, as some bloke with a high forehead and an earring once put it. Same as the little tiffs Trudi sometimes enjoyed with Fang. Not that the poor cat would always necessarily agree.

*

From the outset, Percy and Poncey couldn't help liking one another, even though as rival leaders they weren't supposed to. Something to do with both being pretty good-natured, more than a little camp, and not even that far apart politically. Both parties being, after all, relatively broad churches.

At this stage, however, they were at odds about the Chinese trains. That much became clear a few months earlier when a phone call between them led to an uncomfortable admission from Poncey.

'Ever so sorry, old boy, but I've discovered a few inconvenient truths since your lot left. Mostly about money. Costs of the high-speed project have already spiralled crazily out of control, you won't be surprised to learn.

'Besides, that pandemic screwed us. So did Brexit. Yeah, yeah, that was all our bloody fault, but buying British is a luxury we can't afford these days.'

They agreed to disagree. Still friends, even though Percy was spending much of his time publicly tearing chunks out of the Tory government's approach to the problem. But Biff's warning that the Chinese were getting serious about it did drive the stakes up a bit. Which was why Viv opted for direct action.

A long-running correspondence started by chance had always made Fanny Tiddledick laugh. And came in jolly handy at one point in the past, when Percy got wind of a party funding scam that could have done as much damage to the Tory government as it did to his own. His difficulty being, he didn't know how to handle the situation, while Ponsomby's was that he hadn't noticed there was anything wrong.

It took the intel back-channel between Viv and Fanny to solve the problem of men spotting everything except the obvious. And once again, Viv's casual tone masked a spot of bother.

'Darling! How's jolly hubby? Still wick-dipping for the green and pleasant? Might want to watch his naughties with yellow peril and the chuffers!'

'Chuffed to hear it, darling!' Fanny sometimes means more than she says, Viv knew. And, sure enough, there was a postscript.

'Might tickle his fancy, darling! Or give him screaming habdabs! Will listen out! And scream if he creams!'

Viv smiled. Fanny would keep her word. The memsahib mechanism worked wonders. Though, with a bit of luck, it wouldn't be needed this time.

The friendship between the two women is as unlikely as their husbands'. Passionate and powerful though Viv is, she's also grounded, while Fanny's head is up in the clouds. Which could be why she spends so much of her time on horseback. Brings her that little bit closer.

There could be another reason. One day, just before Trudi met her, Viv got out a photo of Fanny side by side with her favourite thoroughbred, and the little girl gazed, amazed. The woman's long fringe and high-slung pointy ears fascinated her, plus there was something about the nose that seemed to complete the ensemble. As is her way, Trudi spoke her mind.

'But which one is your friend, Mummi, the one on the left or on the right?'

Viv fell back on the default position of grown-up solidarity and suggested little Trudi was being a little disrespectful. Though Percy, who's made it his mission in life never to grow up, had a different take.

'Perfectly straightforward, dear. Count the legs. The human's the one with only two.'

At this, Viv shot her husband a look that was meant to be a telling-off but didn't really work. Percy pretended to be rather ashamed of himself, but that didn't really work either. Trudi turned her big blue eyes from one to the other, then skywards, her way of reminding them for the zillion zillion zillionth time that grown-ups were just silly.

Fanny Tiddledick thought her husband's becoming PM was, more than silly, jolly annoying. Shacking up in that beastly little flat above the shop was hardly her style, but she managed to make herself reasonably comfortable at Chequers. Still a bit pokey, but room for the horses. And when hubby came home, he could frighten them with the racket he made, with a little help from her pink-tasselled tennis racquets. Or whips. They liked a bit of variety.

Ponsomby Tiddledick's complexion has been pink from birth. But when Fanny dons the dominatrix gear, it turns purple, like her prose, which matches the costume. No question, she's a striking-looking woman. Though when she gazes at portraits of her top steeds, Ponsomby sometimes comes down on Trudi's side regarding her looks. Facial similarities and all that; not that he'd ever dare say so.

To this day, when the Tiddledicks head for their holiday home in Cornwall, they swing by Penislow Palace for a catch-up, followed by a spot of sport. In their separate bedrooms, that is. There's swinging and swinging.

A high spot of the year for everyone, including Nanny. As the couples couple and the chandeliers tinkle, her lady garden tingles. Next day, she's so bleary-eyed she can hardly see where she's going. Not far, generally, as she has difficulty walking too.

The poor love's never had much luck with the boys. A pity, as she's a sweet young thing. Perhaps too sweet. She's even out of her depth with Trudi, for some reason. Her problem, Nanny's, that is, not Trudi's, is that she's a frightfully good girl. And because she was brought up to believe it's a sin to fib, she was startlingly honest when she gave Tinder a go.

Stating plainly that she couldn't get enough tended to give the blokes the wrong idea. And all those rude pics they sent left too much room for the imagination. Would be nice to know what other bits looked like too. Their faces, for example.

She gave up in the end, and deciding to love oneself is the beginning of a lifelong romance. With a bit of help from her friends. Lovely little plastic toys. Some quite big, actually, but all of them perfect for the purpose of self-help.

These sessions can last for hours and hours. And even someone as nice as Nanny isn't at their best on hardly any sleep. Not that she's under any illusions about her own problem, which she solves, most of the time, with a regime of rigorous rationing. Taking all the batteries out and popping them into a box in the attic, out of temptation's way.

To Trudi, Nanny's always been a sort of hybrid. Not really a grown-up, but not a child either. Worthy of closer examination. And, as time went on, she clocked the connection between Nanny's trips to the top of the house and her strange mood swings. Further investigation revealed the contents of the box, which baffled Trudi totally. The batteries in her little pink girl's hairdryer didn't do any harm. She wondered if poor Nanny was allergic or something.

Given what she had to go through during off-days, like always having to hunt her own food when the silly creature fell asleep, she eventually took matters into her own hands. Probably an act of mercy, Trudi decided, as she tipped the entire contents of the secret box into the loo and pulled the chain.*

Strangely, Nanny didn't seem all that grateful.

Daddy looked rather cross too, and stayed that way till the fat bloke with the hairy botty had finished doing odd things with his odd things to pipes in the bathroom. And halfway round the house.

So unfair, Trudi thought; she was only trying to cheer everyone up. Same as that last time the Tiddledicks came round to dinner. All she did was crawl under the table when the men were sozzled and tie their nice long shoelaces

---

* Author's note. Trying this at home is not recommended.

together, to give Fang some fun. All good, until they staggered to their feet and took such a tumble, they both knocked themselves out. And broke a number of priceless antiques on the way down.

Inexplicably, that didn't play too well either. Trudi felt very hard done by.

CHAPTER FOUR

Percy regularly went to London just so he could tell the House of Lords how foolishly the Tiddledick Tories were behaving. Always made him smile, that, given it was Poncey who'd given him the life peerage in the first place, as a thank-you for solving the party funding problem he didn't know he had.

Another thing that made Percy smile was Trudi's suggestion she come along too, except *suggestion* may not be the right word. While it wasn't presented as a command, the inference was that no one would get any peace until it happened. So it did, quite often, though there was the small matter, when they got there, of keeping her amused. One of the many ideas Percy came up with was showing her where he once lived.

As a working peer, he had clearance to get into Downing Street, but Trudi didn't. The coppers at the security checkpoint could in theory have got awkward about that, even though she didn't exactly look like a terrorist. That said, the enormous pink glittery tiara she was sporting for the occasion marked her out as deadlier than the male, and the early signs of a quivering lower lip was full fair warning of potential trouble ahead.

Tough call then, but the sergeant knew when he was beat. And as she marched purposefully down the road as though she owned the place, Trudi had one or two relevant enquiries.

'Why have they got great big gates, Daddi? Do they ever open them, Daddi? Why haven't we got them at home too, Daddi? Who lives here now, Daddi? Did you like living here, Daddi? Where was I when you lived here, Daddi? Did you have lots of friends when you lived here, Daddi? Why don't you live here anymore, Daddi?'

Percy scratched his head, as one does when one doesn't know where to start.

However, the last two questions seemed the most straightforward, and linked, though he was more focused on enemies than friends, particularly two vile Chinese men, Fyok Yu and Hon Ki. Approaching the famous black door of Number Ten, he felt like it was only yesterday they had fired the opening salvo in the nuclear imports scam that finally did for him.

His brow furrowed at the thought that these nasty people might be up to their nasty tricks again. Maybe minded to go one step further. A pretty big step, in fact, as any murder victim would tell you. If they got the chance, which they wouldn't, obviously.

Though Trudi kept her mother waiting for forty-eight hours before putting in an appearance in the maternity ward, the boot being on the other foot always strikes her as rude. It's only polite, surely, to answer questions quickly. But she is a rounded human being. Occasionally, Trudi Truculent, but more often, Trudi Truffles. Which is why she gave Daddy a break.

'Penny for your thoughts, old man. Better out than in.'

Hearing his daughter doing the Viv talk calmed Percy. A little.

'Well, you see,' he began, falteringly, 'once upon a time, there were two not very nice men who asked me to do something, and when I said no, they did it anyway and we got in a pickle.'

'Is that why you don't live here anymore, Daddi, because you got in a pickle? Do people always have to move when they get in a pickle? Would you send me away if I accidentally set fire to Fang's whiskers?'

'Of course not, darling. But, er, I would rather you didn't. Daresay if you did, Fang wouldn't exactly have you down as the cat's whiskers either, actually. Er...'

'But that's silly, Daddi, if I set fire to them, he wouldn't have any whiskers.' Trudi's logic was flawless, but Percy wasn't sure she was ready for the concept of the metaphor. So he had a crack at the easy way out.

'You're quite right, darling. Daddy is just silly.'

His mind strayed to all those Prime Minister's Question Times when, right up to the closing weeks when things got really sticky, he'd always had an answer to everything. Yet here he was, stumped by a child.

'Funny how Hitler wasted all those millions of *Reichsmarks* on the Wehrmacht and Luftwaffe,' he said, absent-mindedly, 'when all he had to do was send in a load of kids. They'd have ripped the empire to shreds in minutes.'

Before she'd even crossed the three threshold Trudi

had perfected the art of raising one eyebrow while staring ferociously and placing her hands uncompromisingly on her hips. Percy looked back at her nervously, with absolutely no idea what to say next.

Fortunately, help was at hand in the form of a fox, ambling up the road. Not an everyday occurrence, it always creates a diversion. Right now, a particularly welcome one. The fundamentals of justice, the workings of democracy and the crisis which finished off his government, and him as well nearly, ceased to matter. This was much more interesting.

Percy was always a lot more charmed by the sight than Fang when he was the Downing Street Cat. But he still couldn't get the two not very nice men out of his head.

Their names weren't really Fyok Yu and Hon Ki, but when they rounded off their studies at Harvard, they came in for loads of racist abuse. And got so bored with saying 'fuck you, honky' to annoying rednecks posing as clever young people that they devised the nicknames as a kind of displacement therapy.

It turned into a good laugh, at the expense of and behind the backs of these idiots. Often in front of their faces as well. Made them feel ahead of the game, like a kid that gets a smack and is then told it can go out and be naughty, on the grounds it's in credit.

Which is how come they stuck.

They had fun sometimes doing caricature Chinese voices, and learned how to weaponise English. Posh talk is as powerful as a kick in the whatsits if deployed in the right way with the right people, and Charlie Chancery was a particularly easy target. He'd been their useful idiot in the failed surplus uranium scam, and was going to be again in their high-speed train campaign. Meantime, as if to prove how idiotic he was, he married the polar opposite of Trudi.

Tiny Spleeny wanted to kill Father Christmas because he was giving presents to other children as well as her, while toddler Trudi felt so sorry for him having to climb down all those chimneys that she lit a bonfire in the hearth, so he'd have a nice warm bottom.

Mummy and Daddy could see the plan's drawbacks but didn't have the heart to tell her. That often happened in her early years, though it got progressively harder to hide their smiles. Trudi did love to laugh but tended not to appreciate jokes at her expense. Especially when she couldn't see what was so funny. Though when she did giggle, it was hard not to join in.

Spleeny's sense of humour was infectious too, but more like the Black Death or Spanish Flu, or Covid-19. She'd only agreed to marry Charlie because she found his particularly unusual feature, five fingers on each hand, handy. None of her smelly ex-boyfriends had spotted the connection between any of their four fingers and any form of foreplay.

To celebrate how relatively well they got along in the early days of their marriage, Charlie copied Spleeny's fluffy haircut. Reminded him of his pre-marital gay days, when he was camper than a Volkswagen, though not as nice to look at.

However, when he got the email from Fyok Yu and Hon Ki suggesting they team up again, to get the prime minister to buy their trains whether he wanted to or not, Charlie remembered it hadn't ended well last time and didn't want to go there. But Spleeny had other ideas.

'Fink abaht it, doll, we can, like, take aht dat plonker

Penislow while we're at it. Bottle dis and I'll, like, mash yer face and, like, flush it dahn da bog.'

Only when he's sure she can't hear does Charlie call her the trouble and strife.

*

Percy, meanwhile, had another good reason for wishing he hadn't set himself up as de facto leader of the hashtag No Chinese Trains faction.

Not only were his old enemies ganging up to silence him and force Ponsomby Tiddledick to buy the wretched things, the president of the United States was prepared to go to any lengths to make sure he didn't. What with the US junking America First in favour of America First, Last and Everywhere in Between, China was getting black looks from the White House.

President Michelangelo Ulises Gwump the Third, Mugwump for short, lives up to the name. Democratic dialogue? Hooey. His threat to nuke London if we went ahead with the purchase was only withdrawn when he thought of potential negative effects on his business interests in Northern Ireland.

All of which put Percy in everyone's sights. Ignorance is bliss? Only if getting shot, hacked to pieces or vaporised counts as having a nice time.

Still, at least he got one thing right that afternoon. Convincing Trudi that scampering after the Downing Street fox, giving him a sweetie and coaxing him to come back to Cornwall with her may not be such a good idea. Not that she was easily persuaded.

'But why not, Daddi? He looks like a very nice fox. He could sleep in my bed, with me and Fang.' A simple 'no' wasn't going to do it, then. Daddy had to do better than that.

'Because there's every likelihood he'll take one look at Fang and eat him, darling.'

Trudi considered this from every angle. She loved her cat lots and lots and lots, but the fox was ever so pretty. His tail was much bushier, for a start. In the end, though, loyalty lucked out, as did Fang. The fox did not become the new Penislow Palace Pet, and Percy did heave a sigh of relief.

CHAPTER FIVE

While it's true that Trudi did live for well over four and a half years in the world with very little to distress or vex her, she has had a few surprises in her time, she'll have you know.

One such came the day she found Daddy throwing things at the television. Quite big things, considering the relative fragility of the target, though neither the shoes nor the bunch of grapes had the destructive power to bring it down. In the end, he settled for glaring at the screen and snarling: 'Bollocks to you.' This was duly noted.

Percy was watching a documentary programme, drawing on tweets, speeches and interviews over the previous few years, about the president of the United States. It seemed when commie bastards said no to his second term as president, it really got to him, and it was not until God-fearing citizens said yes four years later that shithole America became great again.

Not all of it, mind. Mugwump was miffed when they dissed his plan to euthanise all African-Americans with patchouli oil and toffee pudding. But at least he got those yesterday's men carved into Mount Rushmore blown up and replaced with five five-mile-high sculptures of himself.

Interestingly, his complexion turns green when he's on about the Old Country, and even glows in the dark. Researchers trying to find evidence of primitive life on Venus have suggested there might be a connection.

Trudi managed to calm Daddy down by clambering onto his lap and pointing out that Mummy wouldn't be best pleased if he smashed the telly to smithereens, and eventually got just as interested in the programme. Particularly the bit about aliens. From a surprisingly early age she'd been fascinated by the subject, and was pretty sure by this point she was one of the world's foremost experts in the field.

'You mustn't be cruel to poor Muggle-Wumpelstiltskin, Daddi,' she protested. 'He can't help being not like us. You wouldn't tell Fang off for not being able to read my *Winnie the Pooh* books, would you?'

Percy pretended to take her point but remained convinced the man was a million-carat carrot-head that the universe would be better off without.

*

Fyok Yu and Hon Ki felt much the same about Charlie Chancery and his *Yìcháng fánrén de qīzi*†, but useful idiots are all the rage where they come from. The Chinese call a man like him a very confused worm, which can at least be dangled as bait.

---

† Translated from Chinese (simplified): Unusually annoying wife

For reasons that will become clear, they had temporarily based themselves in Belfast, which is where they wanted Charlie and Spleeny to join them at their earliest convenience. And, the very next day in the Belfast Europa's elegant piano lounge, they did. Charlie knew he could say yes to their invitation or be torn into small pieces, swallowed up and spat out by his *Yìcháng fánrén de qīzi*, but that was as far as his understanding went.

'Wot I don't get, me old china, pardon me lingo, is wot we're doin' 'ere in dis bleedin' 'ovel. Blobby end o' nowhere, innit?'

Fyok Yu and Hon Ki started as they meant to go on, by putting Chancery straight about his duties, and his place, in the pecking order.

'You see, my dear chap,' Hon Ki intoned suavely, 'there is method in our madness.

'Her Majesty's secretary of state for Northern Ireland happens to have attended the same ancient hall of learning as the cabinet secretary. Thus may we by indirections find directions out.'

Long pause. Charlie scratching his head. Playing havoc with his fluffy hairdo. Finally, a follow-up question.

'Wot?'

It worked then. Chancery and Spleeny were intimated. Both by how these la-di-das were talking, and the quote they didn't recognise.

'You sayin' some government geezer woz at school wiv 'ooevvah sorts fings for da prime minister? So we nobble da monkey to take aht de organ grinder?' A surprisingly astute deduction on Chancery's part, though Fyok Yu wasn't prepared to admit it in so many words.

'Hole in one, maestro.'

He did a perfect imitation of a patient infants' school teacher faced with a kid that can't even plead severe learning difficulties but is just plain stupid. A look Trudi would have recognised, always directed at others, mind, never her. She could hardly be elitist, as she didn't know the word, but did at times feel Sir's pain.

Fyok Yu settled for waiting for the moron to blunder on.

'But woss wiv dat bleedin' great jam jar I saw on da way, outside Mega-Mugwump Titanic Towers? Don't tell me da Yanks are knockin' arahnd an' all.'

'Overpaid, oversexed and over here, old boy.' Hon Ki carefully considered his immaculately manicured fingernails. 'For reasons only they can fathom, they've chosen to surface in the port of Belfast. At least it means we can torpedo them.'

While this was true, what he didn't realise was that he and Fyok Yu were also under surveillance, by radical elements in the local community.

Because the Europa was the IRA's target of choice during the Troubles, the lads often drop by for old times' sake, though these days they go for foreigners, potential contacts now that so many of their comrades have diversified into drugs, people and weapon smuggling.

Of course, they weren't fussed about imported trains, but any talk of killing Brits made them feel sentimental. Which was why their ears pricked up at something Spleeny said.

'Dat ponce Penislow, I wanna, like, gaage aht 'is eyeballs and, like, feed 'em to da pigs. Not dat I, like, got any time for da filf, mind.'

'As you wish, my dear,' Hon Ki murmured mildly. 'We wouldn't be sorry to put flowers on his grave either. Come to think of it, we wouldn't in the least mind helping him into it.'

Coded though the words were, and bright though the lads weren't, it was this fragment of conversation that led to Biff's warning to Percy about Mental Orientals being out to get him.

*

For Trudi, life has always been a now experience. Any decision at any moment can be reversed a moment later without a qualm, and any command can be countermanded every bit as quickly. Also, conclusions can be reached on the flimsiest of evidence, if any at all. Perfectly reasonable in a four-year-old, less so in the president of the United States.

No one with any knowledge of geography or geopolitics will get why Mugwump sent his boys to Belfast. Nor did he, for more than a nanosecond, but it led to a scenario somewhere between West Berlin during the Cold War and a low-budget spy spoof. Mental Orientals who had reason to be there hanging around round Yankee spooks who didn't.

No wonder Chancery was muddled, same as Biff's boys.

Silly though they were, though, they had heard of Percy, and reckoned Hon Ki's threat to murder him could be worth a gallon of Guinness in the right quarters. After their breathless call, Biff waited for them curiously in his cluttered office, which looks so different from Trudi's nice little bedroom.

She has Barbies carefully positioned on quite high chairs, while Ken's seating and head are lowered, thus indicating who's winning and who isn't. Biff's place, by contrast, has only got room for losers, as it's stuffed with memorabilia from ancient failed liberation struggles.

But as the lads shuffled in, stumbling over their hobnailed boots and nervously scrunching up the baseball caps that seconds ago they were wearing back to front to show how cool they were, he was struck by their wide-eyed excitement.

'Bejasus, the fecking cow squealed like our saviour when the nails went in.

'Mother o' Mary, I wouldn't be in Penislow's clogs for all the tatties in Tipperary. That colleen, she doesn't, like, like him, like,' young Paddy grinned, proud of how well he'd got her way of talking.

'Yes, but what are they planning? Exactly? How do they mean to murder him? When? And why? Go back and listen harder.

'Oh, and while you're there, you can have a wee half on me.'

The boys shambled out, reflecting sadly on the seven and a half pints they wouldn't be getting. They had the sort of look on their faces that Fang has when Trudi seems to be offering him a dollop of fish paste then exercises her woman's prerogative. The difference being, she nearly always changes her mind again, quite quickly.

As the door closed behind them, Biff turned to his customary confidant, his parrot, Sir Roger Casement, named after one of his country's most famous martyrs. The man tried to arm Irish revolutionaries in 1916 with imported German weapons, but was hanged after the fascist pig Brits unexpectedly caught him red-handed.

Equally unexpected was the parrot proving he was a she, not a he, a few years down the line by laying an egg.

'Well, Sir Rog... er... Lady Casement,' Biff enquired, 'we may or may not have a new situation here. What should we do or not do about it?'

The bird, always grateful for any attention, fluffed up her crest, bobbed from side to side and said what always goes down well.

'Brits out, Brits out, Brits out.'

Biff's all for that, but did not find it hugely helpful.

CHAPTER SIX

It's a woman's privilege to change her mind. Trudi had heard Mummy say that enough times before she'd even turned four to be convinced it must be true, and enjoyed exercising it extremely often.

Came in handy during one of those London trips when she announced two days in that she was really, really, really missing the sea, and Mummy and Daddy were a little bit cruel taking her away like this. She was always the soul of tact, which was why she didn't think it right to remind them she'd insisted on coming with them in the first place.

Percy couldn't just take her back, as he had appointments to keep, but there was a gap in his schedule, long enough, as good fortune would have it, for a day by the seaside. That's if you call the mouth of the Thames Estuary the seaside.

Both he and Viv were curious to know what Trudi would make of it. Also, there was her cultural education to consider. After all, Southend-on-Sea did boast the historic Kursaal Amusement Park, and the full-sized replica of the ship Francis Drake sailed round the world in.

Bit of a disappointment then, to discover all that was left of the Kursaal was a Tesco store, and the ship had long since gone, God knows where. Still, there was always the beach. Except that the tide was out. Trudi tried to cover her disappointment with an interesting question.

'Have the people drunk it all up, Mummi? Is that why there's all this horrid sticky mud instead of nice wet water like at home? In England?'

'But we are in England, dear, why do you think we aren't?' Though she had noticed the little girl nodding off once or twice in the car, Mummy was confused. Trudi set her straight.

'But everyone's talking in a funny way. You can hear them. They can't possibly be English.'

Percy was intrigued at his daughter's take on the Essex accent, so different from what she was used to in Cornwall. And couldn't resist deviating from his always-tell-the-kid-the-truth policy.

'People can't help what happens to them because of where they are. In a town called Birmingham they talk in a funny way too, because all the smoke from the factory chimneys clogs up their noses and throats.'

Thinking back to her parents' snobbery, shelling out for elocution lessons to cover her regional accent, Viv disapproved of what Percy had just said. And not just because it was nonsense. But Trudi found it very interesting.

'I feel very sorry for the poor people here,' she said, not sounding at all sympathetic.

'Their mummies and daddies must have made them drink lots and lots of smelly, muddy water. Clogging up their mouths and making them miss out bits of words all the time.'

Percy sniggered. Viv snorted.

On the way back, they saw signs pointing to Canvey Island but gave the place a miss, as it looked more Isle of Dogs than Treasure Island. For that same reason, Charlie Chancery hoped it might calm Spleeny when he bought a house there.

What he wanted and what he got were as far apart as the sploshy Southend mud is from Cornwall's golden sands. Trudi had strong views about which was nicer, but didn't forget the one interesting thing she did learn during her day out, which she'd find instructive when she finally got to meet Charlie.

*

It's for the best, however, that Trudi never did get to meet the Northern Ireland secretary, or the cabinet secretary. Especially given the contrast between the respectability of the public positions they held and how they behaved when no one was looking.

The sweet, innocent little girl did come dangerously close to them on a fair few occasions, however, as Primrose Hill is one of Percy's favourite spots in London, and from time to time he'd take her up there.

Because he usually puts her on his shoulders to make the climb, she's fond of it too. The best bit is grabbing hanks of his hair and using them as reins, which she enjoys more than he does. Mistaking his grunts of pain for gasps for breath, she once told him off for smoking too much. In the mummy voice she's got off to a tee.

'I despair of you sometimes, darling. It'll so shorten your

life, and you know I want yours to be the last face I see when my time comes.'

When Viv said that to him, he was rather touched, in spite of himself. But, coming from Trudi, it seemed problematic, as he was fifty-something and she was only four at the time. The and-a-half-and-a-bit bit would not bridge the gap. But when he got to the top and hoicked her up to look across London through the telescope, his bad habits were instantly forgotten.

'It's a very big town, isn't it, Daddi?' Trudi was impressed. Genuinely. For once. 'Do all the people who live here like living here?'

'They liked having me as their prime minister,' Percy said, ever so slightly sadly. 'For a while at least.'

'Never mind, dear, never mind. All good things come to an end.' Another one of Mummy's sayings, that, the one she uses when it really is time to stop trying to teach Fang to play the piano and get tucked up in bed.

In the more leisurely and, for Percy, less painful walk down the hill, now that Trudi was happily skipping along beside him, he decided humanity wasn't so bad after all. If others were a tenth as nice as his lovely little daughter, they'd do just fine.

If he did but know it, barely a hundred yards away were two specimens a million times less nice than Trudi. The Northern Ireland Secretary Dame Fantasia Fealstite OBE, and Cabinet Secretary Egeria Erewego, at that moment talking high politics, after a bout of high jinks at the flat they shared.

It wasn't far from the main drag in Camden, and looked from the outside quite like Peter Pan's house in Trudi's illustrated copy of JM Barrie's book. The inside, however, was very different. Trudi would have found some of the fixtures and fittings excruciating, especially the dominatrix dungeon, complete with fully equipped torture chair.

The one and only thing she would have liked, had she ever set foot in the place, was the mini menagerie, consisting of two dear little otters called Bubbly and Squeaky. The sweet way they had of juggling with their toys softened Fantasia's heart, and sometimes even Egeria's. Not very much, though, as hers was a good deal harder.

Contrastingly, the rest of their bodies were extremely squidgy. The only detectable difference between them being roughly a foot in height. One day, when Trudi spotted in the *Telegraph* a picture taken from behind of Erewego, she made what was, to her, the obvious connection.

'It's Mr Potato Head!'

Percy carefully considered the flowing robes, ankle-length skirt and hair knotted up on the top of her head, and decided his daughter had got a point there.

Trudi would at least have loved her car, a delicately sprayed pastel pink Mercedes SUV, though she'd have felt sorry for it when the ladies clambered in. As Egeria heaved herself up to the driver's seat, the reinforced springs would yield alarmingly. She sometimes worried she'd got a puncture, until Fantasia heaved herself in on the other side and balance was restored.

When Ponsomby Tiddledick made Fantasia Northern Ireland secretary, he thought of copying a special feature in the Cabinet War Rooms. A semi-circular shape hewn out of one of the tables specifically to make space for Winston Churchill's gut.

A senior member of the Cabinet once suggested she looked like an overblown lavatory door. And his ghastly yobbo of an assistant was just as rude, saying she and Erewego weren't really Little and Large, but Large and Fucking Enormous.

Unfortunately for him, Trudi wasn't there to hear that, given that she had by then, in her own special way, learned how to render unto Caesar the things which are Caesar's, and unto God the things that are God's. That's to say she'd figured out how to save people's souls in a way that benefitted everyone.

The foul-mouthed yobbo would have saved himself years in purgatory by shelling out a quid. And Trudi's pretty little piggy swear box would have proved itself yet again to be a nice little earner.

Everybody happy then. Though God and Trudi perhaps more so than the ghastly yobbo.

CHAPTER SEVEN

It's not necessarily true that Trudi has superpowers, though Percy's often wondered. Not least during their visit to Primrose Hill.

As he sauntered and she skipped back in what he hoped was the direction of the car, he left it to her to find it. Distinctive enough, in sunny yellow with pink roses painted all over the bodywork, but you have to be able to see it. As usual, Percy had forgotten where he'd parked, but as always, Trudi hadn't.

'How in God's name do you manage that, darling?' he almost grumbled, as Simone-Sitrouenne, Viv's elderly but much-loved Citroen 2CV appeared round the next corner and the little girl clapped her little hands.

'My dear, it's a woman thing,' she answered breezily, in the voice Mummy uses when Daddy can't for the life of him figure out how she's done something that strikes her as absurdly easy. Viv is too kind to point out that being obtuse is a man thing, though she often thinks it.

Of course, Daddy's frightfully clever, in his way. His PhD thesis did, after all, prove to his professors' satisfaction that the answer to the Schleswig-Holstein question lies in the root causes of the War of Jenkins' Ear. But Viv's master's degree in applied mathematics was more directly useful to someone planning to be a pollster.

Percy does recognise that his head and the clouds are on more than nodding terms, and, to his credit, even owns up to it occasionally. But there are moments, like when they got back to the car and the thing started for once without needing Trudi's superpowers, when he is truly flabbergasted by stuff she comes out with.

'Daddi, where does Mr Potato Head live?'

Though he didn't know exactly where Erewego's flat was, he did know that it was nearby, and at that precise moment was asking himself precisely that question. What he really could not fathom was what brought that thought into his daughter's mind. He wondered whether telepathy's a woman thing too.

Lucky for the two nasty fat ladies that the general public isn't generally telepathic, or there'd have been an awful lot of gossip. There had been mutterings in the gutter press, however, and Fyok Yu and Hon Ki were no more particular about their sources of info than the tasks they'd set their useful idiots. Chancery's not too particular, either, about doing bad things for good money, though he felt the need to double-check his instructions.

'You mean I gotta make aht I'm totty? An' get it off wiv de ugly old bag?'

Though his two soon-to-be co-conspirators shared a thought about pots and kettles, they nodded approvingly.

Their plan was a bog-standard honey trap. Chancery would seduce Fealstite in a warm room where duvets were surplus to requirements, though a surplice might add spice, and speedy camerawork would do the rest.

He glanced nervously at Spleeny, not sure how she'd take to the idea. But she set his mind at rest, as only she knew how.

'Give it one, Charlie. An' two, an' free, an' four, an' five. I'll be, like, like 'avin' a norgy. Not like yer actually, like, doin' it.'

Offensive though they found the disgusting little tart, they were more convinced than ever that she had a point about eliminating Percy. Even after they'd convinced Fealstite to convince Erewego to convince the prime minister to buy the trains, that infuriating man could still convince him back.

Biff's lads struggled with the Chinese guys using words they didn't understand and the others mispronouncing ones they normally would have done. Also, annoyingly, much of the conversation was conducted in murmurs.

As they struggled to make any sense of any of it, visions of rows of frothing tankards grew dimmer by the second. They even wondered where the next halves would be coming from as Lady Casement smeared both their notebooks with poo. Nonetheless, Biff was confident enough to bang off another email to Percy, which included the boys' detailed description of Fyok Yu and Hon Ki.

Bejasus, looks like it really is our old chums from the Orient who've fluttered back. Piddling in our nest again, and wanting to push you off your perch.

At this point, Lady Casement, who'd positioned herself on the desk next to the computer with her head to one side, stared at the screen, hopped up and down and nodded vigorously. Biff looked at her quizzically.

'Don't tell me you can read as well as talk?'

By way of an answer, she did another poo, this time all over the computer keyboard. He wanted to clip her round the ear but didn't, because he'd no idea where to start looking for it. Birds are cunning in that way.

*

The Trudi Nanny brought home from musical theatre classes that selfsame evening was a bird in full song, ship in full sail, Fred Astaire in full pirouette and Ginger Rogers in a fabulously full bowl of cherries. Gone was hopping, skipping and marching with swinging arms. In their place, Roald Dahl's leading lady, Matilda, who was on a mission to prove being small was no bar to being bad.

In a nutshell, the hell with doing as they're told, little people sometimes just have to be a little bit naughty. Also, in Trudi's case, very, very noisy.

Percy and Viv stared at this now rather breathless apparition, and at the framed photograph of Karl Marx that responded to the vibration caused by the little girl's stamping feet by falling off the wall. The glass didn't get broken, though after a fair few gasps, the silence did, by Trudi.

She patiently explained that Juliet was no longer right for her, as she really was a bit too mature for the role, then ordered Mummy to order the sheet music for her new repertoire so she could accompany her on the piano. This, she pointed out, would be a great privilege for Mummy, though she'd better put in the work, as she wouldn't put up with mistakes.

Amazing how abruptly and totally calm can be shattered. Seconds before the Grand Entrance, Percy and Viv had been taking a moment to take in the sun, setting exquisitely over a tranquil sea. It was casting long and lingering shadows through the Georgian windows of Percy's office in Penislow Palace, while the brandy decanter and balloon glasses were glinting merrily on his pretty little Victorian rolltop desk.

But seconds after the Grand Entrance, the prima donna swept out of the room gripping Nanny firmly by the wrist and demanding instant access to one if not two sticky buns. A departure from Trudi's usual dietary regime, but she'd read somewhere that opera singers often have fuller figures and didn't want to be left out.

Unfortunately, however, the restored equilibrium only lasted until Percy turned to read Biff's email on his computer. Viv, leaning over his shoulders and massaging them sympathetically, gave something between a sigh and a snort.

'Might have known those vile men would be getting up to their old tricks again, darling. Maybe it was only a matter of time.'

Then she stiffened.

'Our friend across the water mentions the ugly women they were talking to. One older than the other. What if they aren't both female? That disgusting creature Chancery was a master of disguises, wasn't he? And he knows where we live.'

Percy looked up at her, and down at Fang, who'd chosen this moment to start trying to rip the Elastoplast off his big toes. The cat's savagery felt like a bad omen as he yanked back his legs, catching the underside of the desk and knocking both drinks to the floor.

'Shit,' he grunted. This didn't take things any further forward, but he felt better for getting it off his chest.

Trudi, who'd somehow got through not two but three

sticky buns, chose that moment to skip back into the room. She looked at him in pretend horror, making her eyes as wide as dinner plates and as narrow as arrow slits at the same time. Yet another superpower.

'Naughty, naughty Daddi,' she squealed, holding up her dear little pink Saviour of Souls/Nice Little Earner. 'You must pay your fine if you don't want God to smack your bad boy's bottom.'

Percy slipped a quid in the slot, trying to look ashamed, while Trudi tried not to look delighted. Resisting with difficulty the temptation to give her daughter a high five, Viv settled for making a constructive suggestion.

'Tell your man to tell his snoops to get their calculators out. Get the feeling they're not all that bright, but you remember that bastard Chancery had odd hands. Well, an odd number of fingers on them. Get them to look out carefully and do the bloody sums.'

She was distracted once again by a small person clearing her throat meaningfully. And duly coughed up another two quid.

From the age of three onwards, mental arithmetic had been another of Trudi's amazing accomplishments. Totting up her latest haul, she wondered what had got into her mother, who was normally not a sweary kind of woman at all.

With a bit of luck, she'd keep up the good work.

CHAPTER EIGHT

Shortly after Trudi turned four and began her formal education, poor Percy couldn't understand why Fang, who'd become less feral by his psychopathic standards, had a severe relapse. As usual, it was Viv to the rescue.

'They say men are stupid and women are crazy, my dear. You know why?'

Percy didn't.

'Well, that's the reason. Women are crazy precisely because men are stupid.'

Percy nodded, resignedly, and waited.

'Little Trudi's out for hours each day now. And who's the cat's favourite playmate?'

'Ah, of course.' Percy held up his hands in mock surrender.

'Who's a clever boy then?'

The young lady in question, who'd just skipped in, with Nanny, as usual, struggling to keep up with her in the half-mile hike from school, caught the tail end of this conversation. And, as always, decided grown-ups needed help. Selflessly setting aside her own urgent need for R and R, a sticky bun and, in an ideal world, lashings of ginger beer, she set about setting everyone straight. Wasn't going to be easy, but it had to be done.

'Silli, silli Mummi. Men are stupid because God forgot to give them brains. And women are crazy because he made theirs too big. I know that because mine is so huge. Means I'm cleverer than anyone. Didn't you even know that?'

Viv didn't, and pretended to consider the matter carefully while actually thinking about her husband's features.

The high forehead, strongly defined cheekbones and firmly set mouth all implied determination and intelligence. Though there was something lurking deep in the eyes, suggesting secrets he daren't share with anyone else.

Frailty, self-doubt and plain straightforward silliness, for heaven's sake.

She thought about this man she first married. Trying so hard back then to play both the working class hero and impeccably bred gent. Then came that whizzbang of a letter from the grave, penned on his deathbed by his aristo father, revealing Percy was as top drawer as they come. Not even the second born, but heir to a title.

Not all good, though. As well as an irresponsible, reckless and generally disgraceful streak, the old rogue had a streak of callousness. All thanks to the public school system? Discuss.

'It'll make a man of him,' Percy's pater's pater had told his sobbing wife as they left him, lips quivering and struggling with the trunk his housemaster refused to help him carry. Back in that golden age, boys didn't blub, and if women did, they'd soon say they were perfectly all right really and apologise for making fools of themselves.

Viv made it her mission after Percy got the letter, just a few short years ago, to find out who he really was and let him in on the secret. He'd never get there on his own.

'Your father was a fool but not a knave to pass you on to a married couple when your mother died,' she told him. 'People like him hadn't got a clue about tinies. Too busy being overgrown babies themselves.

'Besides, it gave you a better break than if he'd hung on to you. How would you have liked to be packed off to boarding school, same as him, at the age of five?'

The very thought of doing such a thing to Trudi made Percy want to cry, though he was grateful at least that chaps are allowed these days. Viv was grateful to the bottom of her heart that her parents were against private education on principle. Different for the man Percy grew up believing was his dad. Forget principles, he simply didn't have the money. Of course, Viv knows no more than Percy about his birth mother, though she does have a hunch.

'What about the old line?' Percy once wondered. 'All women become like their mothers, that is their tragedy. No man does, that's his. Think that's me?'

'Have a feeling you passed on that, dear.' This didn't take a lot of working-out, given how effeminate he could be, behind the boyishness. Not to mention how out-and-out gay he was back in the day. When it all came out, manner of speaking, husband and wife had a lot of time to make up, and a lot of new things to talk about.

'Those girlie genes in your jeans hit the spot for me just as they should. Must be why we make rabbits look so lazy,' Viv murmured archly.

Percy loves it when she talks dirty, well, relatively, but for the moment couldn't help focusing on her thoughts about who those vile Chinese men might have hooked up with.

'Hell and damnation,' he began, careful to keep his voice down for fear of having to cough up yet more expensive protection against, well, hell and damnation. 'I'd forgotten that bastard Chancery had paid us a visit. Didn't much matter then. Does now there's a child in the house.'

Trudi had been too busy trying to persuade Fang to eat a raw aubergine to pay much attention. But, her vital interests at stake, she made a couple of points.

'You don't need to worry, silli Daddi. I've got a much bigger brain than this silli man, because I'm a girl. Because he's a man, he's only got a titchy-witchy brain.

'Oh and by the way, I heard what you said. Naughty B-word, naughty Daddi.'

She held up Nice Little Earner; Daddy coughed up the pound coin. Viv smirked and he agreed his daughter definitely is cleverer than Chancery. Against that, the ugly brute knows how to kill people and she doesn't.

'A word with your friend and mine, dearest? Okay, I'm not going to cross the Irish Sea all guns blazing. But he can, if he's feeling trigger-happy.'

Viv shuddered at the thought of ex-Sergeant Monty White, previously Percy's Downing Street bodyguard, now her partner in the polling company she runs from home, getting the Sten guns out again. But maybe needs must.

'All right then,' she sighed. Though, as a warning to Percy to keep the tempo down, she leant forward and bit him on the nose. Gently enough, but it made the point.

Odd, considering words are the main tool of both their trades, how often they don't need them at all. Trudi just thought it odd he doesn't seem to mind. Whenever she tries it on Fang, he hates it.

*

Monty stared across the scrubbed pine dining-room table in his neat little stone-built Cornish cottage at his Kazakhstani wife, Bakyt. She and Viv could be sisters, as they're of a similar age and build, and blessed with the same blend of formidable charisma and delicate features. Also, Bakyt has a way of striking poses entirely naturally that'd send tremors down the spine of any self-respecting heterosexual man, as well as an awful lot of ladies of lavender tendencies. Though they've been together for nearly five years, Monty feels a little thrill of excitement just looking at her.

However, his inner bloke also felt a little thrill of excitement at the thought of locking horns again with Chancery. Happy as he was charging up and down the motorway to do Viv's bidding at her London office, it could be a little humdrum, unlike drumbeats of war. Bakyt, clearly, was of a like mind.

'Filthy scum still alive and making wrong kind of whoopee? We cook gander. Put in washing machine dry out hanging. By toenails, by God. Give good seeing-to.'

Though Bakyt's English has come a long way in recent years, handy for a nuclear scientist at a top British university, the smell of blood brings out something deep in her ancestry. But she puts it on sometimes to make Monty smile, while Trudi maintains she rides around on a broomstick, though Fang is her familiar not naughty witch lady's.

It was agreed Monty's best disguise would be the cropped hairstyle Irish rebels once went for, along with dark glasses and a droopy moustache. By lucky coincidence, it made him look like the Yankee spooks he'd have reason to hope wouldn't notice him. The one difference was his must-have special hat, of a type referred to in an old rebel song as the broad black brimmer of the IRA.

Bakyt thought he looked so sexy that she gave him a nicer sort of good seeing-to.

As a sideways salute to the old comrade in the Met who slipped him two Sten guns and a police pistol as a leaving present, he got hold of a natty nineteen fifties Wolseley, complete with bell. But it's one up on the cop cars lumbering around in old movies. Monty's a sensitive soul with as healthy a dose of camp as Percy, but he couldn't resist squeezing in an Aston Martin engine. Goes like the clappers now.

Trudi gets so excited when he takes her for a spin that he sometimes drives faster than he should as a responsible adult with a child on board. He also indulges her by making the bell go ding-a-ling-a-ling, though he draws the line at screeching to a halt next to old ladies so Trudi can jump out and arrest them.

*

Monty got a lot of looks as he roared into the Belfast Europa car park, and plenty more as he sauntered into reception. Not sure his violin case had thrown everyone off the scent, he tried humming *Danny Boy*, but might as well not have bothered. The racket from the piano bar would have drowned out the Wolseley doing sixty in first, and the bell.

Overcoming his natural fear of a blinding headache, he edged closer to a bunch of guys who, astonishingly, looked just like him. Sat round a table, they were bellowing at the tops of their voices about something supposedly top secret, but actually shared with everyone in the building.

'Eliminating hostiles. Shock and awe.'

'Alert POTUS positive. You read me? Roger?'

'I read you. Roger. Over.'

'Roger and out. God bless Murka.'

This suggested two things. One, these Yanks were ready to do something nasty to someone. And, two, the president of the United States would be pleased to hear it.

Monty had no idea who these guys were, what they thought Mugwump would like to know, or whether he needed to know as well. After all, he'd come to check out the Chancerys and the Chinese, and they were two tables away.

Though the one nearest was already occupied, by a couple of dozy-looking youths with small pencils, big notepads and caps on back to front, they afforded no protection from the noise the Yanks were making. Monty found himself missing those long drives between Cornwall and London, after all, listening to nothing louder than Beethoven sonatas on the CD player.

He suddenly felt less sorry for the great man's rotten luck, however. Deafness had a lot going for it.

CHAPTER NINE

Deafness struck Percy and Viv as a plus too, when Trudi first started tinkling the ivories. Bashing the Bösendorfer, more like. But then, after what seemed no time at all, she was tapping out recognisable tunes.

This was why, the day she did her little-bit-naughty prima donna display, they weren't surprised how good it was. Deafening, yes. But melodic? Yes also. Though Trudi had swept out of the room before they had a chance to applaud, then they'd got distracted by that beastly email about those beastly men, they did discuss the matter later.

'You're a mathematician, darling, so it's not to be wondered at you're also good at music,' Percy suggested.

'And you're a natural-born performer, so it's obvious where she got that bit from too.' Viv smiled, though her tone implied the compliment might be a teeny bit backhanded.

Trudi, who had by then already been put to bed and been read a story or two, or three, or it might have been four, had been so flushed with her West End triumph that she couldn't possibly sleep. So she'd snuck downstairs, and at this point felt it appropriate to remind Daddy of one of his favourite sayings.

'The only thing worse than being talked about is not being talked about.'

For the two of them, snuggled up on the comfy sofa with even Fang for once contentedly purring at their feet, this was a Banquo at the banquet moment, though Trudi saw it as yet another triumphant entry. On this stage at this stage she was dressed down, in nothing but pink frilly jim-jams and pink fluffy dressing gown, though she felt her pink sparkly tiara was a nice complement to the ensemble. She also expected, and received, a nice compliment about the show she'd put on earlier.

'Yes, dear, you seem to have inherited the best of both of us,' said Daddy.

'And let's hope it doesn't get you into as much trouble as it often has for Daddy,' Mummy added, just a shade tartly.

'Oh and by the way, it's well past ten and you should have been asleep hours ago,' she added. The sharp words, though, tempered by an affectionate smile.

'Okay. Night night, daffy old farts.' Trudi fluttered out as soundlessly as she'd fluttered in, satisfied she'd made her point.

*

In spite of their Irishness, Biff's lads had not inherited the musical genes or talent of either Viv or Trudi, nor would they have taken to Beethoven if they'd heard of him, but they did share Monty's interest in the Chancery/Chinese chatter.

However, sandwiched between the murmuring foursome and the roaring Yanks, they were struggling to untangle which conversation was which.

More than once, they took off their caps to scratch their heads. At one point, Paddy was in such a muddle that he put it back on with the peak pointing forward. He jammed it back on again the right/wrong way round, hoping nobody had noticed how not cool he'd been.

Had Trudi been there, she'd have told him in no uncertain terms that it looked stupid back to front. She knew young men were even sillier than old ones because Daddy once showed her a photo of some of his schoolmates sporting the same fashion all those millions of years ago, explaining boys always think they've invented everything and are always wrong.

'I'm so glad I'm different,' Trudi had replied. 'My Barbie dolls are lovely and new, aren't they, Daddi?'

Percy grappled with his always-tell-the-kid-the-truth policy versus Barbies having been around before he was born. In the end, he hit on a compromise, involving that other thing kids think are cool.

'So they are, darling. Same as dinosaurs.'

Trudi gave him her I'm-sure-your-nose-is-growing-but-I-can't-prove-it look and went off to discuss the matter with Fang. Percy gave her his what-do-you-mean-of-course-it's-all-true look and went off to have a sneaky fag.

Biff lit up too when Paddy and his mate showed up at his office. At least they'd lost the idiotic hat look when Lady Casement told them they looked like fecking eejits. Though, as they seemed to be getting more and more of their facts back to front, he wondered whether upping their Guinness allowance to two halves per hour had been a mistake.

'One of them keeps saying something about crucifying that bleeder from Cornwall, and we fecking know where he lives,' Paddy announced with a not very successful attempt at a flourish.

'And we know his name, begorrah, it's Roger,' his friend added. 'And the other one's called Andout.'

Against all odds Biff finally got enough out of them to pass on more intel to Percy in Cornwall, unaware both of Monty's presence in Belfast and of how useful his disguise was. Because the spooks' glasses were so much darker than his, he'd managed to squeeze in unnoticed among them to find out whether they had a bearing on his mission.

On the way back to his little hotel, Monty stopped at a corner shop and bought a large packet of frozen peas, for medicinal purposes. Sitting on his bed and pressing it against his forehead, he rang Bakyt, in the hope she could help make any sense of any of it.

'Think I'd better brush up on Stateside blarney,' he admitted.

'Stateside? What that mean?' Bakyt was alert, if puzzled. 'And Blarney? A castle somewhere, no?'

'Er, yes, but our Elizabeth, Good Queen Bess to her fans, got so fed up with the nonsense talked to her by the lord of that manor that she made the word into something meaning, well, nonsense.' Monty couldn't resist showing off, but, equally, Bakyt couldn't resist winding him up.

'You god of know-how. I kowtow. Supreme excellent man. Ignorant Kazakh slave person kneel and lick boot.

'You keep wits and bits about you, lover boy,' she added,

more seriously. 'I want to lick more than boots when we next in same room at same time.

'We have ancient saying in my country. He without scimitar laugh only when it hurts. Last laugh not last long.'

Monty followed her logic and knew she was talking sense, though he had a strong feeling she'd made some of that up. He's not always sure, though, especially when she and Trudi are discussing broomsticks. Because he was in London the day the joke got going, he's often puzzled when they discuss Fang's extraordinary powers, which include making the university's irritating vice-chancellor drive his car over a cliff.

One afternoon when Trudi was setting off home with Fang, who, incidentally, wasn't struck on the pink collar and lead she insisted on using, Bakyt's farewell was weird.

'When we three meet again? Thunder, lightning or when cats sheeting dogs down?'

Monty knew Bakyt had always been fond of the witches in *Macbeth*. So that monstrous misquote didn't come as any great surprise. Trudi's answer did.

'When the burly hurling's done. When we've won. Or lost. Or something.'

Every bit as wrong, but to Monty an astonishing display of learning for a four-year-old. He wasn't to know Bakyt had taught the child the line ten minutes earlier. Mistakes and all.

Like Percy, however, Monty has a healthy respect for the kind of witchcraft he's always believed gives women the edge over men, so had high hopes his wife could help him out here. Though her profession is all about empirical reasoning, scientists do have lightbulb moments, like when one of them notices that circular things help you get around.

Because Bakyt followed the news fairly carefully and had long been interested in Mugwump from an anthropomorphic perspective, her imagination did a quantum leap. Too late to invent the wheel, but that sort of thing.

'You not see, you not clever clod of tiny police plod brain, idiot not human president want British government not buying official Chinese travel transit trash.

'He slice short of cheese pickle portion, he think make volume noise make different subsequent thing outcome.'

'Sorry, Bakyt, darling, you've completely lost me,' Monty answered, truthfully.

'Okay, dumbo.' Bakyt dropped the funny talk and spelt it out. 'Mugwump's trying to force Tiddledick to say no Chinese trains. Why spies Belfast-based? No logic. Remember, he know nothing. Maybe he think safe distance but close enough. Maybe not even know North Ireland in United Kingdom.'

Monty thought about conversations he'd had with Percy about Mugwump's apparently bottomless pit of stupidity, and about his wife's apparently bottomless well of wisdom. It happens she has a particularly shapely bottom, and he suddenly had a lot of particularly impure thoughts.

'Did you know the brain is the body's most erogenous zone, darling?' he said, seemingly apropos nothing at all.

'Crazy small-brain flea-creature, why you think my lady cave like your man monster machine?' She was thanking him, in her funny way, for thanking her, in his roundabout way, for her cleverness. Theirs was a marriage of true minds.

The mutual attraction was so strong that Bakyt had never needed any of those special toys Nanny was so fond of. But as she lay back after the call ended, she could have been tempted.

*

Her analysis was uncannily accurate, as Mugwump knew for a fact that Washington set the Brits free centuries ago, and they were so grateful that they did the same for the Paddies, and named many of their shithole townships after great cities in the US of A. He'd learned all this from an extremely potted history of Murka provided by one of his chiefs of staff.

'Honkies arrived. Slaughtered natives. Imported slaves. Got rich.'

Somehow, this also confirmed that cowboys created the Land of the Free by smashing indi-bum redskins with a beautiful wall and intercontinental ballistic missiles, so sending the guys to Belfast was obviously the right thing to do.

Totally wasted journey, as all they did was pore over British political news websites, though had they ever heard of the Charge of the Light Brigade, they'd have agreed "ours not to reason why". Not that they ever really knew where they were, thanks to the sunglasses they never took off, even in the dark.

Conversely, the identical crew cuts, droopy moustaches and blunderbuss-sized bulges under their jackets made them highly visible to others. Just a shame neither they nor Mugwump ever got the chance to hook up with Trudi. She'd have set them straight on all sorts of things.

By the time she was three, she had some idea what countries belonged where, and why. By the time she was four, she had pronounced views about the slave trade. And when she hit five, she'd have style tips at her fingertips.

Only one problem. With someone like Mugwump, it'd be difficult to know where to start.

CHAPTER TEN

For some reason Percy couldn't work out, Trudi had a bee in her pretty pink bonnet about ugly Mr Potato Head.

All the way back to Mayfair from Primrose Hill, she was firing questions. More sustained barrage than quick burst, given that even really short journeys like this take longer in Citroen 2CVs than in other cars. Less because of traffic than nought to sixty acceleration, problematic as fifty's top whack. At least she started this time, leaving Trudi free to collect her thoughts in the nice bouncy seat as the car bounced nicely along.

'What does Mr Potato Head do, Daddi?'

'Well, she helps the prime minister do what he wants to do, darling. Sometimes she does it for him, if he's feeling lazy. Which is quite often, actually.

'And sometimes she does what the prime minister doesn't want to do. I think that's quite often too,' Percy added, thoughtfully.

'Why doesn't he send Mr Potato Head away then, Daddi? Or put him in a great big pot, boil him up and eat him?'

'Perfect solution, Trudi. I'll suggest that next time I see him.'

Funny thing was, Daddy wasn't being funny, as he knew Poncey was so dependent on the ghastly old bag that he'd take some persuading to get rid of her, even by the old-fashioned method of just firing her.

Boiling her up in a great big pot and eating her would have struck both men as better still, if they'd known quite how keen she was to get the Chinese trains deal done and dusted. Poncey had admitted she seemed to be in favour, but he had no idea, and wouldn't for a while yet, how far she was prepared to push it. Meantime, Trudi was getting creative.

'If your friend Mr Poncey doesn't think Mr Potato Head would taste very nice, maybe he could put him in a submarine and send him somewhere horrid, where horrid people would keep him forever and ever. What do you think, Daddi?'

Daddy was all for it. He loved Trudi's ingenuity, though did wonder what she'd been watching on her pretty little pink television when she was supposed to be tucked up in bed like a good little girl. Also, it struck him that her idea of sleepy-time and the way she often reacted to being woken in the mornings might be connected.

He'd have been struck dumb had he found out what finally happened to Egeria Erewego, not that he ever did. Nor, at this stage, did it occur to him she had very particular reasons for treating the Chinese trains as her own personal crusade.

*

Blackmail counts as a very particular reason, as much for Fantasia Fealstite as anyone. Her encounter with Chancery had started innocently enough, or so it seemed. Hotel corridor one minute, bedroom the next. The fluttering eyelashes were too much to resist.

He smiled in silent satisfaction. So what the blobby old bag was so no oil painting any self-respecting art critic would put his boot through it? He'd convinced her he'd play the man, and the role play would get the good times rolling. Besides, he guessed, rightly, Fantasia never could resist a bit of rough.

The room had been chosen carefully. No windows, and the bedside lamp switches exactly where he wanted them to be. Fantasia must have no idea anything was wrong. That way, nothing could go wrong, from Chancery's point of view.

'Can only do it in da dark,' he grunted in a voice he imagined was pure pantomime dame. Impure, more like, but by now Fantasia couldn't care less.

As they got down to it, he found to his surprise he was rather up for it, and tried to think about Spleeny. Which wasn't difficult, as she was hiding in the wardrobe just a few feet away, ready to pounce, on his signal.

The sound when it came, excuse language, was both involuntary and exceedingly embarrassing for Chancery, while its immediate sequel was exceedingly embarrassing for Fantasia. Spleeny had already turned on the light with one hand and the camera with the other. And, as she was filming over Chancery's shoulder, all anyone could see of him was the tousled hair and all too clearly visible proof that he'd been in the mood.

In an ideal world, Fantasia would have hacked the bimbo to bits with a machete, or tied her to the front of a large artillery piece and pulled the trigger, or maybe just dropped her from a very great height out of an aeroplane. But, annoyingly, she'd scuttled out. Leaving her vile accomplice to be, well, vile.

'Oo d'ya fink's gonna love dat more? Da missus, nudge nudge, or da boss? Or dem filfy fellers in da papers?' Chancery had dropped the pantomime dame bit, not that he sounded any different.

Fantasia did a better job with dropping the ooh-you-are-awful-but-I-like-you bit.

'Filthy, you say? Or try to say, ignorant brute. Filthy yourself, I say, and say properly, unlike you. What do you want from me, you blackmailing blackguard?'

Chancery couldn't miss the put-down, straight out of the Fyok Yu and Hon Ki playbook. But if revenge is a dish best served cold, this was straight out of the freezer.

'You're gonna make good 'n' sure dat prime minister bloke of yours signs da contract on da Chinese trains. Or we'll take aht a contract on you. You get mah drift?'

Fantasia tried not to let the relief show, as the idiot was pushing at an open door. However, as Egeria who wasn't to know she wasn't to know she'd nearly got to know a man in the biblical sense, she rightly predicted what happened might take some explaining.

*

'Listen, daaaahling,' Fantasia murmured with just the tiniest trace of urgency, 'we must get that ponce Ponsonby to stay firm and not go flaccid on us.

'You know what he's like, always bearing the impress of the last person who sat on him. Needs to be you, daaaahling, not that Penislow fellow. I know and you know you know best, don't you, daaaahling, daaaahling heart.'

Of course Egeria knew that, but suddenly had a feeling there was something she didn't know, because her lover wasn't telling her.

'We both agree those Chinese trains are a no-brainer,' she began. 'Everyone knows made in England is a luxury we can't afford these days. But why does it matter quite so much to you, may I ask?'

Fantasia's heart sank. Of course, the torture chair was only meant to be a bit of fun, but it did work. And when Egeria's eyes had that steely glint in them, it wasn't very nice being strapped down in it.

A tricky story to tell, Fantasia knew that. She had been taken for a ride, manner of speaking, and stories like this can be a turn-on if the partner is in the right mood. But not if she isn't. Or even if she is, her mood might change. A snatch of dialogue from an old funny book came into her head as she tried to steady herself by breathing deeply.

'Doctor says, "Big breaths." Female patient replies, "Yeth, and I'm only shicksteen."' Fantasia did not smile.

*

Chancery didn't smile either when he learned what Fyok Yu and Hon Ki wanted him to do next. And where.

Suburban to the core, he was scared of having to operate out of central London. Years ago, he'd got more front than Harrods, but Spleeny had pulled his shutters down. Her teenager's foul mouth, puppy fat and hair tied in random knots were no threat, and the fluffy barnet that came next was rather nice. But the platinum hair dye, false eyelashes and drawn gangster's moll look? It'd take a better man than him…

Worse, she'd discovered that bursting into tears wasn't as persuasive as screeching in his face. So was what happened in the hotel bedroom an accident? He'd have to lose his hearing to hear the last of that.

'You fancied a bit with that fat old bag. Face it, Charlie, you'd 'ave it off wiv a radiator.' Spleeny goes more for dramatic impact than making sense.

Still, it got Chancery thinking. How would you do it with a radiator?

CHAPTER ELEVEN

Back at Penislow Palace, there was an air of timeless and contented calm, which was odd, as the threat of being murdered normally unsettles people. Then again, an air of calm is not the same as the real thing, and besides, there was the matter of getting Trudi to school.

Percy wandered over to Simone-Sitrouenne, wondering as always if the beastly thing would start, or if he was going to need Trudi's help, again. At least the dear little girl was motoring along nicely, hair plaited in neat pigtails, all ready for the day. As ever, Fang was stalking them, waiting for his chance to leap up and grab the child by at least one of those enticing dangly bits. Not exactly shoelaces, but they'd do.

Percy straightened the badge on the bonnet that spells the motor's initials. He'd had it made specially to make Viv smile on her last but one birthday. She did not point out SS wouldn't have played well with the French on their national car during the war, but hoped one day the Blu Tack would give way and it'd be lost forever.

Annoyingly, she noted for the millionth time, it was still there.

Equally frustratingly, Simone-Sitrouenne wouldn't start until Trudi did her superpower thing. Tapping the dashboard in exactly the right spot with the tiny hammer she always has handy when she's supposed to be going anywhere, she smiled knowingly at Daddy as the engine spluttered into life. How does she do that? Percy will never know.

He watched her clamping on her preposterously oversized but rather pretty pink helmet, and told her yet again he really must get a child's seat. The idea didn't go down well. Never does. If she's told him once, she's told him a hundred times that the car's so slow, it'll never catch up with anything, let alone bump into it.

'Yes, but, darling, it's the law,' Percy always tries to explain.

'Silly Daddi, the law's an ass, didn't you know that? You're a silly ass too, by the way.' More than once, this has got him thinking.

'Do you ever tell teacher he's a silly ass, darling? I merely seek information.'

'Course not. He knows he's a plonker. And you're a daffy old fart, by the way.' Having heard that expression once before, Percy wondered where it came from, and hoped she hadn't heard her mother saying it. At least not if she was talking about him at the time.

On the way home, he dropped into the chemist's to get Nanny's regular supply of special jelly. He once nearly asked her where the hell she put it all, then worked it out for himself and went all red. Nanny was amazed, as she thought only women have menopausal flushes.

Next stop the pet shop, where he explained Fang's need

72

for something to do now that Trudi wasn't around to play with during term time. The best the bloke could come up with was five budgies a week, wings pre-clipped, which didn't do it for Percy. Not even on generously discounted terms, it being a bulk order. When he got home and told Viv about it, she was not impressed. Bakyt, who'd dropped by for coffee, was even less so.

'He brute and savage. We clip his wings also, with meat cleaver, and serve to dogs. And snails.' The way her lips curled back as she spat out the words confirmed she wasn't joking.

*

Unfortunately, Biff was also deadly serious, in his latest email, which began with a nasty parody of Lord Haw-Haw's broadcasts to blitz-hit Britain.

Belfast calling. Belfast calling. Digit alert. Digit alert.

'Yeah yeah, very funny. Not,' Percy snorted.

As Viv read on over his shoulder, her lips pursed, as it destroyed all remaining hope that there wasn't too much to worry about really.

Me lads aren't the sharpest bayonets in the armoury, but they can count. Up to five at least. And bejesus, Percy, the fecking swine is on your tail.

'Thereby hangs a tale,' Percy muttered savagely. 'We should have roasted the pig when we had him penned last time.'

Though she accepted he had a point, Viv didn't like her husband's tone. Or the way his fists were clenching and unclenching. More a measured-and- proportionate-response-than-wildly-lashing-out sort of girl, she wasn't greatly struck on Bakyt's take either.

'My man fix bayonet. Fix all. Shining armour knight, tear entrails, head on pike. Ahead on points, yes?'

'Night of the long knives,' Percy added grimly. 'We can take out that disgusting little shrew he hooked up with while we're at it. Make sure she never comes of age. She's had her last night at the proms. No sympathy there, her symphony's atonal.'

Viv noticed her husband's analogies were getting convoluted. A good sign; meant he might be ready to listen to reason instead of trying to plan a massacre.

'Perhaps better await confirmation from Monty, dears, and take it from there?'

Even Bakyt, who'd been nodding too vigorously at Percy's approach, lost the Dracula look. Her eyes refocused as Viv gently patted her arm and soothingly carried on.

'Also, it might be an idea not to do anything until we know for sure exactly what this horrid man has in mind for the world in general and us in particular.

'There's also the question of why Belfast is swarming with Americans. How, if at all, they fit into the picture. And, if so, whose side they're on.'

Percy's proud of how good he is at the beyond blokeish thing of multi-tasking, like listening to Viv at the same time as slipping on heavy duty gardening gloves. He bought them in self-defence when he swapped his sandals for Chelsea boots, knowing full well Fang would regard the lack of laces as an act of war.

'*Beware of entrance to a quarrel,*' he mused. '*But being in, bear't that the opposed may beware of thee.*' In his slightly on-the-spectrum way he was rather pleased with how that fitted both to his quarrel with Fang and any humans he might be up against. But Viv, who knew him all too well, rounded off the quote with some emphasis.

'*Give every man thy ear, but few thy voice. Take each man's censure, but reserve thy judgment.*'

Percy looked at his wife carefully, noting how low sunlight blazing through arched Georgian windows highlighted her cheekbones, which over time had become more distinctive and even sexier than when he first met her. That happy thought put him off pointing out that the bloke who came out with the lines they'd been quoting came to a bloody end anyway, behind an arras. He switched mode, and plays.

'*Age cannot wither her, nor custom stale her infinite variety.*' Only when both women turned and stared at him did he realise he'd said the words out loud.

Viv gave him a smile somewhere between gratification and a kind of maternal indulgence, delicately laced with lust. Picking up on the vibe, Bakyt seemed soothed, though Fang would have none of it. Wrapping his hind legs firmly round the left boot, he managed to prise enough of it open with his teeth to get one paw in, claws unsheathed.

'Bugger budgies,' Percy screamed. 'What that animal needs is birds of prey. Better still, cat-eating pterodactyls.' Trudi, who'd just got back from school, did not agree.

'Tear-y-duck-tails will eat you too, cruel Daddi. That cat is my cat, and he's a cool cat. Only playing with you because he loves you. And I love him more than I love you today, so there.'

To emphasise her point, she lovingly gripped Fang's tail with one hand and fastened several clothes pegs to it with the other. She was sure he'd like that because they were pink, and couldn't understand why he leapt in the air and went round and round in circles.

*

Across the Irish Sea, by contrast, Monty was getting straight to the point.

Slithering in on the CIA guys' chit-chat had been unexpectedly easy. He's tall and slender, and fit enough for any assault course, while the Yanks only carry off their much fuller figures thanks to their height. They'd manage the shouty sergeant major bit, but that's about it. Happily, the dark glasses glossed over obvious differences.

It struck Monty that they were dumb, in the other sense, as well as blind. When one or the other looked in his direction, he could convincingly answer their question, which was nice and short, and never varied.

'You read me?'

Monty wondered if the bloke was so stupid that he actually mistook himself for a book. Then realised it was just his way of saying he wanted to be agreed with. No problem there. The snappy stock answer always worked.

'Copy.'

Against that, their endless acronyms, POTUS for starters, turned their bellowing into a kind of cipher that no one could be bothered to decode. The general assumption in the Europa was that they were travelling salesmen, touting snake oil, financial products or gadgets that don't work, as if you could tell the difference.

Took Monty a while too. When a person says his mate's MIA, it's not immediately obvious all he's saying is he can't find him. Similarly, after one of them had cocked up more spectacularly than usual then announced he planned to plead the fifth, it wasn't immediately obvious he meant he was going to keep his mouth shut. If only.

But, eventually, the mists began to clear, and back in the blessed silence of his room Monty tapped out an ADL for the benefit of the CCTT. That's to say an Authorised Data List for his Command and Control Team Trainer. Meaning need-to-know stuff to pass on to Percy. Or, better still, Viv and Bakyt.

Monty was suddenly scared that Yankee jargon might be a form of transmissible and incurable brain disease. He tried marching round the room a few times humming *Rule Britannia*, then did a couple of headstands in the hope these silly words might just fall out. After raiding the mini bar, he felt a lot better and got on with it. In English.

'Looks like the Americans really are fixated on preventing Tiddledick from buying Beijing rolling stock. And they're prepared for the long game, if needs be,' he began.

'Hmm, slow boat to China,' Percy muttered as he read, thinking of the origin of the phrase.

'What you mean?' Bakyt demanded.

'The saying comes from poker. As one player slowly loses, the other one scoops up his winnings, equally slowly. But gets there in the end.'

Glancing at his feet, Percy was reassured to see Fang had slowed to a halt, for the moment. But there was more from Monty. Lots more.

'Stupid as they are, the damn Yanks have taken their president's crazy scheme and run with it. Even though he only stumbled on the idea by mistake.'

'Same as Christopher Columbus, discovering the New World by setting off in the wrong direction,' Percy mused. 'Talk about starting as they mean to go on.'

'How about not talking at all, for the moment, dear?'

When his wife gives him that look, he knows to shut up and concentrate. Viv is by nature a patient person, but Vivienne's nose-nibbling isn't all that affectionate.

Trudi sees it as all the fun of the fair, or unfair, in Daddy's case, as men can't help being slow on the uptake. She starts her little pink stopwatch when she can see he's in trouble but he can't. And squeals with delight when he finally catches on.

By this point, he may well have squealed too, but not in the same way.

CHAPTER TWELVE

It turned into a long night at Penislow Palace. Only ended when Bakyt announced she really must be getting home before Genghis started fretting and taking it out on the furniture. The one time she'd tried bringing him round, it took smelling salts to bring Fang round. Percy loved it.

'So he's met his match at last. Serves the little bugger right.'

'Now, now, magnanimity in victory, dearest,' Viv protested.

'Not your bloody feet he goes for,' Percy grumbled back.

Glancing at the Elastoplast still wrapped round his big toe, Viv decided not to tell Trudi about his bad language in the morning. It was justified in the circumstances.

Hard to tell whether Fang had been scared out of his wits or simply overwhelmed by what looked like millions of shoelaces, Afghan hounds being unusually hairy. Though Genghis makes a point of hiding the grooming brush in ever more inventive places, Bakyt always finds it in the end. Tempting just to eat the wretched thing, but he's picky about his diet. Cushions, shoes and carpets are delicious, but that nasty plastic thing? Maybe not.

He once tried burying it at the end of the garden, but the wretched woman sniffed it out somehow. It's a dog's life, he grumbled at the time, though if he'd had any idea what Trudi puts Fang through, he'd have cheered up no end. This evening, however, the humans' focus was on Monty's long and carefully constructed email.

Mugwump's rationale for planting his spies in Belfast is as mysterious as how he keeps his combover in place. But he struck lucky, as scumbag Chancery's been working on the Northern Ireland secretary, who shares a London home with the cabinet secretary.

The idea is Fealstite leans on Erewego to lean on Tiddledick to ignore your sensible advice and buy the Chinese trains. Crazy. You know what kind of public backlash it'll cause.

'Yes, of course I know,' Percy snarled. 'But how does Monty know all this about Chancery? That's what I want to know.'

'Gather and surmise, my love. How about we just read on?' Spotting once again his cue to put a sock in it, Percy continued scrolling downwards, and didn't even dare nod at the next paragraph, that began:

You may be wondering how I know all this about Chancery.

The fact is, like Mugwump, I struck lucky. All the time I've been pretending to be one of the Yankee goons, Chancery was on the next but one table.

Not only that, he's in cahoots with that vile Chinese duo who gave you so much grief when you were prime minister. They've reinvented themselves as polyphonic prodigies, but they're up to the same old tricks on behalf of their nastily persuasive government.

Wish I knew more, but what with the Americans' demon decibel count, plus the half-witted paddies who're always at the table separating us, it's hard to hear all they're saying.

Still, could be worse, these Irish lads hardly say anything. Too busy licking the ends of their pencils and scribbling on great big notebooks.

Terrible writing, incidentally, but at least they're literate. All credit to Martin McGuinness when he was in charge of education here. Oops, sorry, going off the point a bit.

'Actually not,' Percy heard himself saying before he had time to stop himself. Trying to ignore the look on Vivienne's face, he carried on, now that he'd started.

'Sounds like they're Biff's boys, spying on Chancery, as he promised. Certainly fit the description. His parrot says they're fecking eejits. Smart bird, that. Or maybe no one's told these lads smartphones work as tape recorders.'

Vivienne's features relaxed slightly as she followed this up with the obvious question.

'Isn't it about time Monty and Biff put their heads together, dears? Shared intelligence, and all that?'

'But he only arrive two days ago,' Bakyt pointed out. 'He like to take his time, at all times.' At this, a dreamy look came into her eyes, causing a definite return of the Viv look as her mind also began to stray a little.

So you lovely people have as much fun as Percy and me, do you? she thought but didn't say. Girlie talk that, for another time. Anyway, Bakyt hadn't finished yet.

'Also good to confirm finding independently. Peer review absolute essential, or evidence suspect. Suspect everything. Absolutely.'

Percy nodded sagely. 'Of course, you are a scientist. But

liaison will be essential, and probably sooner rather than later.'

'Same as me leaving,' Bakyt said, draining the last of her vodka. 'Soon not soon enough. Bored dog bite everything. I bite him too, but he take no notice. No sense, no feeling, brainless brute.'

This was too much for Trudi. She'd only got out of bed for a wee-wee but had got distracted by the sight of Percy's silver cigarette box, which made a perfect naughty step for Ken. Unnoticed by the grown-ups, she'd slipped it onto the floor and placed her Barbie dolls all round him as a punishment for being brainless. He deserved it because he's a man. But a dog, even a man-dog, couldn't help it.

'Of course he's brainless, silly Bakyt, he's a boy. But that's not his fault, because he's a dog, not a brute. You've hurt his feelings, because dogs do have feelings, you know. And they have teeth too. All the better to eat you with. It says so in my book.'

CHAPTER THIRTEEN

Daddy may have screwed up in politics, but, though she hesitates to admit it, Trudi has her moments too. Like that time just before her fourth birthday when she left Fang shut up in a room for too long.

He's a fastidious little creature and pretty good at holding on, but the moment finally arrived when he just couldn't. Happily, there was a big enough bit of bare boards to limit the damage, but unhappily, he ended up like a castle hemmed in by a moat. And when Trudi finally remembered him, he still hadn't figured out how to escape without getting all wet and smelly.

She instantly read his distress, arising as much from the indignity as anything else, but couldn't be sure Daddy would be as understanding. What if he got so cross that he sent poor Fang back to where he came from? That place in London he was always promising to take her to, one day?

Though she was pretty sure she could talk him round, that wasn't the same as being absolutely sure. And, as bad luck would have it, Mummy was feeling in an unusually devilish mood.

'Oh, I don't know, dear, you never know with that daddy of yours. That naughty cat is always trying to eat his feet, and you know he doesn't like that very much.'

Because Trudi ran out of the room without a word, Viv didn't realise her joke had misfired. In fact, the little girl was choking back tears, scared out of her little wits. Knowing Daddy would be home in ten minutes, she took matters, and Fang, into her own hands. Shutting herself in the downstairs toilet, bolting the door and grabbing several sheets of loo paper, she set to work with her pink pen. Tricky, as she was still clutching the bemused cat. She began writing. One word per square, which she passed under the door. One by one.

Ime. Nott. Kumming. Owt. Evver. Untill. Yoo. Pomiss. Knot. Two. Sendd. Fangggg. Bak. Evar.

Percy was puzzled. First by Trudi's apparent disappearance off the face of the earth. Then by the slips of paper all over the floor in the hallway. Because they'd been blown about by the breeze caused when he opened the front door, the message now read: *Untill. Nott. Sendd. Owt. Evver. Evar. Ime. Fangggg. Bak. Yoo. Pomiss. Knot. Two. Kumming.* Which was even harder to decipher than the original.

At least it gave him a clue where his at times somewhat eccentric daughter might have got to, an impression confirmed by the occasional sniff from the other side of the locked door.

'Any idea, dear, what seems to be the trouble?' His question took Viv by surprise, though when she looked down and worked out exactly what the trouble was, she couldn't decide whether to laugh or cry. In the end, she did a bit of both before placing her face close to the door, which remained resolutely locked until she'd promised, absolutely, word of honour, bottom of my heart, Fang wasn't going anywhere. Ever. Because Daddy was a very nice daddy really and loved his little cat almost as much as he loved his little daughter.

There was a sound, suspiciously like a harrumph, then a decisive click as the bolt was pulled back. Phew. Crisis over then.

'Poor Fang hasn't got a voice,' Trudi explained patiently, when Percy and Viv gently tried to tease out of her exactly what she'd been thinking. 'So I had to act for him.'

Just this once, both her parents realised their daughter really wasn't acting. And were both rather impressed.

*

No question Trudi's a million times better than President Mugwump at giving a voice to those who haven't got one. When his chief spook explained there was no point hanging around Belfast, he fired the whole team. Next, true to form, he hired another bunch of highly trained operatives and told them there was no point hanging around Belfast.

After thorough consultation with the State Department, carefully bypassing the White House, the new top spy accepted that Northern Ireland was a kind of British colony. Also, London was the capital of England, which he'd always thought was a village near Paris. So, by a process of elimination, it was decided they'd better head there next.

Mugwump was on the point of unleashing a twitterstorm on the lines of: *Always new Belfast was waist of time! Kill cheefs not nativess*! Then remembered it's best to keep quiet about top secret operations.

Enjoying the peace that had descended on the Europa piano bar, Monty decided to check out Paddy and his mate. Worth a try, as the notes he'd compared with Biff read like a whodunnit minus the bit saying who actually did do it. Not that he was terribly hopeful, as the young heroes were sitting pert and poised for action, notebooks and pencils at the ready, even though there was no sign of the Chancerys or their Chinese comrades either.

'You can put the scribbling pads away, lads. Have a pint on me instead.'

The two Irishmen were suspicious of Monty's cultured English voice but liked the idea of a proper Guinness instead of the measly halves they'd been getting up till now. Easily bought, Monty thought, seeing as he hadn't even said who he was.

When he did, the boys were in such a muddle that they went through the caps on wrong/right right/wrong wrong/right way round routine all over again. Yes, he was a mate of Biff's, but no, he had worked closely with a British prime minister. It was like the Angel Gabriel teaming up with Heinrich Himmler or Hermann Goering. Against that, a pint's a pint.

'Those five fingers, on each hand, the work of the devil to be sure to be sure,' Paddy began, having no idea that the froth from the Guinness smeared across his top lip made him look like an ancient walrus, minus geeky teeth, obviously.

'Bejesus, could hardly believe it. The colleen said she wanted to prick Penislow's eyeballs and drink the juice. If she's not the devil, the pope's a Proddie.'

Monty suppressed a yawn and tried to look on the bright side. At least they weren't shouting.

'They said something about looking for fires somewhere. And everything going west. Didn't get that bit, didn't seem worth writing down.'

'You certain they didn't say they were going to the Smoke? Heading up west?' Suddenly Monty was all ears.

'Same difference, to be sure, to be sure. Er, to be sure ..?' Paddy wasn't.

Monty smiled and ordered three more pints. Of course they'd have moved on to London. They'd done what they needed to here; Biff had already got that bit from these lads' ramblings. And the Yanks had almost certainly gone the same way, whether or not they had a clue what POTUS had in mind. No one ever did, least of all POTUS.

*

Things had calmed down a bit in Primrose Hill. Bubbly and Squeaky were carrying on as normal, though Fantasia was disappointed she couldn't get them to eat the torture chair's thumbscrews. She took an Uber all the way to Islington to pick up lashings of salmon paste from the fishmonger's in Essex Road, but smearing it over the wretched things didn't do the trick. Otters aren't that bright, but they can tell the difference between their favourite food and an instrument of torture.

Still, Fantasia needed to keep up the pressure on her partner to keep up the pressure on the PM, because Chancery was keeping up the pressure on her. And though she'd failed to paste up the otters, she hoped at least to butter up Egeria.

'You see, people like us, you know, ministers and whatnot, we only think we're running the show, but it's people like you who are actually in charge.' Her simpering tone, and theory that flattery will get you anywhere, worked. Just this once.

'Tiddledick's idea of intelligence gathering consists of little more than asking yours truly what's best for Britain. As he leaves boring graft like reading the papers to Fanny, who rarely gets past *Penthouse, Mayfair, FHM* and *Razzle*, yours truly truly rules the roost.'

Egeria followed this up with the look a brilliant public speaker would give an enraptured audience, that said *no need for applause, ladies and gentlemen, it was nothing, really, nothing at all.* Though it's very much for the best that Trudi never met her, she'd have been interested in that technique and would have practised it for hours in front of a mirror.

That said, even at only four-and-a-half-and-a-bit, she would have recognised it helps to get your facts straight. Fanny Tiddledick was extremely well read, albeit about everything except politics. Erewego was spot-on with Ponsomby, however, and rejoiced in her infallible sifting system for keeping him in the dark.

Stuff like recommendations that top civil servants get huge pay rises and super-gold-plated pension schemes went into a red box marked "Essential". Ordinary things, like recommendations that top civil servants only get large pay rises and generous pension schemes, went into a red box marked "Important". And really annoying guff, like recommendations that top civil servants settle for inflation-linked pay rises and bog-standard pension schemes, were jammed into a red box marked "Boring".

Any hint that any section of society is less than a hundred

per cent in favour of buying cut-price Chinese trains with the electronic capacity to infiltrate and control the nation's security apparatus and hence potentially take over running the country would be at the very bottom of the "Boring" box. Or in the bin.

*

Percy had long suspected as much, so wasn't terribly hopeful about Viv's idea of posting to Number Ten the findings of carefully targeted polls specifically worded to put the fear of God up people. Or rather, the fear of a Chinese takeover of Britain's security apparatus and thus the government of the country.

'I wonder which is worse,' he wondered. 'The pissy Almighty does have a lot to answer for, when you consider the fall of man and all that, but those Beijing bastards must be at least a close second.'

It was Viv's turn to wonder, as she glanced down at the Almighty's representative on earth, what Nice Little Earner's tariff was for two rude words and blasphemy in the same sentence. She also wondered whether the child had a system of multiplying up the penalties, like shifting from simple to compound interest, if there were multiple sins.

In the event, Percy got lucky, as Trudi was too busy to trying to teach Fang to play chess to notice. And getting very cross about the stupid animal's transparent attempts at cheating. Whenever she moved a piece into a really threatening place on the board, he dabbed it onto the floor, with a really smug expression on his face.

Every time he did this, she stamped furiously, and, it being an old house, the effect was felt everywhere. Percy thought about the particularly nice time he and Viv had had the night before, which must have got the chandelier immediately below their bedroom shaking and tinkling. What if Nanny had heard? What on earth would she have thought?

Just then, the young lady in question limped into the room, the expression on her face an odd mixture of inward satisfaction and outward discomfort. She wandered out again a moment later, having first asked Percy not to forget her special supplies next time he popped into Boots, which she hoped would be soon. Also, a first for her, she wondered if he wouldn't mind getting her some nice soothing ointment.

Percy had an uncomfortable feeling he knew why she was feeling uncomfortable.

CHAPTER FOURTEEN

Having rogered and copied their instructions to keep their mission extra top secret, the fresh spooks covered their tracks before they'd really made any by taking a roundabout route via Vilnius in Lithuania and touching down at London Southend Airport.

A secure beachhead, albeit horribly pebbly as well as getting on for forty miles off target. Though if they'd taken off their sunglasses at the terminal, they'd have spotted the purpose-built railway station just a hundred paces away.

But they didn't, so they didn't.

Trudi would have pointed out that Southend and London are very different places, culturally as well as geographically, as the locals' habit of drinking the nasty water meant they missed out bits of words. She'd have found the spooks' Texan drawl rather peculiar too, but more English than Southend language. If they'd asked what the nicest bit of the town was, she'd have recommended the road out.

But they didn't, so she didn't.

Had they told the taxi driver to take them to Southend Central railway station, they'd still have made it to Fenchurch Street in about an hour. Alternatively, he'd have been well chuffed if they'd asked him to drive them all the way to the City.

But they didn't, so he wasn't.

Instead, they demanded to be taken to the town centre, then called the cabbie an ignorant Limey for not knowing where Primrose Hill was. He shrugged his shoulders and dropped them at the top of the High Street, where no one else could tell them how to get there either.

'Pimwose 'ill? Wossat when it's at 'ome den? Ne'vah 'erd of it, mite.'

'An' anuvvah fing, can't you keep yer bleedin' voice dahn? Yer givin' me a right bleedin' 'eadache, arse-ache.'

The team's spokesperson, or, rather, shoutsperson, Hank, who'd got the job on account of his outstanding people skills, handled the situation with due delicacy. Mindful of his orders not to compromise top-secret missions by gunning people down on sidewalks, he went no further than fumbling in his shoulder holster, releasing the safety catch and cocking his pistol. He forgot certain obvious precautions as an idea struck him.

'Aw, shucks, guys, let's get outta here and relax by the Thames.' He'd got the right river, though the bit they headed for was about five miles wider than at Tower Bridge.

*

Trudi would have told them the second least worst place to check out in the Southend area was Leigh-on-Sea. Her until then not very successful seaside trip had ended up in the amazingly unmessed-up historic fishing village called the Old Town, where she'd enjoyed looking at the pretty little cockle boats bobbing about.

She was only sorry they hadn't brought Fang along for the ride, as all those seafood sheds everywhere would have got him thinking he'd died and gone to heaven. She begged Daddy to buy a little tub of prawns for him to try when they got home, but Viv told her by then his little treat would have so gone off, he would certainly die. But not go to heaven, Percy added, with a lot of feeling.

Remembering the rude and, as it turned out for Daddy, expensive things he said last time Fang playfully got his claws out, Trudi had decided it was time for a little sermon.

'But doesn't that boring man with the funny clothes on say you're supposed to forgive your enemies, Daddi?' Though she was giving him her special wide-eyed butter-wouldn't-melt look, he spotted the wicked crinkle and wasn't having any of it.

'To my certain knowledge, the vicar does not have a cat,' he hissed. 'And if he did, I'm quite sure he would not turn the other toe every time he got attacked.'

Viv patted Percy sympathetically on the arm but couldn't help smiling all the way to the car, which, as was so often the way, refused to start until Trudi got her little hammer out. When the engine spluttered into life, the racket drowned out all thoughts of Fang's minor misdemeanours and Percy's mortal sins. And by the time they'd wobbled past Canvey Island, the little girl was curled up in the back, fast asleep, having sad dreams about Daddy not using any swearwords about the vicar.

*

While the Penislow day out had started badly but gradually picked up, the same went for Hank and his chums. Wandering along the London Road got them no closer to the river, but it has so many car showrooms that they actually took off their sunglasses and suddenly felt at home. The Harley Davidson motorbikes they'd been peering at were actually four classic Ford Mustangs, coolest wheels on the planet. As the spivvy salesman had no idea that the Mustang's stateside nickname was the Pony, he didn't realise how good his offer sounded.

'Take da lot off me 'ands and I'll knock off a pony. Aah's dat sand?'

Sounded so much better than the twenty-five pound discount for bulk the spiv had in mind that Hank decided the Director of National Intelligence would agree his team was upholding the finest American traditions. A fast buck is what you get in a Pony. Real fast.

The bloke was so gobsmacked at how many fast bucks he'd made that afternoon that he went to the trouble of marking the route to the nearest half– decent beach on a map, and even toyed with actually giving it to them for free. It didn't come to that, but he did knock twenty-five pence off.

As an alpha male, Hank isn't hot on multi-skilling, though even a woman would struggle to read a map while driving ridiculously fast on unknown roads in an unknown car. Somehow, he found the beach, but struggled when Leigh Old Town's cobbled and only roadway abruptly stopped. A violent handbrake turn onto the little harbour slowed him down and he came to a halt by nudging a couple of parked cars. Over the edge.

The other skidding Ponies brought the total to eight, which, unlike the cars, didn't go down well, though the geezer in the café cheered up when they ordered, by American standards, not much food at all. Only eighteen portions of chips, eighteen pints of prawns and eighteen full English breakfasts, as they didn't want to look greedy.

*

Trudi's never wanted to look greedy either, though things have a way of turning out right for her, like whenever Daddy uses inappropriate language, she's always got her pink piggy handy. Because it's too big to carry around in her pocket, and Fang doesn't just drop it at her feet like a dead birdie trophy, Percy once asked the obvious question.

'What is it with you, Trudi darling, this extraordinary knack of knowing before I do when I'm going to bloody well swear?'

Oops. Silly Daddy. Done it again. Viv sniggered and Percy paid. Having no idea his clever daughter could read from the lines in his face when he was about to go off on one, he put it down to coincidence.

Wrong.

That's not to say things never just come right. Take the Yankee spooks showing up at the same place as the two horrible Brits tasked with shafting them. For Charlie and Spleeny, it made perfect sense, as the direct flight from Belfast to London Southend Airport landed them conveniently close to their home sweet home, on Canvey Island. This meant they could have a spot of R and R, and relieve the sitter of Caligula, Charlie's sweet little whiskery pet. Spleeny had never taken to the animal but had come to accept that if she cooked it for dinner, her husband would smell a rat. Literally, in this case.

Eventually, they'd have to hammer up the A13 to the Smoke, but at least they could do it in the comfort of their own car, a classic Mustang, as it happens. Though he's slow on the uptake, Charlie likes travelling fast, including in his speedboat.

Terrorising water skiers and sailors was thrilling, and Spleeny had worked out a points system for the different classes of victim. Lowest scores went to able-bodied adult males, highest to defenceless children, with a bonus if they had any physical disability. The police once set off in hot pursuit in one of their high-speed launches, but it got too hot for them when Charlie poured a tank of petrol over the stern and put a match to it.

Today felt just right for a quick round trip to Leigh Old Town, taking in a pint or two at his favourite pub, the Crooked Billet. Or, as he fondly nicknamed it, the Crooked.

'Woss all dat caper?' Spleeny was puzzled by the upturned cars, some on the decks of fishing boats, others just bobbing around aimlessly.

'Well, strike a light,' Charlie muttered, thinking of the day he torched the police launch. He was more interested, however, in the jammy jam jars on the harbour.

Because she's a girl, Spleeny hadn't noticed them, but when Charlie pointed them out, she was on it. Even if the keys weren't in the ignition, he knew, but she didn't, that they'd be easy to hotwire. And as Canvey's only a twenty-minute drive away, they could have the lot stowed away in the barn behind their gaff in under three hours.

Once again, everybody happy then. Apart from the Yanks, in this case.

CHAPTER FIFTEEN

Trudi's been figure-conscious since her third birthday. After blowing out the candles and making a secret wish that Daddy would swear more often, she rounded off the performance by tucking into three slices of the really yummy cake. But then it all went horribly wrong. Though she rarely took much notice of the silly things silly grown-ups come out with, something Mummy's cousin Bertha said got to her.

'Goodness gracious me, you'll get fat.'

Viv, who's never much liked the woman but had to invite her because she was on holiday in Cornwall, thought she was one to talk. It struck her the name was well chosen, though how Bertha's parents could tell what their baby would turn into remains one of life's unknowns. Likewise the connection between that throwaway remark and the conspiracy between Trudi and Fang that would last right through her teen years.

She'd eat up some of what was put in front of her like a good girl, but set aside what she knew the cat would probably go for. Then she'd deploy her dazzling repertoire of cunning tricks, getting any adults present to look out of the window, behind a flower vase, up one another's noses, anywhere except in the direction of her plate.

Fang had quickly learned to position himself under the table, and how to eat quickly and quietly. It was years before Percy and Viv figured out how come a cat who was so picky with the food they gave him could always look so glossy and healthy. Trudi was smart enough to cover her tracks by heartily tucking in when she was really starving after school, then looking surprised that people looked surprised.

That day in Leigh Old Town, Hank and his henchmen did, as they did all the time, what Trudi did, a good deal more moderately, just once a day. And the bloke in the café couldn't resist bulking out the plates with one of an English breakfast's less expensive ingredients. Three large cans of baked beans per person? Better for profits than guts.

The Yanks were relieved, in more ways than one, that they hadn't splattered the public toilets on the harbour as well as all those cars. Also handy for Charlie, as the cubicles' doors remained locked long enough for him to get the first Pony rearing off to Canvey and himself back via speedboat in time for the second. Almost. As Hank stepped out into the open air, he stopped feeling much better when he spotted what was going on.

'Hey, you, asshole, get your thieving hands off my Pony!'

Chancery's not great on reading but does dip into American criminal history. Which is how come he was able to quote what a relatively eloquent Chicago gangster said when the Feds caught up with him.

'This is a helluva time to be caught without a gun.'

Only one thing for it; Charlie leapt headlong into the

back of the speedboat and screamed at Spleeny to step on the gas. Not that that would have guaranteed they'd have got away, as they were very much in range of a very cross Hank. Against that, a fat slob heaving a whopping Smith and Wesson XVR 460 Magnum from a shoulder holster is not like Clint Eastwood whipping out a Colt 45 revolver. Hank fired quickly, but unwisely.

Never a good idea to leave pistols in shoulder holsters cocked with their safety catches off, because when you're trying to get them out, the trigger finger can get in the way of your own safety. The expression *shoot oneself in the foot* isn't often meant literally, and, as Hank was about to discover, it's not a nice sensation.

*

There was a whizzbang moment too in the House of Lords, where Percy had tabled an urgent question concerning the threat to national security posed by the potential purchase of Chinese trains for the High Speed Two project. The government's security spokesman wasn't up to high speed, or even a gentle amble, on Ponsomby Tiddledick's thinking on the subject, as he was ninety-five and suffered ninety-five per cent memory loss.

'Over my dead body,' he harrumphed.

Percy liked the sound of that, and would have blown the not quite dead body a kiss, if it hadn't felt like necrophilia. Meantime, forgetting he was in the chamber, not Annie's Bar when it was still open, the ancient buffer boomed on.

'Bloody disgrace if you ask me. Never trusted those rotten rats since the fall of Shanghai.'

Fellow peers started dozing off, and when he got on to teaching Johnny Foreigner a lesson, preferably with gunboats, the only hack in the press gallery did too. Pity, as subsequent speakers agreed that the Chinese trains would be worse than a meteorite taking out London. Quite a scoop for the *Railway Gazette*, as well as a handy hint for Tiddledick.

Or would have been, if he'd got to hear about it. Percy had a feeling he wouldn't, at this stage, given how he suspected Egeria Erewego operated, but thought it worth a try.

After heavily underlining the fruitiest sections from the Lords' official verbatim record, he addressed an envelope to *Number Ten, attention the prime minister.* There was a neat bit of irony from an ex-head of the secret service, who never misses anything, except a mixed metaphor. He said Beijing taking over the job was a delicious idea, as they couldn't do worse than the spotty dicks making such a dog's dinner of it now.

There was also the suggestion from a one-time Tory leader of a certain age that horses are the only reliable way of getting around. At that point, Percy couldn't resist pencilling in a caricature of Fanny. Because he was rather proud of his work, he regretted showing it to Viv and Trudi, though for the little girl it was a cue she'd been waiting for for a while now.

'I love my little pussy…' she began, brightly, in a tone of voice that clearly indicated she hadn't finished. Percy and Viv exchanged a glance, hoping this wasn't a lead-up to the birds and bees routine, again. But it wasn't.

'The problem with Fang is, he's not big enough for me to ride on. Was probably too little even when I was little, and certainly much too little now.'

Mummy and Daddy could hardly argue with that, though Percy secretly thought it wouldn't be such a bad thing if Trudi did squish the little beast; it'd save him a fortune in Elastoplast. However, it was all too obvious what was coming next.

'I was thinking,' Trudi wasn't given to wheedling, but she gave it a go now, 'I was thinking maybe if you got me a little horse, I could become a champion jumper and make lots of money.' The great big eyes were only an opening gambit. They had a steely glint as she played her trump card.

'I could buy you a nice new car, Mummi, that would start all by its own. Then I could make even more money by selling my little hammer, and use it to buy you lots of lovely dresses. You'd like that, wouldn't you, Mummi?'

Mummy thought that would be splendid, but wasn't sure a small plastic hammer would fetch enough at Bonhams to get her very far in Bond Street, though Daddy thought Trudi's oversized helmet would make a great riding hat.

It was no surprise that Mummy closed the discussion with the annoying "when-you're-a-little-bit-older" patter. Pester power it would have to be, then, starting with fake tears. In time, she'd get the hang of the actors' special way of really crying, but for now dabbing her eyes and making weird wailing noises would have to do.

It didn't occur to Trudi that Viv meant exactly what she said, but she wouldn't have been that impressed even if she had. When you're four-and-a-half-and-a-bit, the day after tomorrow is a lifetime away. Everyone knows that, silly.

Meantime, there was the matter of Percy's picture of a human looking like a horse, and Viv's strongly held belief that while Ponsomby might think it was funny, Fanny might not.

'Think about it. Would you laugh at a *Spitting Image* image of you looking like Fang?'

He did think about it, and so did Trudi, who by now had cheered up enough to dry her eyes, which weren't the slightest bit wet in the first place, and gently set him straight.

'You're a very nice daddi, Daddi, and I love you very much. Especially as you're the only daddi I've got. And you're quite clever too, which is surprising, considering you're only a man. But you have to face facts, Daddi. Fang is prettier than you.'

Percy looked at his daughter, and his wife, in a resigned way. And got the rubber out.

*

Back in Cornwall two days later, Percy and Viv awaited developments.

So did Fang, though he knew it wouldn't take long. The lovely hot day meant those annoying Chelsea boots would soon be replaced with something more comfortable, and more suitable, from his point of view. He pounced, Percy recoiled and Trudi giggled hysterically, before she remembered she was Daddy's Little Helper and got out the rolled-up newspaper.

As Fang clawed his way up the nearest weeping willow tree, which seemed fitting, as he was bored to tears by always having to run for his life, Viv smiled contentedly. Everything felt just as it should.

'Savage, psychopathic and strangely soothing, don't you think, darling?' she murmured to her breathless little daughter. Trudi, who always liked loads of words that started with the same letter, or at least sounded as if they did, answered back in kind.

'Silli sod's sodding scarpered!'

Viv raised her elegantly expressive eyebrows and toyed with hunting for the pink piggy swear box and demanding a refund on Percy's behalf, but remembered she'd got rather more important things to do. Like switching on the computer and banging out what she hoped would be just the right form of words to Fanny Tiddledick.

Happy hubby still, darling? Corpsing at corpses chewing over chuffers? Better dead than red! Read any good books lately? Red benches blaa-blaa!

A bit cryptic, but Viv calculated that if Ponsonby had seen the Hansard extract Percy sent him, he'd have had a moan about it. And about the stupid old farts who'd be better off six feet under Primrose Hill. Not of course if he hadn't. Fanny's answer confirmed as much.

Sweet Fanny Adams, darling! Poncey's in the pink. Except when I whip him into shape! Goes red in the rectum then! Wrecked 'em? Do my best!

Percy and Viv were too busy smirking at Fanny's way of putting things to notice a young woman and a small person peering over their shoulders at the screen. For Nanny, the words caused a nice sensation in her lady garden, while Trudi thought, and indeed stated clearly, that grown-ups are just weird.

'Wibbly wobbly wankers, one-and-all.' She wasn't clear what all these words meant, and had no idea at all that "wanker" and "one" only sound as if they start with the same letter, but don't really.

What Viv couldn't understand was how come Trudi and Trudi alone always knew exactly where to find the swear box.

CHAPTER SIXTEEN

Trudi had often heard Percy use that rude-sounding word that rhymed with anchor, usually when he was talking about someone he didn't like very much. But the way he tried to suppress a giggle when she said it suggested maybe she'd crossed a line somewhere. Though, when she asked Nanny what it meant, all she got by way of an answer was a dreamy sigh and a faraway look, which didn't help much. But she had good works to do; saving Daddy's soul and making Fang more comfortable at nights.

The look on the cat's face as she fished the swear box out of its latest hiding place confirmed he hadn't much liked that lumpy piggy thing thing under the mattress in his basket.

She'd recently devised a new strategy with Daddy. Rather than making him cough up every time he said something rude and thus discouraging him from repeating his mistake, for the moment at least, she went for jotting down all the suspect words, then hitting him with them when he'd got over his hissy fit.

There had been some debate within the family as to whether the word "fart", as in "daffy old", counted as a suspect word. After batting the matter to and fro between them, they settled for a points draw. But in the end Trudi did have to cough up a quid after she'd tried to give Fang a high five. He'd responded by getting his claws out and she'd called him a stinky bloody mog.

She got her own back, and the quid, and a fair few more when Percy and Viv got down to analysing Fanny's odd emails. Shame she couldn't clap her hands, but even someone as skilled at multi-skilling as her couldn't do that at the same time as trying to write things down.

'Of course prime ministers don't open their own bloody letters,' Percy grumbled. 'Their sodding strap-on brains get there first.

'The buggeration is, we don't know whether the fat cow buried my stuff at the bottom of the "Boring" box or bunged it in her crappy bin.' Scribbling like a girl possessed, Trudi almost asked him to slow down a bit, but thought better of it in time.

She'd have managed wealth beyond dreams if Percy had realised his ploy had given Erewego an idea. Yesterday's man wants to meddle? Two can play at that game! After shredding the letter, she dug out a research document that looked respectable but was as even-handed as Hitler's take on Jews, gypsies and gays. The snappily titled *Anglo-Sino Solidarity Helpfully Offering Legitimate Expertise* claimed to have conducted detailed in-depth analysis, and its conclusions made David Cameron's idea of a golden era in UK-Chinese relations sound almost like a declaration of war.

It argued that if we linked arms with the brilliant Beijing

government then never mind roses in Picardy, a trillion flowers would bloom in Piccadilly. It'd end our post-Brexit isolation and put the damn Yanks in their place. Right the wrong inflicted by that upstart Washington when he insisted on not being a British colony anymore.

Erewego set aside all thoughts of useful idiots, nobbling or out-and-out corruption as she copied and pasted the whole thing, printed out a hard copy and carefully placed it in splendid isolation in a new, specially devised red box marked: "Absolutely vital to the nation's wellbeing".

She did spot that after the heading, the title *Anglo-Sino Solidarity Helpfully Offering Legitimate Expertise* was shortened to the acronym A.S.S.H.O.L.E., but was pretty confident Tiddledick wouldn't.

*

It is possible, just, to not notice a small child slipping her food under the table for the good of her figure, if not necessarily her cat's. It's also vaguely plausible that a person clever enough to become prime minister could somehow miss the acronym A.S.S.H.O.L.E. But it's out of the question that any human being, no matter how stupid, could fail to register a bullet in the foot.

What happened to Hank on Old Leigh Harbour was a painful reminder never to leave the Wesson XVR 460 Magnum cocked with the safety catch off, and guaranteed a spell MIA. And when the ambulance arrived, the other spooks accidentally did Chancery a huge favour by clambering into the back, hands in their shoulder holsters, in case this was some slimy Limey trick to kidnap Hank.

Charlie couldn't believe his luck when he popped back on the off-chance. Goodbye, armed Yanks with troubled guts; hello, shiny Ponies with dented bumpers. By bedtime, he was the proud if unlawful owner of five classic Mustangs, which dear little Caligula couldn't wait to customise. Those seats would beat the Last Supper, even though the leather did look a tad chewy.

After a couple of days in Southend General Hospital, the spooks returned to Old Leigh to find in place of their Ponies a notice tied to a lamppost that read: *Pssst, anyone wanna buy a Pony? Fore goin' beggin' darn da rowed. Discahnt four bulk perchus. Fone dis numbah.*

When he heard an American voice on the blower, Charlie decided he'd better wear a wig, change the plates on the motors and daub the interiors with jellied eels, to put the buyers off the scent. Not that they'd recognise the vehicles anyway, thanks to Caligula, who was very much an eat-anything-within-range kind of rat.

*

By this point, schools were out and Cornwall was doing its usual give-the-summer-holidaymakers-a-hard-time thing. It was unseasonably cold, the wind had got up, white horses were scudding across the bay and Fang was being even madder than usual. So Percy decided they all needed a break from the little brute, and, anyway, it was time for everyone to put their heads together.

There'd be ample space for his little lot, plus Biff but mercifully minus crazy cat, and cat-sitting nanny, in the flat attached to Viv's Mayfair office. It happened that Monty's old flat in Kentish Town was temporarily between tenants, meaning he and Bakyt could stay there and share tender memories of their first nights together. And relive them with gusto.

Up till then, everyone had relied on Zoom meetings, but they'd been liable to distractions caused by one animal scratching screens, another endlessly serving notice the Brits should get out and a third regularly running off with a computer mouse clamped in his jaws. Besides, Percy reckoned it was safe to assume all the people they were trailing had by now all decamped to somewhere near Westminster.

Unfortunately, he'd failed to factor in Fang's fiendish cleverness. All that packing could only mean one thing, and he had no plans to be left behind with boring annoying Nanny like last time. As a result, when they made it to Mayfair they got a shock, on opening Trudi's case, to find a cat comfily curled up among the pretty pink knickers, opening one eye and purring smugly.

The little girl was delighted, unlike her parents. But Percy was philosophical enough to accept he'd be safer here than back home, as he was hardly going to be wearing sandals in London, whatever the weather. In the event, Fang had other things on his mind, thanks to Biff, who'd become a tad more eccentric since he left Downing Street. Apart from his Belfast accent becoming more pronounced, his waistcoats becoming greener and his hair longer, he'd made it a rule never to go anywhere without Lady Casement.

Having decided to kill and eat the creature immediately, Fang was shocked to learn that feline fecking eejits were worse than unfeeling fecking Brits. Quite apart from the racist and cattist aspects of what he was hearing, he was struggling to work out whether this was a bird at all. They don't as a rule talk, at least not within his experience.

Still less do they follow up a string of insults with a nasty nip on the tail, which got him hopping mad, or, rather, madly hopping, and suddenly wishing himself back home with lovely, interesting Nanny.

Tired but extremely happy, Trudi dreamt of pterodactyls and tigers slugging it out, but didn't know which horse to back. She didn't know about mixed metaphors either.

CHAPTER SEVENTEEN

In the morning, Trudi was up bright and early. Amazingly so for her, but she was a maiden on a mission. Like turning five, it's not every day a girl gets to meet a real live, talking pterodactyl. Or even an African grey parrot.

If Fang could have talked, he'd have said hell hath no fury like a cat scorned, or at least a cat of his sensitive and delicate disposition, not that Percy would recognise the description. But the unhappy pussy hadn't clocked that life for girls of four-and-a-half-and-a-bit really is a now experience; neither did he realise the only way to beat 'em is to join 'em.

His tail really hurt too.

In his jealous rage, he clawed his little mattress out of his little basket and dabbed Trudi's horrid, nasty, smelly piggy bank onto the floor. Because cats get out of sorts on less than seventeen hours' sleep, it was a minor victory. While for Viv, finally getting her hands on the wretched thing was like winning the battles of Agincourt, Waterloo and El Alamein. Amazing how childish grown-ups can be at times.

But her masterplan would have to wait until she'd studied the results of her poll. It confirmed that the British public weren't so dozy as to want to be trampled on by an autocratic communist superpower, while potentially dire consequences for vulnerable minorities, like pigeon fanciers, trainspotters and Morris dancers, didn't bear thinking about. Viv's skilfully framed questions almost always produced the right answers.

Annoyingly, though, respondents' thumbs-up to hols in bracing Skegness, drinking warm beer in musty marquees and scoffing fish 'n'chips wrapped in carcinogenic newsprint meant the British public were pretty dozy after all. Biff's instinctive reaction, that you didn't need a poll to work that out, didn't go down well.

It was agreed that Tiddledick should be spared the boring detail and just given the main finding: that hardly anyone wanted the Chinese trains. So what if British rolling stock made High Speed Two slower and costlier? You get what you pay for, and besides, the tortoise did beat the hare.

Useful ammo for later, but, meantime, new intelligence had come to light by chance, confirming Egeria Erewego's vested interest in the Chinese option. When Paddy's mum interrupted a debriefing session with Biff to tell him it was teatime, he did what he always did. Only this time instead of finally letting him take the call, his special technique of prodding and swiping his smartphone's screen at random led him somewhere he never knew existed: the record/playback function. The sound was fuzzy, but the message wasn't.

Got da footage, like wot you wanted. Dirty? I should coco. De old hag 'ated it. Right cock-up for 'er. Or would've been, if she'd got dat lucky—

At this point, a shrill voice interrupted.

Lucky for you, more like. If you'd got yer end away, like, I'd a chood yer goolies off and, like, fed 'em to yer rat, yer rat.

Next, the first speaker could be heard again, sounding angry but anxious.

Button ye lip, yer lippy tart, or I'll slit yer bleedin' froat. An' it will be bleedin' bleedin' an' all—

But this exchange was cut short by a cultured voice with a hint of a Chinese accent, clearly trying to move the conversation on.

My dears, perhaps you'd care to refrain from philosophical contemplation of the ethical connotations of intimate interplay, and save your sweet nothings for the privacy of the boudoir.

The next sound on the recording seemed be a male and a female in unison, giving a brief and inconclusive response.

Wot?

Undeterred, the cultured voice pressed on.

Gratified we now have the incriminating incentive at our disposal. Kindly hand it over. Handy it will certainly be if the lady shows even rudimentary recalcitrance.

The conversation seemed about to wind up as a second cultured voice, again with a faint oriental inflexion, sounded a note of triumph.

Most unlikely, old boy. I'd say the trout is tickled.

Cultured voice number one, however, was clearly determined to have the last word. It oozed smugness.

In this case, surely, you mean old trout, old bean.

*

Percy shuddered. Last he heard of trout tickling was when a couple of his so-called friends were stitching him up. They got there in the end, which is how come he was no longer prime minister. Viv stroked his arm sympathetically, and though Bakyt didn't know what it was all about, she bared her teeth in solidarity. Even Fang looked up and twitched his tail, grateful, come to think of it, that he'd still got one.

'Chancery's obviously gone to ground somewhere,' Percy snarled, long-suppressed hatred and bitterness bubbling to the surface. 'We're going to have to dig him out, so I can bury him again. This time, hopefully, for good.'

Trudi, who could make no more sense of any of this than Fang, or Lady Casement, if she were honest about it, did pick up on Percy's apparently rather negative take on events.

'Poor Daddi,' she murmured. 'Having a bummer of a bloodi day, are we?'

Hah! The moment Viv had been waiting for! All this time she'd had her trophy/hostage/weapon hidden in her desk drawer. As she whipped it out, Trudi couldn't miss the triumph in her eyes, and gave up without a fight.

'All right, Mummi,' she sighed, holding out her hand. 'Give it to me.'

Seconds later, as if by magic, she'd opened the lid just below the little piggy's botty. Next, she shook out a couple of pound coins and handed them over. It was a fair cop.

Viv hadn't planned to actually take any money off her, but changed her mind when she realised the thing was brimming with cash. Besides, Trudi's expression as good as said she'd lost a skirmish, not a war, as Daddy was the gift that kept on giving. Also, infuriatingly, how she opened the piggy bank was as much of a mystery as how she started Simone-Sitrouenne.

*

At least Percy was able to get to the bottom of one mystery pretty quickly. It only took a few phone calls to old contacts to establish Egeria Erewego's precise address, and confirm that Fantasia Fealstite lived with her.

'Hmm,' ex-Met Monty muttered, 'isn't it high time I upped my game? From gamekeeper to poacher? Did a spot of in-house investigation?'

'Call me old-fashioned,' Viv objected, sensibly. 'I always thought breaking into people's property was against the law.'

Because Bakyt thought so too, she found the idea thrilling. While Trudi, who wasn't quite getting the gist, shuddered at the thought of anyone breaking into Nice Little Earner. How much she'd got stashed away was for her to know and nobody else to find out. Not that she'd have mentioned that bit, even if she'd got the chance. Which she didn't, as Percy had the bit between his teeth.

'Never mind what might or might not stand up in a court of law,' he said, 'if we wire the place up for sound, we'll probably get all we need to force Tiddledick to see reason. He might even get the pigs, er, sorry, Monty, your former colleagues, to nail Chancery for blackmail.'

Trudi was about to point out that pigs worked better as private banks than private armies, but again Percy got in first.

'You never know, it's always possible the woman's got an inside track on the Yanks trying to interfere in British domestic policy as well. Mugwump's face? Smeared with egg? Should make for a tasty omelette.'

'Problem is, he wants what we want, surely,' Monty and Biff pointed out.

'Yes, but Tiddledick will want to think it's something he wants, not something he thinks someone else wants him to want.' This, Viv's second sensible point, was backed by Bakyt, who has a degree in psychology as well as a PhD in nuclear science.

'Of course you right,' she said. 'You one smart lady, Viv. You blokes scruffy suits, not good fitting size.'

Though the words sounded odd, Trudi thought she got the idea, vaguely. And, as this struck her as a battle of the sexes, she decided to even the odds, with the help of Lady Casement.

The two were already best buddies, as the bird lapped up learning as much as the girl loved teaching, and parrots and four-and-a-half-and-a-bit-year-old humans are pretty compatible mentally. Besides, Trudi was much more fun than Biff, who always sounded like a record that had got stuck and wasn't that good in the first place.

So, unbeknown to him or any of the other grown-ups, Lady Casement now had a whole new vocabulary, and after a few whispered words in her ear, wherever it was, she gave them a piece of her mind. And her mentor's.

'Girls are great, boys silly billies. Girls are great, boys silly billies. Girls are great, boys silly billies. Girls are great, boys silly billies. Girls are great, boys silly billies.

'So there.'

CHAPTER EIGHTEEN

Though Fang had had his first decent night's sleep in ages, he was no more cheerful in the morning. Unable to forgive Trudi or that shouty, cattist, tail-biting monster, he sprung onto Percy's lap and glared at Viv as though it was all her fault.

Biff was feeling just as bad. Not least as he suspected his horrible pet had taken the trouble to figure out what some of her new words actually meant. Unlike the stuff he'd taught her, which he was sure she just parroted, in her beastly parroty way. Because she found him boring? Awful thought, that maybe in his case she simply couldn't be bothered.

'Bejesus, no wonder me fecking wives left me,' he muttered miserably. The ladies in question, had they been present, would have wondered what took him so long. Viv tried to look sympathetic, which was tricky as she thought he'd got a point. At least confirmation didn't come till he'd popped out for a pee.

Lady Casement started behaving alarmingly. Rotating

her head in a peculiar fashion, she was making a horrible noise that could have been a human in extreme distress, maybe even dying. Some sounds can be deceptive, and Viv and Trudi didn't manage to decode this one until the bird actually spoke.

'Biff is sooooo boring!'

Suddenly it was sooooo obvious. When people's boredom crosses a certain threshold, the way they yawn can sound as though they're ready to pop their clogs.

Trudi clapped her hands and Viv gave her a high five. Then sorely regretted it. Having been taught her manners from a very early age, she had tried at all times to get her daughter to show some respect for grown-ups, even boring ones. Fat chance, now she'd let her guard down. Amazing how quickly children learn to see through their parents. Viv knew from then on any nonsense on her part would be demolished with no more than a look.

Sometimes, she almost wished she'd had a boy; that way, she may have got a few years' more grace. It might also have helped, though she hated to even think it, if the little one hadn't been so scarily clever, talking in short but complete sentences before her first birthday. Handy for Percy, mind, as it meant when he fumbled with her nappies, she could tell him how to do it properly.

He freely admitted a PhD in political science was more useful for stuff like being prime minister than the everyday practicalities of life. Nappies being a prime example, as he never did get his head round getting the Velcro the right way round. The fact that Trudi definitely did, it having such a bearing on her own comfort, convinced Viv that the child had inherited enough of her genes to get her started. It was still Percy's fault she'd far too many brain cells, though if she was on a spectrum of some kind, at least she wasn't as far up it.

Right now, however, the poor man was demonstrating his downside by missing a warning sign from Fang. Consolingly stroking him was good; not spotting the narrowed eyes and faint hissing was not. Hard to tell whether the animal suspected he was being patronised or was simply feeling irritable, though either way the vicious bite on the hand was a reminder of the need at all times to stay alert.

'Not only could the nation find itself under cyber attack, facilitated by Chinese trains, there's also Charlie Chancery gunning for us, literally,' Percy grumbled. Not that Biff needed reminding. Back in the room now, he'd remembered the note to self to wash his hands to make himself less repugnant, but had forgotten to break the habit of boring on about historic Irish struggles.

'True, we managed to outsmart him last time we got the guns out, but we have to keep our guard up at all times. He only needs to get lucky once.'

Percy had heard that line from Biff so often that he could see why Lady Casement fancied someone else to talk to.

*

A plan, of sorts, had been cooked up, at least for the day. Monty and Biff would fit up Erewego's joint, Percy would sniff around parliament for confirmation of a rumour that Fyok Yu and Hon Ki had been cosying up to the Intelligence and Security Committee, and Bakyt and Viv would keep the peace between Fang, Trudi and Lady Casement. Though the women's task, at this stage, wouldn't directly further the cause of keeping Chinese trains off British tracks, they'd probably got the trickiest job.

Picking locks, disabling alarms and planting bugs are a doddle for Monty, who spent much of his time in the Metropolitan Police Force nudging the limits of the law. Biff does too in Belfast, though often from the other side of the fence. That habit of his at Westminster, throwing stones at the statue of Oliver Cromwell outside parliament whenever Monty's colleagues weren't looking, was nothing to what he gets up to these days.

So he had no problem now with letting off a small smoke bomb on the pavement near Erewego's house, so no one would notice Monty slipping in. There was plenty of time, as members of the cabinet who weren't away on holiday were meeting, and the woman would always sit in, to make sure her underlings taking notes didn't misunderstand conclusions. Or, rather, didn't fail to misrepresent them if they weren't to her liking.

She found something almost balletic in the way the tiniest tweak to cabinet minutes could set the civil service pirouetting off so far wide of the intended direction. Leaving ministers unable to alter the course once it'd been set. Fair or otherwise.

Well, Ponsomby was going to be set wise whether he liked it or not, because it was for his own good. Same as that time Percy really had to insist Trudi didn't eat the cake she'd made out of shredded stinging nettles and mud, topped off with pink shoe polish. It was months before she finally admitted it might not have tasted very nice.

*

Safely inside Erewego's elegant-looking pad, Monty was gobsmacked at the contrast between the oh-so-best-behaviour street view and the oh-so-naughty-naughty interior. He wondered what Bakyt would make of the torture chair, and muttered a line from his favourite Ibsen play. '*But good god, people don't do such things.*'

Not being a great reader, Chancery would have gone for "cor blimey, strewth, stroll on", but Monty prefers to put things more delicately, even though what he'd just said meant pretty much the same thing. After careful consideration, mainly consisting of asking himself what Bakyt would have suggested, he hid a bug in earshot of the infernal machine.

There was also the obvious option of the whopping four-poster bed, though when he noticed the room was full of prints from the Marquis de Sade's spectacularly pornographic book *120 Days of Sodom,* he went all Chancery. 'Cor blimey, strewth, stroll on.' Even for a gent as civilised as Monty, there are times when needs must.

Naturally, he had a quick nosey round the fat perv's desk drawers while he was there, and couldn't believe his luck. Recent correspondence from the Chinese Embassy, with subtle but unmistakeable references to tasty little sweeteners to come, suggested Fyok Yu and Hon Ki had been busy shoring up the blackmail rap already sorted with her lady friend. Nothing definite, but the progressively warmer tone of the incoming material revealed clear if circumstantial evidence of yet another tickled trout.

'Percy will love this,' he murmured as he photographed each page. 'Tiddledick won't.'

A quick text to Biff and the street was suddenly all foggy again. By the time it cleared, the two of them were well on the way to the garage in Pratt Street where the Wolseley had been discreetly tucked away. Not that anyone would have suspected them of any wrongdoing, thanks to the extra large nuns' costumes Viv had dug out from her dressing-up box before leaving Cornwall.

Monty thought disguising himself as a woman was rather a laugh. But Biff didn't fancy making a habit of it.‡

---

‡ The reader must decide if that dreadful joke was even more dreadful than the last really dreadful joke.

CHAPTER NINETEEN

Trudi was starting to feel sorry for Fang. From the moment she'd been old enough to realise he'd got more legs but fewer arms than her, she'd adopted him as in all other respects her other half.

Now that Lady Casement had become the little girl equivalent of her latest squeeze, she wondered if that might explain his new habit of biting her favourite dollies and sitting in front of her, pointedly facing the opposite direction and twitching his tail. He even once did wee-wees on one of her books.

Her remedy, after first chasing him all round the flat with a rolled-up newspaper, was to save him the trouble of always having to wash himself by filling the sink with lovely soapy water and popping him in. She couldn't understand why this didn't cheer him up.

It seemed a pity Mummy and Daddy weren't keen on going back to that quite nice place near that horrid place they'd once visited. They could have taken Fang with them and given him those prawns that would have made him so happy.

At that very moment, and in that neck of the woods, Chancery was managing to make what was left of Hank, and his friends, every bit as happy as Fang would have been. Admittedly, the four gleaming Mustangs he'd just sold them had slightly damaged seats, but in all other respects were so perfect that they surely owed him a drink. After all, he'd done them such a good turn, turning up at exactly the right moment, with exactly what they wanted.

Besides, he found their company as reassuring as Trudi did when she met a child twice her age who didn't know how to tie his shoelaces and thought America was somewhere in Devon. She had found someone less totally brilliant than herself; he had stumbled on people more totally stupid than him.

He was on a roll, as well as eating one that was oozing the sort of seafood sauce that would have driven Fang frantic. All courtesy of his customers, and nicely topping up the hundred per cent profit on the jam jars and free jars in the Lobster Smack.

The pub, in a nice spot not far from Chancery's home, was usually referred to as the Smack, which always appealed to Spleeny, given her business interests. Canvey's easy-going ways don't extend to open sale of heroin in the shops and this had created a stimulating gap in the market.

In the hope his new customers would become new friends without realising they were actually old friends, of friends at least, Chancery had made adjustments. The stubbly skull certainly changed him, though his nose was as stubby as ever.

Spleeny had spluttered she'd sooner die than dye, then

remembered Hank's huge pistol. If he managed to point it at her head instead of his foot, her wish might come true. Charlie wasn't struck on the lairy hair, though it did remind him of a song his old mum used to sing to him in his cot when she'd run out of brandy to shut him up. *Somewhere Over the Rainbow.*

Turned out their disguises were a waste of effort, as Hank's colleagues' dark glasses meant they couldn't have passed on any descriptions, even if they'd been given the chance to. But it was obvious to Chancery who they were, thanks to the racket they made and the fact they all looked the same. Also, he'd picked up enough of their bellowed conversation to figure out exactly what their game was. Neatly summed up by Mugwump on Twitter.

So diserpointed our frends and alyce in Ingland gottit all rong with Kung futile trayns. Shood no hoo there frends are by now!! Dumbo dedbeet lymeys!!

Percy once showed some of this stuff to Trudi, and when he told her who'd written it, she was jolly relieved that America was further away than Devon, as it was frightening to think such a big country could be run by such an obviously little person. She could only hope his mummy remembered to do up his shoelaces for him.

*

Though Chancery had yet to have his life changed beyond all recognition by meeting Trudi, he'd have given her a high five if she'd been with him that day. Though the Yanks probably could have found America on a map, they'd never heard of Devon.

Stupid though he knew he was, he was convinced he could do what Trudi did to more or less everyone. Wrap them round his little finger. With the buying business done and froth from his beer smeared all over his, sad to say, rather weak little chin, he began to tentatively probe.

'Fing is, me ole cocker, dat Penislow geezer don't know wot's good for 'im.' Charlie's tone was intended to imply he'd no idea who any of them were, but was just making conversation, as one does, with oversexed and overpaid tourists who happened to be over here.

'My bosses wanna set 'im straight wiv dose Chinese trains your geezer don't want 'im to buy. Nah wot 'ee really needs is a spot of persuasion.'

In what direction he needed to be persuaded, Charlie didn't specify, as that would spoil things. But he'd said enough to convince these highly trained professionals that he could be of use to them.

'Hey, buddy,' Hank shouted, 'sounds like you're our kinda guy, and we sure could use a little help. We wanna know how come the Thames is so wide here? And how many goddam miles is it to Primrose Hill?

'London Southend Airport gotta be near London Southbank, right? You got a music hall there, right? Where your Shakesbake dude hung out, right?'

'Cor blimey, strewth, stroll on.' Charlie's favourite expression was surely the appropriate response to these drongoes, even though the nearest he'd ever got to classical theatre was panto. Once, with his mum. Two things about that day felt relevant: the sweeties he nicked from the kid sat next to him and the show's name: *Babes in the Wood*.

'So 'appens I'm goin' dat why meself tomorrah. Meet me

and da missus in de old tarn in da mornin' and I'll show ya da why.' They were all so grateful that they pretty much told Charlie what they were up to. Also, they got the introductions out of the way, though Wayne, Shane and Duane said with a smirk that their colleague was Hassidy.

Hopalong Cassidy got the name after he too took a bullet in a lower limb, but a lot more heroically than Hank, who got the hump and threatened to plug the lot of them. Knowing he was crazy enough with that goddamned shooter to spoil everyone's day, they didn't say he was a spoilsport.

*

At eleven sharp next morning, four Mustangs confidently roared onto the harbour in Old Leigh, while a fifth spluttered uncertainly. A strapped-up left foot doesn't make driving impossible, but it's tricky in a manual car. Lucky for Hank, he was a non-smoker, as Spleeny's specially rolled treats would have finished him off.

Wayne had kicked the baccy years ago, and Charlie knew better than to go there, in the circumstances. But minutes later Shane and Duane were wonderfully jolly and happy to share every single thing, including what their moms and pops did in the bedroom. Charlie listened intently, if selectively. So did Hank, who thought he really should be allowed to gun people down on sidewalks.

Half an hour later, three Mustangs roared off the harbour, one of them rather uncertainly, onto the cobbled street. Two more roared onto the decks of boats moored below. A visiting anthropologist, who was researching the behavioural habits of Essex people, watched with interest. 'And then there were three,' she mused to the man in the café. 'Very Agatha Christie, don't you think?'

When the bloke answered 'Agafa 'oo?', she stared at him intently, opened her notebook and did a lot of scribbling.

Giggling hysterically, Shane and Duane clambered up the steps back onto the harbour, and somehow found their way into the rather chewed passenger seats of Hank's and Wayne's motors. It took a while, giving Charlie time to arrange with the furious fishermen to drop their uninvited cargo off at his place. A bit knocked about now, as well as knocked off twice, but still worth a few bob. Charlie chuckled. Hank didn't. But Spleeny did, for reasons of her own.

Turning on her iPhone's tape-recording function during Shane and Duane's confidentially comprehensive briefing had been a coup. Fyok Yu and Hon Ki would think so too, like.

*

When they all finally made it to Camden High Street, none of them noticed two unusually tall nuns striding along the pavement looking extremely pleased with themselves. But Hank was gobsmacked as they approached the Holiday Inn. He'd no idea London was so big, as well as having miles and miles with hardly any houses on it. Also, when he stepped round the side of the hotel, he couldn't figure out how come the Thames was suddenly so much narrower.

Trudi would have raised her eyes skywards in a perfect imitation of someone who really can't believe anyone in the world can be quite so silly, and then explained very slowly, quite loudly and very clearly, in the shortest possible words, that it's the Regent's Canal.

She'd have gone on to tell him, again in the tone of an exasperated mummy whose toddler seems unable to grasp the difference between a plastic spoon and a carving knife, that the canal and the Thames are not the same thing, and London and Southend are not the same town. Very likely she'd have gone on to suggest he wouldn't be ready for kindergarten just yet. And Spleeny, though she knew less about anything than Trudi when she turned four, was at least ahead of the game with this lot.

'Fing is, like, we're on da same page as you,' she screeched.

'We fink you should, like, put da screws on our prime tosser. Show 'im 'oo's da boss, like. Not 'im, it's your geezer in da White 'ouse. Dat's right, like, innit?

'Fing is, like, we're on a secret mission too, to stop dem bleedin' trains. We gotta special contact, like, at da top of government. You tell our mate wot yer doin' next. 'Ow yer plannin' to, like, stop our prime plonker in 'is tracks. Railway tracks, like, geddit? An' we promise we'll do da rest.'

Charlie stared, dumbstruck, as Spleeny opened up an empty fag packet, carefully gripping her tongue between her teeth as she slowly scrawled on it an email address and handed it to Hank.

It read: *honkiroolsok@fyokyu.com*

'Why thank you, ma'am, forever in your debt. God bless America. God bless you.' Hank's gratitude seemed boundless. Charlie's relief certainly was when he glanced over the man's shoulder, spotted what she'd written and figured out why.

More than relief, it was genuine admiration, hard to admit to about the tart who was supposed to honour and obey him while kneeling at his feet and kissing them.

CHAPTER TWENTY

Trudi's not one to get cross. Or at least not often.

You can't really count her throwing her toys out of the pram when she was ickle, as she only did it because it was fun watching Daddy charging around trying to stop Fang snatching them up and taking them God knows where, never to be seen again.

But there was the time at the beginning of her first term at school when she'd set her heart on marrying Sir. Newly qualified, he was in his early twenties, so a couple of decades down the line, a union between the two would have been unusual but feasible. At this stage, however, Trudi was conscious the age gap meant she'd better tread carefully. Her mistake was discussing strategy with Mummy and Daddy.

Their mistake was not spotting that she was in earshot when they had a little giggle about it with Sir at the school gate. And their punishment was summary, if symbolic, execution. Trudi said not a word to either of them in the car, and immediately they got home shot upstairs, dug out her least favourite Barbie and any old Ken and flung them out of her bedroom window.

Of course, Percy and Viv didn't suffer any physical pain but did undergo a certain amount of torment when they heard their daughter's furious scream as the dollies hit the ground.

'That's what I want to do to you, horrid smelly smelly smelly smelly Mummy! And you, horrid smelly smelly smelly smelly Daddy! You've ruined my life, beastly nasty old old old old people!'

It was one of their first insights into exactly how cross, if crossed, their normally lovely little daughter could be. And it took the promise never to do it again, and to buy for her birthday the prettiest electric three-wheeled motor scooter available on Amazon, to calm things down. Also, they had to agree, whatever their private thoughts on the matter, that matrimony with Sir could be an option later.

It was full fair warning that a little person's emotions, however silly they might seem, can be every bit as intense as a grown-up's. At least there were no bones broken. Unlike when Fyok Yu and Hon Ki had a falling-out over Hank's first email.

Because it'd zapped through before Spleeny had had a chance to tell him to expect it, Fyok Yu couldn't decide if it was some kind of joke or just plain weird, but he read on anyway.

Hey, buddy, we ain't taking no shit from doggone limeys. Our Mugwump got plans, right?

He's done historical research, figured out ways to make these dudes see reason. We gonna rent a room somewhere. Deep underground, close to your Congress house. Getta thousand tons of high explosives. Dig a tunnel. Blow the goddamned place sky high if your guy don't get the message.

You read me, right? One big bang, right? Yee-haw! Sure, some guy called Guy fawked up big time one time, but your asswipe PM won't get that lucky with POTUS.

We gonna get our new man on it. He's a halfwit but knows how to get things. He gottus wheels, he'll get the whizzbang for us.

And when we're through, we'll waste him. Geddim to lead us to the Thames, plug him, and drop him in it. Maybe we take his moll as a trophy, put her in a zoo, right?

Gotta special relationship with these dudes, same as between our two great nations. We say jump, you say how high. You read me? Roger and out.

Fyok Yu giggled as his finger hovered over the delete button, and he wondered, when Hon Ki lunged forward and shattered it with a karate chop, if he was the only person in the room not certifiably insane.

Difficult to work out what got to Fyok Yu more. The humiliation he felt at Hon Ki's hands, or the extreme pain he was feeling in his own. But though they were temporarily out of service, both feet, both elbows and his forehead were still fully functional weapons of war.

Chancery wasn't too chuffed either, when he read that selfsame email that Hon Ki had managed to pass on before he passed out.

*

Trudi went off *ring-a-ring o' roses* when she turned four, and Percy decided she was old enough to know it might be all about a horrid olden days illness, like Covid but ever so much worse.

Because Chancery's mum wasn't up to speed with that sort of thing, and he was a late developer, he was still fond of the nursery rhyme when he was twelve. And he'd have liked it all the more now if he'd known that *a-tishoo a-tishoo we all fall down* could well refer to people dropping down dead. Though those Americans seemed almost too brainless to breathe, he really did think they liked him. And really did not think they were planning to plug him and chuck him in the Thames. In desperation, he turned to Caligula for sympathy, hoping a bit of chocolate might win him round.

Unlucky for him, he didn't have Trudi on hand to set him straight. Having tried all sorts of things on Fang in her time, she knew the specifics of small furry animals' likes and dislikes, and their response if they suspected the human was having a laugh.

'I may look 'ard, but I do 'ave feelings, especially when I feel 'ard done by,' Chancery confessed. Seconds later, he had lots more feelings, in several of his ten outstretched fingers, the rat having decided they looked less inedible than the chocolate.

To Spleeny, Caligula's behaviour only confirmed that she was never wrong. Number one first, like, right? Hence, when she read the offending email, her simple solution.

''Oo bleedin' cares wot 'appens to da bleedin' trains? 'Oo bleedin' cares 'ooze side we're bleedin' on, so long as we don't get, like, bleedin' killed?'

'Yeah but no but yeah but,' Chancery began, as he often did when he couldn't think what to say. Fyok Yu and Hon Ki had already let on, in their menacingly softly spoken way, that

133

they'd slit his throat if he didn't neutralise the Yanks, and there wasn't much to choose between a bullet in the chest or a dagger in the jugular. Though Spleeny, as ever, was ahead of the game.

'Penislow didn't try and, like, murder us when we 'ad our differences last time. So we gotta work wiv 'im now. Fink abaht it, ya bleedin' 'alfwit.'

In normal circumstances, Chancery was more thick-skinned than a nuclear reactor, but this was different. What made it feel even more wrong was that she was right.

At least he'd still got Percy's mobile number, from the time they worked against then with then against one another last time round. But instead of calling, he decided a text message would give him a chance to get the tone right. A blend of intimidation and sophistication.

Now sea hear, old been, we have shard interests that mite interest you. Together we can save our grate nation from a frightful fete. Together we can repel all borders. The world is our cloister. But only if you get it rite. Yew reed me? Then wring me!!

Rereading it carefully, Charlie was pleased that predictive text hadn't messed anything up. Proof, he was convinced, that he was great with language. Or grate, maybe.

Though Spleeny agreed, to her own surprise, she flicked off predictive text and added a quick postscript. To leave no room in Percy's mind for doubt.

Yule get on wiv it if ya no wot's good for ya, durr-brain.

*

Percy had never had himself down as a durr-brain, though Trudi had her doubts as she listened to him dribbling on as he read the message.

'*There are more things in heaven and Earth, Horatio,*' he murmured dreamily, '*than are dreamt of in your philosophy.*'

Ten years down the line, she'd have whispered in his ear: '*Hamlet*, Act One, Scene Five.' But was happy for now to keep it simple, if varied.

'Silly billy Daddi. Always bludi blathering. Try lying down, somewhere dark. Pint of brandy, naughty Daddi? Do you good, daffy old git.'

Instead of suggesting his daughter might try being a bit nicer to him for a change, Percy proved her point by staring vacantly into space. Until Fang sorted him out. As anyone at the wrong end of an abusive relationship with a cat will confirm, claws sunk into flesh always bring the here and now into sharp focus. Particularly sharp in this case. Percy shook his foot violently and cursed the little brute.

'*Angels and ministers of grace defend us! Be thou a spirit of health or goblin damned?*'

Again, quick as a flash, the teenage Trudi would have congratulated Percy for managing to stick with the same play, but would have pointed out that Fang had to be some kind of spirit as he'd have died years ago. At this stage, however, the poor little moggy definitely felt like goblin damned, having been so upstaged by Lady Casement.

'The hell with *hell hath no fury* like the wrath of a woman spurned,' Percy fumed. 'What about bloody cats? Especially ones of a sensitive but vindictive disposition.'

Viv managed, somehow, not to laugh, though the little dots on Percy's foot did call to mind the phrase "red in tooth and claw". Besides, the weird text message and weirder postscript left an awful lot of other dots to join up.

'The mountain? Can it actually come to Muhammed?

Seems we'd better put that to the test. Obnoxious though that man is, it's better to have him where we can see him, don't you think?'

'Inside the tent pissing out, rather than outside the tent pissing in?' Percy's good on political quotes, especially crude ones. For the millionth time, Viv wished he'd save them for when Trudi wasn't there. As she skipped out without a word, the glint her eye spoke volumes.

Almost immediately, an extremely loud stage whisper could be heard from the next room, while a parrot could also be heard, squawking at the top of her voice. 'Brits out, pissing out. Eejits in, pissing in. In out in out, pissing all about.'

Viv had a good mind to take a leaf out of Fang's book, and a section out of Percy's nose.

CHAPTER TWENTY-ONE

Everything went quiet in the next room when Biff plopped a tea towel over Lady Casement's head. It stayed that way when he turned on his heel, as Trudi was so angry she couldn't even speak. She did, however, stick out her tongue and make an extremely rude gesture at him, with both hands, which she felt made the point.

Having no idea how thoroughly he'd been told off, Biff rejoined the grown-ups and mentioned his mates in Belfast, the ones with the guns, but Viv insisted that talking to the man might be more constructive than killing him. Unhelpfully, when Trudi leapt up and pulled off the stupid tea towel, Lady Casement launched into a sentimental Irish song ending with the words: *"To the echo of a Thomson gun."*

Preferring to keep his nose intact, Percy sided with his wife, pinged off a message and got an interesting response.

Wot abaht somewhere discreet? How abaht de Outer Hebrides? Or Land's End? Or if dat's too far wot abaht 'Ighgate Semmetry? Feel like I'm arfway dare already. Joke. Geddit?

Percy did, and smirked meaningfully at Biff.

'What is it Thatcher once said about Labour's attitude to fighting an election?'

'Frit,' Biff snarled. His fixation with That Bloody Woman stemmed from her monstrous claim that there was something criminal about IRA freedom fighters' perfectly reasonable policy of blowing things up.

Wondering for the millionth time what it was about men, Viv brought them, for the moment at least, to their senses. 'Just tell him Highgate is perfectly convenient. And suggest straight away.'

An hour later, Percy and Biff were standing next to a large man with a beard who does nothing but glower. But then sculptures aren't big on chatter, and, anyway, Karl Marx wasn't noted for his sense of humour. His claim that history repeats itself, first as tragedy then as farce, was hardly a bundle of laughs.

Ten minutes and five cigarettes later, Percy spotted a couple with dark glasses and wide-brimmed hats pulled low, which made them look rather odd, while their tent-like wraps reaching to their ankles would have been ideal for changing into swimming costumes but seemed out of place fifty miles from the nearest beach.

'Doctor Chancery, I presume.' Percy's greeting was jaunty, unlike Charlie's answer.

'Shhhhhh. Keep yer voice dahn. Someone might 'ear.'

'Everybody here will, but best not worry about it, eh? They're all dead.' Percy felt that this should put the two of them at their ease, though the answer suggested not.

'Wot?'

Because Chancery and Spleeny were still gawping at

them as though they'd just clambered out of a coffin and started dancing the Charleston, Percy decided to change tack. Thanks to his pre-politics career on telly, he was good at reading things but pretending he'd just made them up. After a lightning glance at the Marx memorial, he put on his really clever face and spoke earnestly.

'The philosophers have only interpreted the world, in various ways. The point, however, is to change it.'

Not good on smaller typefaces or longer sentences, Charlie and Spleeny hadn't got past workers of all lands unite. So they stuck with their well-worn formula.

'Wot?'

Percy sighed, and got down to business.

'You seem to have changed sides, my dears. How about we compare notes?'

Chancery whipped out a wad of fake fivers in the hope of swapping a few for the real thing, then, realising his mistake, got on with his story, pulling no punches about how he'd like to land a few on these brutes lined to insult and murder him. Though Percy was all in favour of both, he went for the approach he'd adopted with Trudi the day she wanted to spray Fang with pink luminous paint. A tiny touch of diplomacy.

'Dear chap, I quite understand your displeasure.'

Had Trudi asked him if he meant that, he'd have replied yes. But no to what he said next.

'I've always had the highest regard for your integrity and concern for your welfare.'

Chancery tried to look as if he expected nothing less, and Percy shared essential facts, which didn't include the bugging of Erewego's place, Viv's back channel with Fanny and Monty's Sten guns.

Surprisingly, it all got a bit more chilled in the end. Biff genuinely found it funny that Chancery had managed to nick the Mustangs three times. Gave him one or two ideas to pass on to the lads back home. And they could all safely agree that the Yanks were brain-dead, though Percy had to fake a violent coughing fit when Charlie moaned about them thinking he was a halfwit.

*

'D'you think it's the light that's attracting them? Or is it something in the air?' Seemed to Percy perfectly logical questions, as, barely a minute after Chancery's Mustang finally roared off, two more appeared from the opposite direction.

Biff, who didn't really get either joke, did admit it was strange. No less so when two burly goons in dark glasses clambered out of the first, and one clambered and another hauled himself with difficulty out of the second. This one was struggling with his crutch because of the huge bulge under his left armpit. But he managed somehow to hobble towards the entrance to the park, with the others in tow.

Percy muttered out of the side of his mouth, in the manner of hammy actors in old cops 'n' robbers B-movies, 'Follow those goons.' Biff looked at him despairingly. But they did anyway, ending up at the next table, in the café's outside area.

Having got the lowdown on the first bunch of Yankee crazies from his spies in the Europa, Biff was forearmed. Percy wasn't. The noise was such that other nearby tables were empty in no time, with one genteel old lady grumbling something about the dead being awakened. Her friend was so temporarily deafened that she settled for nodding sympathetically, as only genteel old ladies know how.

'Bloody hell, it's enough to awaken the bloody dead,' Percy shouted at Biff. While his words weren't as genteel as the old lady's, they were every bit as wasted. So he settled for banging off a text to Viv. It was quite clever, but not very informative.

Battle of the Little Bighorn? Custer's last stand? Last of the Mohicans? You won't believe this.

Back in Mayfair, Trudi watched with some concern as Viv pursed her lips and stroked her normally unlined forehead. Nothing odd about Daddy's baffled frowns; different matter altogether with Mummy. She'd no idea that even the superior gender sometimes struggled with things. But it was all over in a flash, as Viv just got on with it and suggested, in a terse text, that Percy did the same.

'Try me.'

He did. And the conversation started to flow.

'Yankee loonies. Here in Highgate.'

'I don't believe you.'

'Told you.'

'Sound them out?'

'Sound advice.'

Percy had a feeling, however, that it wasn't going to be that easy. He was used to putting things reasonably simply with Trudi, but this looked to be hugely harder. Apart from having a bigger vocabulary of useful words, his bright little daughter was also almost certainly a lot better at thinking.

Even the first step wasn't as straightforward as it should have been, after the waitress remembered to put sugar on the Yanks' table, but not on his and Biff's.

'Sorry to trouble you, gents.' Percy pointed meaningfully at the dish full of little white cubes. 'Might we trouble you?'

Not liking the word "trouble", Hank started fumbling with his shoulder holster and snarled 'reach for the sky.'

Percy decided Oscar Wilde was right about England having everything in common with America except language, but Biff got round the problem neatly. The shortcut to every Yankee heart ever since a million half-starved Irish folk fled to America in the 1840s and began vigorously breeding never fails.

'But to be sure you're a lovely man to be sure,' he crooned. 'Holy mother of Jesus, blessings of blessed Mary upon you if you'll koindly pass the sugar, to be sure.'

There's something so irresistibly caressive about the caricature Irish brogue that even if you're telling someone their mother's about to die a slow and horrible death, it sounds comforting.

'Why, howdy pardner!' Hank, Wayne, Shane and Duane shouted in a rather improbable unison. 'With guys like you, we share and share alike.'

Splendid. What's yours is ours and what's mine's me own, Percy thought but didn't say.

'We couldn't help but overhear, sorry about that, that you're concerned about the brazen Brits wanting to buy Chinese trains,' he did say, loud and clear.

'I'll have you know we think it's the stupidest idea ever. And all right-thinking folk this side of the Pond agree with us.'

Percy was concerned that the word "brazen" might have been a bit sophisticated for this bunch of throwbacks, but was right in thinking that "stupid" was in their vocabulary.

He also guessed correctly that they were so spectacularly self-centred that it wouldn't strike them as odd a complete stranger should launch straight into their pet topic, same as the halfwit. Hank waved his crutch around like a heavy machine gun mowing down hundreds of marauding commies, and spoke frankly, if not very interestingly.

'Well, I'll be doggoned. And may God bless you two. Too.'

Percy and Biff tried to look frightfully meek and grateful as they waited for the moron to tell them something useful. He got round to it in the end, though not without a lot of moronic blather first.

'We're here to check out that filthy Russki Marcus. We know he's holed up somewhere. Wanna make sure the critter ain't gonna go trying to change the goddamn world again.'

Once again, Percy thought it best not to say what he was thinking: *The Russki in question, in point of fact a German Jew, you pea-brained nincompoop, is not on the verge of changing anything. People don't when they've been dead for nearly a century and a half.*

But he did admit that "holed up" summed up Karl Marx's situation rather well.

'If you like,' he added, 'we'll be happy to show you his tomb. Which, we grieve to confess, is in consecrated ground. The British are impervious to impropriety.'

Concerned that Percy was getting carried away, using words with far too many syllables, Biff stamped on his foot under the table. Discreetly, but hard. Then added a few reassuring words.

'But mother of Jesus, the man was surely the very devil to be sure to be sure. His remains may be buried here but his soul is surely rotting in hell. God forgive me, it's a sin to hate,

143

but I cannot forgive his wicked ways, to be sure to be sure.'

Percy gasped. Partly because of the pain in his foot, but more thanks to Biff's stupefying hypocrisy. In their Downing Street days, he'd campaigned to put a statue of the man on Parliament Square and fly the red flag on all public buildings.

CHAPTER TWENTY-TWO

The walk down the hill to the tomb took a while, as Hank insisted on stopping every few steps to moan about Limeys not letting Mustangs onto public footpaths. Percy tried to look sympathetic, not very successfully.

At the sight, eventually, of the Great Satan himself, all four Yanks yanked at their shoulder holsters and started muttering about being better dead than red. Once again, Biff calmed them down.

'To be sure to be sure, ye moight as well be saving your dear little bullets, to be sure. The all-seeing Almoighty's already seen to that, to be sure.'

The crisis was averted. Which was lucky, as the old ladies who'd been at the café were now midway between the guns and their intended target, and wouldn't have enjoyed putting the noise-waking-the-dead theory to the test. Pleased it hadn't come to that, Percy gave them a cheery wave and took up the Chinese train conversation again, but got carried away. Again.

'You were saying, gentlemen? Your magnificent and munificent leader wishes the idiotic English to execute a vehement volte-face and bury any such egregious exercise in the fetid oubliette of history?'

The Yanks reached for their guns again, suspecting the Limey was really a goddammed Russki talking commie lingo, but Biff came to the rescue in time.

'To be sure to be sure, me poor friend was drupt from a great hoit when he was a wee babby. Gets in a moddle with his words.

'What he's trying to say, to be sure, is he'll be wondering what your wonderful president's going to do to get the filthy Brits to see reason, to be sure to be sure.'

Mollified, the Americans revealed how the special relationship between the two great nations could be sealed by blowing up the lesser of the two's seat of government. Percy was horrified, as it took his own campaign to steer Tiddledick away from Chinese trains through the roof, manner of speaking. Even Biff thought it might be going a little bit far.

But, keeping up the pretence of being a lovely soft Irishman, he offered to drive Hank's Pony down to the entrance to the cemetery, to save the poor man the walk back up the hill. Percy offered to get the other one, as he'd always fancied a ride in a Mustang, preferably with Trudi in tow. Because he'd only ever taken her anywhere in Simone-Sitrouenne, she'd have been dead impressed that he could drive faster than fifty.

*

Mummy's troubled expression when she got that last text

from Percy troubled Trudi. Worried that one or the other had got out of his or her depth, she decided she'd better find out for herself what was going on, and, if necessary, sort them out.

Daddy's nappy training, she remembered, had been straightforward enough, but because this seemed a tad more complicated, she carefully selected the cupboard in the living room that'd be just about big enough for her, and her notebook. When Percy and Biff made it back to Mayfair, she was ready and waiting, and surprised at how sweary Mummy could be when she didn't think there was a child in the room.

'It's a bloody disaster,' Vivienne snapped. 'Not only does Mugwump make Stalin look like Father bloody Christmas, he's also, clearly, off his bloody trolley. And if it ever came out that you knew all along about his preposterous idea, you'd be in for the bloody high jump as well.'

Scrunched up in the cupboard, Trudi struggled. Four bloodies in fewer than four seconds! She couldn't decide whether she could charge for each one individually, or whether, because it was repetition of the same word, she'd have to knock a bit off. Either way, she could hardly present Mummy with the bill now, as it would blow her cover completely.

'We'll need to tread cautiously,' Percy began, cautiously. 'Have the feeling we already know more than we should. Need to break the news gently, somehow. Also, there's the minor adjustment to the telecommunications arrangements in the home of the cabinet secretary, which I wouldn't wish to advertise too widely.'

'Yes. Had my reservations about that little jape of yours too,' Vivienne muttered. 'But you went and did it before I had time to think it through.'

'Boys will be boys?' Percy wondered, tentatively, sensing she wasn't quite so sure of her ground now. The intelligence gathered could after all be invaluable.

Trudi made good her escape when they all headed for the drinks cabinet in the next room. She was grateful to get out before her legs actually broke off, while Percy was just longing to get shot of Vivienne. Viv was so much nicer.

*

Satisfied that the bugging device at Erewego's was working properly, Monty moseyed up to Mayfair, leaving Bakyt behind to continue monitoring proceedings through the diamante-studded earphones he thought she'd like. And was as shocked as everyone else at what he learned.

'"Remember remember the fifth of November, gunpowder treason and plot"? This is the twenty-first century, for God's sake, not the seventeenth.

'My old colleagues at Tottenham nick had no inhibitions about pushing suspects down flights of stone stairs, then not very accidentally treading on their heads. I would advise them to push this psycho out of a rocket. Spacesuit not obligatory. And direct him towards the furthest black hole in the universe.

'However, since that's not an option, I suppose we'll have to settle for spiking his guns. My own may come in useful in this instance.'

As they always did at the thought of Tommy guns, Biff's eyes lit up. Viv's didn't, and Vivienne hovered round the room when Percy spoke next.

'Be rather fun to let the loonies build the tunnel, tip off

MI6 in the nick of time, pass the word back to the Senate and get him impeached. Peachy, huh?'

'The man's fans are so blinkered, they wouldn't blink at footage of him disinterring his granny and eating the corpse,' Monty sighed.

'Besides,' definitely-definitely-Vivienne added, 'there's no question people would wonder which of us knew what, and when. And why we didn't speak up sooner.'

But all talk of life sentences meaning life, with no parole, was cut short by the sight of a little girl tripping merrily into the room with a parrot on her shoulder, chanting lustily. The parrot, that is, not the girl.

'Remember remember the bloody November. Gunpowder bloody and plot. Treason remember bloody treason. Treason and bloody and Biff.'

Scared out of his wits, Fang sprung onto Percy's lap, then remembered that birds are supposed to be frightened of cats, not the other way round. But when he tried another hiss, rather a feeble one, no one was fooled. Percy's crack at looking stern was just as useless, while Trudi's triumphant giggle dispensed with Vivienne.

Oddly, only Biff spotted the warning signs. Though cabinet leaks can be a pain, at least you can throw the little black book at disloyal ministers. A parrot would only chew it up and spit it out.

'Keep yer gob shut, gobshite,' he snarled. 'Zip it, shagging eejit. Ye hear me?'

There's nothing wrong with Lady Casement's hearing. Though she doesn't always quite get the message.

'Remember the fifth of Biff. Treason the Biff of plot. Gunpowder bloody and Biff.'

By this point, the parrot was in paroxysms of excitement, hopping from side to side and flicking her crest up and down, something between an Irish jig and a Groucho Marx routine. Trudi started planning her career, probably as a teacher.

When Bakyt showed up, that plan took definite shape. Faced with a classroom full of naughty children or a lecture hall full of disgruntled undergraduates, Trudi would wave her magic wand and cast a spell on the lot of them. Her fellow chief witch was such an inspiration.

The two had a good chat about pointy hats, cauldrons and familiars, and Fang was ever so pleased to be scooped up in his one-time best friend's arms and swept into the bathroom. Less so when he found himself draped in a shawl and made to try out magic potions. A mix of toothpaste, hair conditioner and mascara rubbed on his nose was one of the nicer ones.

At least it was attention, of a kind.

CHAPTER TWENTY-THREE

Trudi was on the point of taking a biggish step in the monumental journey of life. Up till then, she'd always looked out on the world from inside herself. But now she was beside herself, on finding out it can work the other way round too.

Accustomed as she now was to being the teacher, she was surprised to find she'd accidentally passed on the baton, just this once, to Fang. While cats' priorities are easily misunderstood, their intelligence should never be underestimated. Same as their range of feelings, including the desire to inflict death by a thousand scratches, if they're in a certain mood. This applies especially to cats with an F in their name, as Percy knows to his cost.

But, as Trudi was about to find out, they can experience hurt if, for example, they feel mistreated by a certain little girl, naming no names, ahem. And sometimes go the extra mile to put things right, if they really have to.

Fang's reaction to that certain little girl's way of brushing up his skills as a familiar was not to be wondered at, as no cat in his right mind takes to his nose being smeared with nasty, smelly things. Against that, the poor creature had been feeling so left out of things that he was ready to give anything a go. While he hadn't come across the epigram in married life, three's company and two's none, the way forward might be to swallow his pride instead of that nasty bird.

He spotted his chance when Trudi sat on the floor next to his basket with the monster on her shoulder, not parroting abusive, cattist or even just plain catty things for once, but quietly and rather tenderly smoothing out her hair with her beak. Fang tried to make himself invisible as he slithered out of his basket and snuck up behind them. The obvious thing to do next was to leap onto the creature's back, break its scrawny neck and rip its vile body to bits, but Fang had a better idea, striking in its originality.

He reached out the paw of friendship.

And it worked! What he hadn't realised was that Lady Casement was by nature affectionate and playful, and didn't really understand half the things she said. Say your piece first, and then figure out what you meant. Well, sometimes. In every one of those ways, she was just like Trudi, which was how come they got on so well. And now, suddenly, it was cutting three ways, as Lady Casement turned and started gently teasing out the fur between Fang's carefully sheathed claws.

A couple of minutes later, worried that things were too quiet on the wayward front, Viv popped her head round the door and couldn't believe her eyes. It's not every day you see a cat curled up with a bird on a little girl's lap, lapping up her sweet little song about being Siamese whether you like it or not. Though it didn't accurately describe them, it sort of did. Sort of perfectly.

As usual, Trudi was doing the girlie multi-skilling thing, in this case, singing and thinking at the same time. Was it possible, she wondered, that Fang had been the teeniest tad disappointed that she'd so warmed to Lady Casement she'd given him the teeniest tad less attention? Could it conceivably be he'd decided to set her a better example by taking matters into his own hands, or rather, being a cat, paws? Pause for thought first. Then, excuse French, éclairissement.[§]

In Halfwit's shoes, she'd have said 'cor blimey, strewth, well, stroll on.' In the Yanks', she'd have settled for 'I'll be doggoned.' Or, if she'd been Percy, she'd have wowed the fans with: 'O wonder! How many goodly creatures are there here?' Actually, she didn't say anything. But, in the space of a nanosecond, she'd become an older and wiser person.

And Fang had become an older and wiser cat. Now that Lady Casement was a close friend, he felt the poor bird's pain at having to put up with Biff. With his instinctive eye for personal hygiene, he wondered if a good scrub might help. Having often noticed the Guinness and grub blotches on the green waistcoat, Trudi thought the same, though nothing could save the man from being terminally boring.

Viv too had learned a little lesson. Tiptoeing out of the room, she thought about the showbiz saying "never work with children or animals", and wished working with supposedly grown-up humans could be half as straightforward.

*

[§]   A Labour prime minister once used this word in a Commons debate. Though it wasn't ruled to be an unparliamentary expression, MPs on all sides went 'oooohhhh.' Not many people know that.

It was about to become even less so, as Fyok Yu and Hon Ki had arranged to hook up with the chair of the Intelligence and Security Committee of the Commons, in the hope of countering the American gunpowder plot. No point drawing up the train contract if there was no British government to sign it.

Struck them as odd, though, that after they'd thanked Charlie for the intel by tipping him off about the goons' other plan, to murder him, that he wasn't keeping well clear of them. But there it was; he wasn't.

On their way to the meeting, they couldn't miss the familiar figure heading towards them, flanked by four noisy, overweight throwbacks in preposterously dark glasses. Not the same ones as they'd picked out in Belfast, but it was obvious who they were.

'I spy with my little eye something beginning with S,' Fyok Yu muttered.

'Let's see, could that be spies?' Hon Ki answered in an even tone.

'Not racist, is it, to say they all look the same to me?' Fyok Yu smirked.

'Fair point,' Hon Ki admitted. Though they'd never really been bosom buddies, they were remembering to be civil to one another after they both got overexcited when that informative email came in. The severe bruising on Hon Ki's head and shoulders was gradually subsiding, though Fyok Yu's finger would be in a splint for a while longer. He'd no idea what Hank had done to his foot, but felt a spasm of fellow feeling in spite of himself.

*

When Trudi first saw the Palace of Westminster, her only real thought was how big it was. But then, to a three-year-old, even an ordinary-sized bungalow looks as if it's got lots of room in it. By the time she was four, she did suspect lots of things must have happened there and bombarded Mummy and Daddy with questions.

Did Queen Victoria have to climb on the roof to hide from the Romans? Did King Arthur keep his round table there? Did the nasty Norman man shoot someone in the eye from the top of the big tower with the clock in it? And did that poor king who had his head chopped off get told off in the bit that looked really old?

Percy did rather struggle with explaining what happened when, and where, but could answer, accurately, that King Charles the First was sentenced to death in Westminster Hall. And when Trudi demanded to know exactly where he was standing when he heard the bad news, he promised to show her.

Percy and Viv were fascinated by her hunger for knowledge. They could have wished her appetite extended to her greens at dinnertime, but accepted you can't have everything. And Fyok Yu and Hon Ki would certainly have agreed that Trudi ran rings round a lot of adults, when they crouched down among the hordes of tourists outside parliament and earwigged Charlie and the Yanks' conversation. If you can call it that.

'Gee whiz!' was the best Shane could come up with as the building, one of the most iconic in the world, hove into view.

Anxious, doubtless, to remind his colleagues that he owed his position as leader to his greater analytical skills, Hank added thoughtfully: 'Well, holy smoke.'

Though Charlie was in front of them, he was pretty much in step with Trudi. When she was three.

'Big, innit?'

'Well, I'll be doggoned,' Hank replied, before making a valiant attempt to catch up with Trudi at the age of four. 'How come a little country like England has such a stoopidy large senate house?'

'England's also got Scotland, Wales and Norvern Ahhland,' Chancery replied stiffly. 'Used to run Osstrylia, and China and France and Germany, and India an' all. And your country.'

Trudi would have had grave doubts about much of that, while Percy would have pointed out that these days we're only hanging on to Scotland and Northern Ireland by our fingertips. And the Anglo-Saxon migration and Norman invasion meant Charlie had got the German and French connections back to front. Fyok Yu and Hon Ki settled for a sharp intake of breath at the slur against their country, but Hank took his protests on behalf of his homeland to another level.

'Goddam, Limey, don't you know your own goddam history? You never heard of the war of goddam independence? We set you free out of the goodness of our goddam hearts. We are the land of the goddam free, goddam it.'

He found himself seriously questioning whether a Limey dumb enough not to know England's a goddam ex-colony of the US of A would be able to manage an explosion big enough to take out this stupidly huge building.

Charlie already knew the answer to that would be no, but hoped he'd be well out of the way before Hank did too.

*

Trudi wiggled her little pink thermometer energetically and jammed it firmly into Percy's mouth. She ran the back of her hand over his forehead then gripped his wrist and counted carefully, wearing the expression of extreme concern that medical professionals do when confronted with a patient who's clearly feverish.

It was Daddy's pathologically erratic behaviour that got her worried. No one in their right mind looks up lovely places by the seaside when they already live in a lovely place by the seaside, surely? Could be, after a week or so in Mayfair, he'd forgotten he had a house in Cornwall, but if so, it was a bad sign.

When Percy explained that he was looking for a place for someone else, not himself, Trudi breathed a sigh of relief. She thought, as a precaution, his condition should still be closely monitored, but as he printed out details of more and more places, a good time was had by all.

Lady Casement had lots of fun poo-poo-smearing all over the pages, and Fang thoroughly enjoyed dabbing all of Percy's pink highlighters onto the floor and scurrying off with them. Though, when Trudi learned Daddy didn't very much like the people who might live in the place, she got the thermometer out again, in case he was having a relapse.

Percy and Viv had already factored in the possible need of a safe house for the Chancerys and, after speedy research, plumped for Thurso. It wasn't a particularly expensive area and the property would doubtless pay for itself as a holiday let if, for whatever reason, it was surplus to requirements.

But if Charlie didn't end up in the morgue, and the missus in Missouri to blend with other animals in the safari park, Thurso would have a lot going for both of them. Percy

157

guessed the town's fascinating history, dating back to Norse times, probably wouldn't quite hit the spot, but they'd enjoy slaughtering swimmers in the speedboat, while survivors could splash out on Spleeny's spliffs.

What really sold it, however, was location. The northernmost town on the British mainland couldn't be further from Cornwall if it tried.

CHAPTER TWENTY-FOUR

When Percy makes a promise to Trudi, he does not forget to keep it. She makes sure of that. Which is how come he duly showed her the brass plaque on the floor of Westminster Hall marking the spot where King Charles was condemned to death. Her forehead crinkled into a frown for a second, but returned to its usual carefree smoothness as a happy thought struck her.

'Wasn't it lucky that when you stopped being the ever-so-important person, they didn't chop your head off too, Daddi?'

Percy agreed it certainly was, but hadn't got far into explaining regicide is not standard practice in England when they arrived at the central lobby, where Trudi found something else every bit as interesting. The little post office tucked away there so reminded her of the one back home that she suddenly remembered Nanny.

Tightly holding on to their hands, she gave her parents the special, wide-eyed innocent look she knew worked best when she had a question that was a demand really.

'Daddi, can we find a nice postcard to send to nice Nanny? She must be so lonely without me and Fang to keep her company.'

'Keep the poor bloody woman on her toes, more like,' Percy murmured instinctively, under his breath.

'Yes, of course, dear, that's a lovely thought.' Viv was all smiles. Even more so as she watched Trudi carefully gripping her tongue between her teeth and driving home her affection for the young lady she spent so much of her time driving to distraction.

Dere luvly nanni, the card read, *weve so mist you hear in Lundun. Hope yure enjoying a bit of peece and kwiet for a chainge. Weel bring yoo bak a luvly present wen we kum hoam. We promis. Luv from mee and fang. Oh, and mummi and daddi.*

The clue was in the Fang namecheck. Though Trudi hadn't come across the word "empathise", she'd started doing it anyway. That much was obvious to Percy, and the thought made him go all gooey. Seconds later, however, he went all bare-knuckled at the sight of Fyok Yu and Hon Ki bowing in a phoney Chinese fashion to the chair of the Commons Intelligence and Security Committee.

*

To describe the man as an evil sleazebag is like suggesting Beelzebub was a trifle out of order. Percy had Sir Peregrine Verrigreen MP PC QC as a CAUC. An acronym, short for Complete And Utter... something or other that doesn't quite rhyme with "aunt", but isn't far off.

Verrigreen? Very-not-green, more like, bent from birth

as a Romford Rolex. His habit as a kid of dipping into Mater's purse got several nannies the sack, as he'd play the butter-wouldn't-melt card while pointing the finger at these blameless young women.

That same skill had kept him in parliament far longer than he deserved, as he graduated to pointing that same finger at inappropriate parts of loads of other blameless women. When, as happens when blameless women take umbrage at someone trying to dip into something they value even more than their purses, out popped a wrinkly version of his childhood self.

He'd refined his technique at the bar, getting really nasty and obviously guilty people off scot-free and happily picking up a fortune for his efforts. Wearing his barrister's wig made him happy too, as it covered his receding hairline.

How the slimy git got any further up Westminster's greasy pole than cleaning the lavatories had only one possible explanation, Percy thought. To do with an incident the gutter press claimed involved the deputy prime minister, a fellow lawyer with whom he once shared chambers.

Featuring an energetic stripper, a former silk, an uninhibited nun and a close relative, it was straight out of the movies. But an impeccable alibi provided by an impeccably word-perfect Peregrine Verrigreen, kept the DPM's name out of it. Pity, Percy thought, as he'd already adapted the title of the crime drama *The Cook, the Thief, His Wife and Her Lover*.

The Cock, the Brief, His Vice and Her Brother.

Naughty parties are perfectly legal but politically awkward for married family values campaigners who happen to be deputy prime minister. For the best then that it was proved he wasn't at this one. Especially as photographic evidence that might have proved he was really went up in flames along with the entire building. Even more so as the stripper, the nun and her sibling went the same way.

*

Squeezing his family behind a statue of a stern-looking William Ewart Gladstone, Percy watched unseen as Verrigreen smarmed over his Chinese guests before leading them away, presumably to the privacy of his office. A quote from the great statesman popped into his head as they disappeared from sight.

Selfishness is the greatest curse of the human race.

Viv looked at him knowingly, and Trudi cursed herself for not bringing her pink thermometer, as his brow furrowed and he meditatively murmured another Gladstone-ism: '*Justice delayed is justice denied.*'

More to the point, Viv thought, lunch had been delayed too long too, as a decidedly peckish-looking Trudi told Daddy rather faintly not to have a relapse.

'It's not just pooh bears that get rumblies in their tumblies, little girls do too,' she added, meaningfully, before correcting herself quickly. 'And quite big girls, I'll have you know.'

Mummy shuffled her off towards the nearest restaurant, while Percy continued hunting for his old uni friend and now trusted contact, Shurelynott, to gratify another bodily need.

No, nothing naughty, just a fag. And no, not that sort of fag either.

When the man showed up, finally, the two of them snuck off to a little-used outside area, just behind a bit of lean-to roofing that looked like a shed and, obligingly, had a couple of bikes under it. Percy inhaled deeply and grinned. 'Bring back memories?' Obviously did for a bloke sorting the bins, as he spotted what was going on and bunged the roll-up behind his ear into his mouth.

'Boys will be boys.' Percy grinned again, but Shurelynott suddenly went all serious.

'Thing is, me old darling, Verrigreen's dipped his wick once too often and his old lady's finally severed ties.'

'You mean she's cut off his wick. Bet that hurt.' Percy smirked.

'You know perfectly well what I mean. She's cut him off without a penny. Remember, she inherited the stately home from Daddy, so now she's chucked him out, he's stately homeless, so to speak. And he's never bothered to put anything aside for a rainy day.

'The man's practically on the breadline. Well, relatively. London rents, same as London rent boys, frightfully dear, dear. And no knights' discounts from ladies of the night, I'm told.'

It suddenly became obvious to Percy why the CAUC had agreed to meet Fyok Yu and Hon Ki. Of course he wasn't on the breadline, but canapés and champers were more his style. And offering convincing evidence that Chinese trains would never zap out signals via GCHQ to the Pentagon and back via Beijing would be money for old rope. Or, rather, ropey, intelligence.

No problem with credibility. As chair of the committee overseeing the work of Britain's intelligence services, he was supposed to know better than anyone what does and does not pose a security threat. And he was such a clever liar that he'd even managed to persuade his party leader he liked and respected him.

Tiddledick wouldn't have been so easily taken in if he'd met Verrigreen's last nanny. Or the first. Or any of the long list in between, for that matter.

*

By the time Percy and Shurelynott had got through all the brandy in both their hipflasks and a whole pack of Gauloises, Fyok Yu, Hon Ki and Sir Peregrine Verrigreen had sealed the deal. And the unusually nasty piece of work was feeling as smug about it as he was about his unusually nice office overlooking the Thames.

A couple of grand had cranked up to two million, paid into an untraceable Swiss bank account. When Fyok Yu finally got there, Verrigreen still looked terribly unhappy about the risks he faced. Inside, he was grinning from ear to ear but thought better of saying *that'll do nicely, sir.*

The flat he'd now be able to buy in Eagle Wharf, Pimlico, had distinct advantages if he ever got rumbled. As well as having direct access to the river, as wharves do, it had a spare bedroom just big enough for the getaway speedboat that'd whisk him, if need be, to Battersea Heliport.

Verrigreen wasn't going to murder the queen or bed the Duchess of Cornwall, or try any of the other more obvious ways of committing high treason, but he would be giving aid or comfort to the sovereign's enemies. Same caper as got Hitler's little helper Haw-Haw hanged in 1946. Best not be caught then.

Assuming he wasn't, he'd have a nice view of the MI6 building. Which meant, when he claimed to be keeping a watchful eye on the security service, he was telling the literal truth. There's a first time for everything, he supposed.

CHAPTER TWENTY-FIVE

In the Commons restaurant Mummy had chosen, with some care, Trudi was having a whale of a time. Worries that she'd end up looking like one went out of the window when she saw toad in the hole and spotted dick with custard on the menu. And rice pudding with strawberry jam on top.

'What are you going to plump for, dear?' Viv asked, hoping Trudi wouldn't pick up on the word "plump" and ask for a salad. Fat chance, she thought, while carefully avoiding that expression too. But as the last mouthful of spotted dick with rice pudding, custard and strawberry jam on top went the same way as the adult-sized portion of toad in the hole, the hungry girl did turn into a spectacularly full one. Determined though she was not to feel guilty– after all, Fang wasn't there to help her out and it was rude to leave anything on the plate – she did have one question.

'Does everyone here eat things like this every day, Mummi?' Viv glanced at the ridiculously overweight Tory peer on the next table her daughter had just been staring at, and let her in on a little secret.

'Thing is about politics, darling, it's showbusiness for ugly people.' She felt instantly ashamed of herself for saying such a thing to a small child, but Trudi had already figured this out for herself anyway. Though it begged a question.

'But Daddi does politics too. We know he's silly, Mummi, don't we? But he's not ugly.'

'Of course not, darling. Hard enough work being silly, without having to be ugly as well.' Though Viv left it at that, she'd have gone a lot further if she'd been with Bakyt. Not ugly? More drop dead gorgeous, actually. As her mind strayed to some of the things she and Percy sometimes got up to, she went all red herself.

'You all right, Mummi?' This empathy thing was really taking hold.

'Yes, of course, dear, it's something ladies do when they get to a certain age.'

Same as Percy, Viv was all for telling the child the truth wherever possible. But there were exceptions. And as lies go, it was only little. And white. Unlike her face.

*

At that very moment, in another part of the building, Verrigreen was working on whoppers.

He had in front of him a confidential dossier marked: *Potential Threat Posed to National Security by Chinese Trains in the HS2 Project*. It sounded as absolutely impartial as it absolutely wasn't. All he had to do was make it look like the product of a considerable amount of in-depth research and analysis on his part. Which, again, it absolutely wasn't.

He had done some digging, but only into exactly which

flat and which speedboat he'd pay for out of his enormous new Swiss bank account. The rest was wonderfully simple, thanks to the miracles of modern technology. In an earlier age, he'd have had to laboriously copy out the entire dossier. All 20,000 words of it. Now a few clicks and it was copied and pasted into a neat new document on his Microsoft Word account.

Not that he was lazy, mind. His training as a barrister had taught him that stones should never be left unturned. Especially when they might have all manner of unpleasant life forms lurking beneath them. For this reason, he spent a fair few hours carefully reading it through, making sure there was nothing the slightest bit pidgin about the English.

Disappointingly, he discovered that the Chinese Government had people on its payroll every bit as good at lying as him. Worse, the language, grammar, phraseology and syntax were faultless. Detailed and densely argued though the document was, it was clear and concise, a surprisingly easy read.

He sighed and rolled up his sleeves. It was going to take a lot of work knocking this lot into shape. Again, all down to his silk's training. Any official document that anyone other than a fellow lawyer could make head or tail of really wouldn't do. He felt as duty-bound to keep the proles in their place as those doctors who kicked off about Labour oiks creating the NHS. By the time he'd finished adding the necessary frills, unnecessary words and preposterous sesquipedalianisms,⁵ it was more than three times its original length and utterly indecipherable. Job done then.

---

⁵ A sesquipedalian word is annoyingly long, but not as bad as flocci-naucinihilipilification, which says a thing's totally rubbish. It's what it means, and what it is. Handy for scrabble, though.

Then, of course, there was the final touch.

After making a hard copy of his revised version, which might as well be in Chinese as far as Tiddledick was concerned, he printed out and attached the original text. Then he got out his fountain pen and wrote the following in clear italic calligraphy.

Hi, Ponsomby. Thought you might like to see this. Hope it'll help set your mind at rest regarding Chinese involvement in HS2. As you'll see, I've put a lot of time and effort into it.

I've also appended a summary, which could save you some time. You might find it a bit oversimplified but I like to hope it retains the guts of it.

Very best wishes from your very greatest fan, Peregrine Verrigreen.

He smiled as he set down that last little fib. Calmed his nerves at being so honest about MI6.

*

By the time he'd finished, he was heartily sick of the subject, while back in Mayfair, Trudi had been literally sick. Several times. Knowing all about the fat kids' treats they dished up in Commons restaurants, Percy knew better than to believe a word of it when she told him it was all Mummy's fault making her eat it all up. He also knew better than to not nod in agreement when she told him she was never going to eat anything again. Ever.

But he didn't know better than to blurt out his feelings to

Viv about Fyok Yu and Hon Ki's schemes. Or, rather, he did, but forgot.

'Why, in God's name, why, are these shitty Chinese bastards going to so much extra trouble, when they've already got the fat old cow Erewego by the short and curlies?'

Viv gave her husband a Vivienne look as Trudi slowly dragged herself off the comfy little sofa she'd settled in and tottered out of the room. Forget the pink thermometer; this was definitely a pink piggy bank moment.

*

Whether it was really needed or not, Sir Peregrine Verrigreen's get-rich-quick scheme was also working out rather well. No sooner had Tiddledick finished poring over the findings of the independent research group, which shortened its name to ASSHOLE, than Erewego presented him with another splendid memo, this one put together for his personal attention by none other than the trusted chair of the Intelligence and Security Committee.

'Well, Egeria,' he purred when he had her seated in the special chair in his office he always motioned her to, because it was the strongest and biggest. 'Well well well. There seems to be an emerging consensus that I've been right all along about the low-cost option for HS2 rolling stock. You agree with me, I trust?'

He doubted it, given her double default position that he hadn't the faintest grasp of anything and that she alone understood the nation's needs. Actually, she was often right on the first point, though the second rarely crossed her mind.

'Well, Prime Minister,' she began, in the vaguely

disapproving tone she always adopted to keep him in his place, 'there are valid arguments for and against. But, of course, advisers only advise, ministers decide. And the PM's word is law.' Erewego particularly liked using the acronym PM, because in her mind it was short for Pusillanimous Moron.

While outwardly playing the just-this-once-let-the-man-think-he-knows-best card, she was inwardly shrieking with delight that he'd been hooked. And lined. And sinkered. As she waddled out of Tiddledick's office, her upper lip curled, making her look like Cruella de Vil, if you missed out the rest of her.

CHAPTER TWENTY-SIX

The next day, Trudi was having problems. For a start, she was starving, which ruled out the food-free breakfast she'd announced would be just the beginning. Would have been easier at home in Cornwall, where the family generally ate off the large, cluttered, scrubbed pine kitchen table. She could always have pointed out something really interesting in the garden, grabbed a few bits and munched away to her heart's content, on the floor.

A lot more compact and ordered in Mayfair. Immaculate shiny surfaces and absolutely no clutter. Not so many hiding places there.

Percy could see her difficulty but was too tactful to notice. Or, apparently, remember what she'd said only a matter of hours before. But he couldn't resist giving Viv a sly wink, and she could resist giving him one too. Bit like what she'd done during the night, which had left them both with a nice, rosy glow.

Goes without saying, Fang and Lady Casement weren't

getting up to that sort of thing, but they had got cosier and cosier, and this was starting to grate, just a little bit, with Trudi. She'd been so proud of herself, getting Fang in the gang, but cats and birds are supposed to have a healthy mistrust of one another, not cuddle up together at night. Nor are they supposed to be forever inventing new games to play, still less when they involve a parrot grabbing a little girl's favourite dollies and fluttering up with them to somewhere only cats can reach.

What's a little girl to do? Apart from worry about what state the dolly will end up being in? And feel left out? Of course, Trudi didn't think she was being selfish or anything, but she worried that tiny tinge of jealousy was unbecoming and didn't go with her new, even-nicer-than-ever-before look. But if she was feeling conflicted, it was nothing to what Chancery was going through, what with the competing demands being made on him by his various sets of masters.

Even Percy's instruction to simply report back on what the opposing factions were up to was a struggle, as he could hardly keep up himself. Also, the promised bolthole in Scotland if things got sticky was problematic, as Spleeny didn't like the look of it. The tasteful blend of soft pastel curtains, carpets and wallcoverings was as far from her idea of attractive as the colour orange was to Trudi. And the prints on the walls? Sunflowers? Chairs? Bedrooms? Nah.

'Van Goff? 'Oo's ee when ee's at 'ome den?' she asked Charlie. Pointlessly, obviously.

He had at least managed to buy time with the Yanks by locating a nifty little ground-floor flat just south of the Thames, though getting anyone to actually build a tunnel from the basement to the Palace of Westminster could be tricky. There was a problem too with the quantity of explosives needed to take out such a large building. Structurally ramshackle though it was, it wasn't going to just fall down all by itself.

He could but hope that Hank was even more half-witted than he was, and be taken in by the stash of replica hand grenades he'd picked up in a military memorabilia shop. The clincher was putting them in a spherical black container with what looked like a fuse sticking out of it and a white stencilled label marked "huge nuclear bomb".

*

Chancery was careful not to mention this part of his plan at their next meeting, which took place opposite the building which may or may not be in danger of getting blown up, depending who you asked.

Satisfied that it sure as hell was, Hank disappeared into the underground car park at Abingdon Green and roared off, leaving Charlie standing there and listening vaguely to a Sky News reporter doing a live report about something or other. He took a bit more interest when the hack highlighted something that once happened a few yards from where he was standing.

A Home Office paper had come out that day concerning the need for stiffer sentences for attempted terrorist outrages. All a bit boring, until the reporter gave his stuff a bit of colour by pointing out the spot where quite a well-known terrorist had met his end.

Although Mr Fawkes managed to avoid having his bits cut off and his insides cut out by jumping off the scaffold, it still struck Charlie as an argument against trying to blow up parliament. Especially as, it's worth mentioning, the scaffold was jolly high. Meaning he ended up with a broken neck anyway, poor Guy.

But though Chancery's cunning plan to not, after all, blow the place up got him out of one difficulty, he still faced another. Even the dumbo Yanks would spot the difference between an undamaged building and a bomb crater. Which was why, as he climbed into his own Mustang and turned the key, he decided to man up. Spleeny might one day escape from whatever zoo the nutters ship her off to, but he wouldn't get that lucky. A bullet through his brain would not be what the doctor ordered.

Fishing out his mobile, he made a point of pulling over before keying in the number. Safety first seemed sensible, even though he was fairly sure people didn't get hung, drawn and quartered for traffic offences.

'Guy Fawkes may have been a bleedin' suicidal maniac,' he bellowed to his astonished wife, 'but I ain't. You got dat?'

Percy, or Trudi ten years on, would have sympathetically quoted the bit in *Hamlet* that referred to the Everlasting fixing his canon against self-slaughter. But Spleeny was not a deep thinker.

'Dunno wot yer talkin' abaht, yer loony. Just 'urry up, I'm 'ungry. Bring fish 'n'chips or I'll eat yer rat.'

Chancery heaved a sigh. Looked like being an uphill struggle, this manning-up malarkey. Even the gentle incline up Farringdon Road felt a bit steep.

*

At least Percy doesn't have that sort of problem with Viv.

Or Viv with Percy. If she thinks what she has in mind is too subtle for the male brain, she just bypasses it. This always strikes him as a good idea, though not always at the time.

Bakyt's variant of this technique is more direct. If Monty strikes her as being particularly obtuse, she gently strikes him with whatever comes to hand and threatens him with the dread of Dracula. Only in fun, though it is in her genes to half believe in vampires.

'I good girl. Promise, never bite anyone,' she explained, to everyone's relief except Trudi's, who thought people who hadn't been very nice to Daddy when he was in charge of the country thoroughly deserved to be eaten up by Bakyt. Who hadn't, incidentally, finished talking.

'Genghis not bite anyone either. Except Amazon delivery person. But serve him right. Dodgy kinky slutbitch insult my man. He die. Good people not deserve. Everyone safe. Except dodgy kinky slutbitch.'

Monty quietly explained that actually it was all the Afghan's fault. His playful way of nipping random people on the bottom didn't strike everyone as all that funny. Least of all the Amazon guy, who still had stitches in his rear from the last time a dog went for him. But he cheered up a bit when Monty slipped him a tenner.

'Then all's well that ends well,' Percy announced. 'Same as in Shakespeare's work of that name. Served the dodgy slutbitch character Bertram right, getting banged to rights for accidentally banging his own wife.'

Trudi, sitting quietly in the corner canoodling with Fang, could hardly be expected to recognise the reference to the blokeish bloke in the not-so-well-known play Daddy was on about. But when Percy pointed out that another man got tricked in the same way in Mozart's *Marriage of Figaro*, she scuttled out of the room to find Lady Casement.

It's his favourite opera, he's got several CDs of it, and birds are supposed to sing, aren't they?

In no time, the clever little creature had got the melody but was still struggling with the Italian. So was Trudi. *"'Sull'aria… Che soave zeffiretto… Questa sera spirerà… Zeffiretto…'"* is a bit of a mouthful.

Dodgy… Slutbitch Bertram… Banged to rights… Banging his wife… was much easier, for both of them. And as Trudi danced prettily into the room, Lady C clinging on with difficulty to her shoulder but effortlessly holding on to both tune and words, Viv came over all Vivienne.

She was irritated that Nice Little Earner seemed to have vanished, as Lady Casement hadn't learned the word "slutbitch" without help. Though little you-know-who had picked up far worse from big you-know-who, aka Daddy, "slutbitch" was definitely refundable, even if Trudi insisted on a discount on the grounds it wasn't her who'd said it.

Viv would have been crosser still if she'd realised Trudi regularly half emptied the little piggy bank into the lining of Fang's mattress, so it wouldn't sound chock-a-block when she shook it in that demanding-with-menaces way of hers. Fang wasn't best pleased either to find his soft bedding making way for hard cash.

Tough call how it'd get spent. Maybe the best-ever pink doll's house, or a spare motorised pink scooter, in case the promised birthday present broke down. Or perhaps, better still, that horse Mummy and Daddy had been so mean about not buying her.

In keeping with her new and even-lovelier-than-before

personality, however, Trudi toyed with buying them a nice new 2CV. Shame Citroen stopped making them about thirty years before she was born; would have been nice to give her little hammer a rest.

But, for the minute, she had more pressing priorities. Teaching Fang authentic Mozart was never going to be easy, though at least 'miaow' sounds the same in Italian as in English.

CHAPTER TWENTY-SEVEN

Before the start of the summer holidays, Trudi had got nicely into the swing of infants' school. Of course, there was stuff to learn, though she couldn't understand how hard the other kids seemed to find such easy things. She felt like she was running a race with both her legs tied up, but consoled herself with the thought it'd be worse for Fang.

At least it left her time to dream up tricks to play on Sir, who she was so over by now that she couldn't for the life of her think what the attraction had been in the first place. So far the best had been teaching the others a more fun version of the assembly song, *Lord of the Dance.*

Instead of dancing all over the place all the time, there was an awful lot of burping.

She was so proud of her creative efforts that she gladly put her hand up when Sir demanded to know who was the guilty party, and couldn't understand why Percy was called into the office later that day. Also, she couldn't help overhearing herself described as a "precocious little madame".

'What does pree-coh-shus mean, Daddi?' Trudi was all wide-eyed innocence after she'd got the hammer out in Simone-Sitrouenne and they were finally on their way home.

Percy got such a fit of the giggles that he nearly crashed the car. The only thing he couldn't work out was how he'd managed to keep a straight face when the boring little prig was going on about how it was all very well Trudi being top of the class at everything, but that was no excuse for letting herself down to the bottom with rude words. When the man looked him in the eye and questioned where on earth she could have picked them up, he'd come dangerously close to a heart attack.

Some fifteen years earlier, Spleeny too had had her moments, though in her case they stemmed from always being bottom of the class in everything. Her favourite trick might have been of some interest to Bakyt, at least from a mythological/genealogical point of view. It involved waiting till Sir had his back turned, biting him savagely in the arm, smearing the face of the kid she hated most with fake blood and dashing out of the classroom. Worked even better if she pinned the blame on the child Sir hated most. Made no odds, as she hated everyone anyway.

More recently, she discovered that while all people are hateful, some are more hateful than others, and it can be useful picking targets. She currently had in her sights Fyok Yu, Hon Ki, Hank, Shane, Wayne and Duane. In no particular order, so long as they all ended up dead.

Charlie had done his best to convince her that Thurso was a lovely place, a perfect retreat, manner of speaking. But his manning-up manoeuvres had not so far got him anywhere, and weren't likely to till the makeover was over. A long job, as it involved covering the walls with woodchip paper, making swirly Artex shapes on the ceilings, installing a Tudor pub-style bar and eighty-eight-inch telly in every room and converting the lounge with the sea views into a sealed-off dope cultivation centre, complete with all the latest hydroponics.

The Van Gogh prints would be replaced with huge reproductions of football stars without their shirts on. Spleeny also had a few choice words of advice for Charlie.

'You gotta, like, face yer demons, and kill da bleeders. You gotta, like, man up, man, even if it killsyer.'

He had a feeling there was a flaw in her argument somewhere, but couldn't quite put his finger on it.

'Ya don't suppose, do ya—?' he began plaintively, but she cut him short.

'No, I don't. Woss rong wiv five against one? Al Capone took aht 'undreds. Ain't ya still got dat machine gun?'

Actually, he hadn't. Any more than his old swagger. Something to do with living with Spleeny, he suspected, though he'd never dare say so. Especially at certain times of the month. Once, when he made the mistake of asking if she'd got the painters in, she gave him the infant school teacher treatment. Which proved he was right. As well as wrong.

So She Who Must Be Obeyed must be obeyed, but he couldn't do it on his tod.

*

Trudi averages fifty brilliant ideas a minute. More than Charlie had managed in his entire lifetime. But something did occur to him which could just turn out to be a lifesaver. From his earlier brush with Biff, he remembered that because he clearly came from a long line of fighting men, he was well up for a scrap. Admittedly, when some of his lads got involved in that last shindig together, they were as much good as a Plasticine blunderbuss firing blobs of blancmange, but they would make handy human shields.

Knowing Percy wouldn't take to the useless drunken layabouts getting in the way again, Charlie decided best not tell him. And at the next Highgate Cemetery rendezvous, he was the living embodiment of tact and diplomacy, by his standards.

'Ya see, me old cock, I'm stuck between da smartarse Chinese and dumbo Yanks. Rock an' an 'ard place, right?'

'Of course, my dear chap, the Charybdis and Scylla syndrome,' Percy purred, pretty sure the ignorant prole wasn't up to speed on Greek mythology, or Norse, or anything that wasn't in the *Daily Star* or the *Beano*. The put-down didn't go unnoticed.

'Wossat s'posed to mean, when it's at 'ome den?' Though Charlie's answer was meant to put the pompous poseur in his place, he did stop slurping his coffee from the saucer. Also, he waited till Percy popped off for a pee before he popped his question to Biff.

'Remember your geezers wot did such brave fings last time we woz 'avin such a laugh togevvah?'

Biff did, though he'd hardly describe the collective near-death experience the halfwit was on about as a laugh. More a fail in every regard, especially his boys' rubbish performance before they slunk back to Belfast. But everyone deserves a second chance, and maybe Irish pigs can be bigger pigs than Chinese pigs, and smarter than Yankee pigs. Hard to be less so.

Of course, Mr and Mrs Chancery might get caught in the crossfire, but Biff didn't mention that, or share any of it with his old boss. He'd only the man's interests at heart, and Percy was looking relieved, as one does after a pee. Shame to get him wanting another one quite so soon.

*

Three hundred and twenty-two miles away, in Falls Road, Belfast, Chopper McMurphy was picking his nose.

It's his brand of Zen meditation, calms him when he's short of people to have bullied, blagged or beaten up, which he's too weedy to do himself. He's needed comforting ever since Brexit failed to derail the Good Friday Agreement and left his old IRA comrades still stuck with drugs and gunrunning. Blowing up checkpoints and army bases was better craic.

It's a bittersweet consolation, when Biff drops by, listening to Lady Casement chirruping on about armoured cars, tanks and guns. But this day, come noon, as Chopper puffed away at his eightieth fag so far, his piggy little eyes lit up. Buried among all the ads for flick knives and baseball bats, there in his inbox was the answer to his prayers. From the man himself.

Fancy a bit of better craic? A crack at crackpots across the water? My mucker Percy's got too many fecking friends. Needs to kiss a few goodbye.

Not wishing to disappoint, he left out the targets' nationalities. Anyway, if they accidentally took out the fecking Chancerys, at least they'd be notching up a couple of Brits.

Chopper, always a fatty, had ballooned since the last

call to arms from Biff, four years earlier. But substituting tracksuit bottoms for jeans and chucking out every mirror in the house had sorted that. He solved his other problem, that he was born and brought up on a scuzzy estate in South London, by bigging up his dad's Irishness. No one needed to know that the old man lived all his life on that same estate unaware of his own ancestry.

When Chopper's early career as a rock star faltered, thanks to his lack of musical ability or sex appeal, mostly sex appeal, he decided being a Fenian felt more cool. Besides, having waited in vain for months for his big break, he felt on the same page as all those freedom fighters who hadn't got lucky in 800 years.

In that same romantic spirit, he hired a tugboat for the twenty-mile journey from Larne in Northern Ireland to Portpatrick in Scotland, instead of just hopping on the ferry like anyone else. Though the suitcases stuffed full of Sten guns were also a factor.

The force-six gale would have made for a vile crossing if the ten-strong squad of hardened professionals hadn't been too bladdered to notice they'd even left harbour. They were in a slightly better state for the next day's rendezvous, at a cosy little Camden pub near the London Irish Centre, because Biff insisted it should be at 10 am. He felt less in control fifteen minutes and forty pints of Guinness later.

'I don't need you to kill people, just scare the fecking daylights out of them,' he said, tetchily. 'Though, if they're not responsive to bye bye, by and by, you can raise the bar.'

Thinking he meant a different sort of bar, the lads gave a whoop. Their girlie side came out as they managed to slurp their drinks and bare their teeth at the same time.

Biff had already made matters worse for himself by following up his email to Chopper with a phone call while Lady Casement was in earshot. Not only that, after putting down the receiver, he'd sung a couple of lines from a giveaway song, all about what young men get up to. In this case joining the IRA.

The clever little bird remembered that this came from the Irish republican ballad *The Boys of the Old Brigade*, which she shared with Trudi. The every-bit-as-clever little girl wondered if two and two might make four, and asked Percy.

'Is boring Biff doing something silli, Daddi? D'you think he wants his smelli Irish friends to come and see us?' Daddy doubted it, but tried to be tactful.

'I think that might be a bit far-fetched, darling. Even Biff is not that silly.'

Because Trudi wasn't convinced, she tried the same question on Viv, on the obvious grounds. A good call.

'Hmm, you're a clever little minx, darling, but it is a stretch. I can only hope you're wrong.'

CHAPTER TWENTY-EIGHT

Trudi thought carefully about what Mummy had said, couldn't see herself breaking the habit of a lifetime now, and looked forward to being proved right as usual. Meantime, she thought it'd be fun teaching Lady Casement a few words from a song Daddy had once told her Biff really hated, all about what great chaps the Proddies are.

It worked dangerously better than expected, as Biff started chasing his terrified pet around the flat with a meat cleaver, and only stopped when Fang sprang to his new bestie's defence.

Nothing like claws sunk into a man's man-bits to make him see sense. Only thanks to his trousers was it a crisis not a catastrophe, as the cat was showing no mercy. Not as if Lady Casement doesn't have an agenda of her own, mind. Bit like Biff with the Sash, she takes grave exception to one particular *Monty Python* sketch.

Egeria and Fantasia know it well. Even quoted from it after they'd got past their tiff about Charlie Chancery by kissing and making up, among lots of other things.

'But, daaaahling, feels like I'm tired and shagged out after a long squawk,' Erewego sighed.

'Oh yes, so exhausted I might have kicked the bucket, shuffled off this mortal coil, run down the curtain and joined the bleedin' choir invisible,' Fantasia smirked.

Given that the script included references to a parrot being nailed to a perch, pushing up daisies and being an ex-parrot, you can see where Lady Casement's coming from. You can also imagine Monty's reaction as he heard what the horrible hags were saying, at his listening post in Kentish Town. Ripping off the headphones, he decided he needed some air. Now. Arm in arm with Bakyt, he strode down Kentish Town Road trying to put together his thoughts, which fell to bits when he spotted a spectacularly nasty reminder of his teen years.

Chopper McMurphy had been a hated schoolmate at his horrible South London comprehensive, and he'd never wanted to set eyes on him again. But there he was, stepping out of the pub with Biff. Suddenly, on the grounds that if you really want something done, you do it yourself, Monty wished he had his Stens with him, to save him having to delegate.

Bakyt demonstrated her kindly concern by making a low-pitched sound midway between the snarl of a tiger closing in for the kill and the hiss of a crossbow loosing a poison-tipped bolt. Looking at her frothing mouth, Monty wondered where in her slight frame she managed to store so much foam.

*

The mood in Mayfair was every bit as not festive when Monty

spilled the beans, though Trudi heaved a sigh of contented satisfaction. Viv got where she was coming from and so did Percy, who wanted to kill Biff.

'You loathsome little people person, you wee willy wanker, you make leprechauns look like sodding giants. Does your diet consist of anything other than tablets marked "eat me and make your brain shrink"? Or do you have me down as the kind of lamb that's so bloody ugly, slaughtering's too good for it?'

On the back of that, Percy was a bit breathless, Trudi was totting up the profits and Biff was a bit put out.

'Ye fecking eejit, my boys may not be Hannibal's herd of elephants, but they're handy cannon fodder when everyone's against ye.'

Monty pointed out that the animals may have scared the daylights out of the Romans when they came rampaging down the Alps, but they didn't win the Punic war in question. This helped calm the atmosphere, as Percy found it rather interesting. But he couldn't just let the matter drop.

'Never mind elephants in the Alps, what about the elephant in the room? These boys are a total liability. As they proved last time, they laid waste to our best-laid plans. As you may remember.'

Biff could hardly forget and, already worrying that history may be headed for a Karl-Marx-farce-style rerun, almost managed an apology.

'Bejasus, Percy, I couldn't just stand by and watch these Chinese slimebags slit your throat while the crazy Yanks try to blow up parliament. Though I still say that's long overdue.'

At this, Percy couldn't help but smile. Fang was disappointed, as he likes a good ruck if he's out of range of low-flying furniture. Lady Casement tried to get them going again with a song about stealing British armoured cars and giving them to the IRA, but it didn't work. Viv, still bristlingly Vivienne, couldn't understand why Percy had suddenly calmed down till she connected the half-empty brandy decanter with her husband's slightly unfocused eyes.

'So what next, then?' she fumed. 'We sit back and watch this bunch of raving drunks mess up everything? Why not get them to blow up the Chinese Embassy while they're here? And Soho? And that nice restaurant on the canal at Primrose Hill, the Feng Shang Princess? Shame to leave them out.'

Thinking Feng Shang Princesses sounded rather fun, Trudi slipped into the next room to hype up her dollies by cross-dressing them. It took the edge off Ken's geekiness, slipping him into a frock, and Barbie looked rather cute with short hair, which would obviously grow back again in a day or so. But she was suddenly troubled, not so much by Mummy's weird words as the way she was saying them. A tone reserved for when someone's done something really bad. Probably Daddy, but not necessarily.

Trudi tried ever so hard to remember all the naughty things she'd done lately, both here in London and before they left Cornwall. Surely they hadn't all been discovered? And she did say sorry to Nanny after she'd superglued together the pages of her book, cutting down *fifty shades of grey* to three or four very chunky ones.

But, to be on the safe side, she hopped into the pretty little ottoman at the end of her bed, having taken the precaution of grabbing the bottle of sherry Mummy sometimes likes a nip of. Wouldn't do to die of thirst while in hiding. Turned out it was rather nice. Especially after the fourth good glug marked her out as definitely more Daddy's than Mummy's little soldier. Getting quietly sozzled calmed her no end, and a thoughtful contribution from Bakyt had the same effect on the grown-ups' discussion.

'Maybe Biff brutes not so useless after all. Fantasia Fealstite Northern Ireland Secretary? Yes? Maybe they stake out horrid hag's hovel. Talking loudly. Ugly men. Nasty accents. Soften her up? Maybe she persuade other fat cow to change mind about trains.'

Monty smiled grimly. With the flat already wired up for sound, he'd know in no time if it was working. His only worry was whether the stupid woman would even recognise a Belfast accent. Biff thought about getting the lads to sing the *H Block Song*, but accepted she probably didn't know Irish freedom fighters had ever been locked up anywhere.

'Provisional IRA? Expect she think PIRA stands for plastic things you store food in,' he grunted.

'No, she won't have heard of Pyrex,' Vivienne sighed. 'Her type just bungs the leftovers in the bin. Wouldn't even think of giving the otters a bite.'

'Talking of greedy little creatures, haven't heard a peep out of Trudi for a while,' said Percy, suddenly concerned at what she might be getting up to on her own. There'd been a minor crisis back home when Nanny had slipped out to Boots, on the pretext she'd run out of toothpaste, which Bakyt hoped she wouldn't muddle with the stuff she was actually short of, as it would sting like crazy. On that occasion, Viv eventually found the mischievous little girl rummaging through her make-up bag and jewellery box, obviously planning something or other.

On this occasion, Fang solved the mischievous-little-girl

problem by trying to prise open the ottoman. Having not managed to get at the brandy, he was after the booze he could smell wafting out of it. When Percy gave him a hand, out of curiosity as much as anything else, there was Trudi, softly snoring away, as happy as a lark, if not as well behaved.

'The little monkey,' Vivienne muttered when she noticed the empty sherry bottle doubling up as a pillow. 'That's so naughty.'

That's my girl, Percy thought but didn't say.

*

Next day, Trudi had the mother of all hangovers, which her mother thought served her right. Percy, naturally more sympathetic, prescribed a spot of fresh air on Primrose Hill. Though he had a feeling he'd end up carrying her down as well as up, it would give them a chance to see if Biff's bozos were doing what they were told.

They were, sort of; lolling outside the ghastly women's home in vivid green patio chairs with a crate of Guinness each, enjoying the summer sunshine. Percy too was looking on the bright side.

'At least they'll make the place look untidy. Knock a few million off the value of the horrible hags' gaff.'

With that same thought in mind, many of the locals hated them. But the arty ones thought they gave the place colour, while one guy who made cult movies wanted to sign them up for his latest grainy and gritty film all about useless, drunken layabouts. Percy, Viv and Trudi happened to be walking past just as he was making his initial pitch, which didn't go down well.

'Go fecking shag yourself, and your mother and all who sail in her, or we'll rip off your kneecaps, so we fecking will.' Chopper emphasised his point by flicking a bogey in his face, and Trudi suddenly felt better. Language like that would buy her a whole herd of ponies, and something even smarter than a Citroen 2CV for Mummy and Daddy.

She didn't get the chance to invite them back to Mayfair, as both parents seemed anxious to whisk her away as quickly as possible. But she kept staring back, and squealed in excitement when a bunch of other weirdos suddenly showed up. Though Percy was grateful for the excuse to put her down and have a rest, he was jolly glad they were safely out of range.

*

Having decided it was high time to see for themselves where the pawns in their game actually lived, Fyok Yu and Hon Ki were surprised to see all these grubby oiks on the pavement outside. They vaguely remembered a bunch of Irish hoodlums from their last brush with Percy but couldn't even put faces to faces. Names didn't come into it; it'd be like christening fleas. But they did notice the accents.

'If the English are an inferior species, the Irish are beyond the pale,' Fyok Yu muttered. 'If you'll pardon the reference to that country's colonial history.'

'Actually, it was never a colony, but one of Britain's kingdoms,' Hon Ki murmured, just to be annoying. The two were agreed, however, that these human stink bombs probably weren't a bunch of navvies who'd run short of canals to build. The only question was whether they were there to protect the ladies or kill them.

From their vantage point halfway up Primrose Hill, Percy and Viv relied on Trudi's ever-so-much-younger eyes to describe the way the two Chinese men put hankies to their noses as they drew closer to the men on the horrid chairs, then suddenly darted behind a huge car.

'Daddi! Mummi! They're playing hide and seek! With the funny-looking monsters walking towards them.'

Percy and Viv could hardly believe their or, rather, Trudi's eyes, though even at that distance they couldn't miss the stonking great motor doubling up as a hiding place. When she described the funny-looking monsters who'd just appeared, they could hardly believe their ears either.

Though the little one leading the way was clearly identifiable as a man, Trudi wondered if the other four were giant insects. Those huge black glassy eyes didn't strike her as the least bit human, while the large and misshapen left leg attached to the noisiest one could well have been part of a dinosaur.

Trudi's not one for overstatement, though the day she told Percy he was the cruellest man who ever lived when he tactfully pointed out Fang couldn't have kittens even if he tried, was an exception. Same as when she said he was the loveliest man who ever lived after he let her feed her ice cream to the birds because she didn't like the taste and bought her another one.

She can also do understatement, however, and the way she set Percy and Viv straight about the drawbacks of not having the eyes of a four-and-a-half-and-a-bit-year old is as good an example as any.

'They look a little bit funny, Mummi. Not sure Daddi would like them very much either.'

CHAPTER TWENTY-NINE

Mr Arty-Crafty bought the Zil-111 because it said in the *Guinness Book of Records* that it was the largest passenger car in the world. Designed to remind comrades in the Soviet Union that some comrades were more equal than others.

Some film directors are more titchy than others too, though Arty-Crafty can just about see to drive it when he stacks up the cushions he has embroidered with bright red hammers and sickles. Dinner party guests don't really believe his story about stealing the motor while in the gulag after the Russian premier of his film *Love Leon Trotsky*.

Fyok Yu and Hon Ki were very grateful for it, though. While Charlie, Hank, Shane, Wayne and Duane were obviously on the same mission as they were, that was no reason for comparing notes. Still less, as Charlie had no more idea than they did what the Irishmen were doing there, while the Yanks with their ridiculous glasses hadn't even seen them.

Trudi asked herself what would happen if they didn't take them off in time, and got her answer in no time, as Hank hobbled straight into Chopper McMurphy and tumbled to the ground. Shane, Wayne and Duane did the same, like a row of oversized and not very attractive dominos. As they clambered to their feet, she again showed how good she can be at playing down drama.

'I think they're all a little bit cross with one another, Mummi.'

She looked on with great interest as the little fat man scuttled off to join the little slender men, the smelly men who'd just had drinks knocked out of their hands rummaged for something, and the fat insects and insect/dinosaur all fumbled under their armpits. The ice-cream van that'd just appeared was tempting, but she thought now might not be the moment.

What Trudi couldn't see from where she was standing was Charlie, Fyok Yu and Hon Ki muttering to one another behind the Zil-111. Though four dead Americans wouldn't make much of a dent in their country's vast population, they thought it'd be a good start.

It's what should have happened, given the odds. Bullets coming out of a Smith and Wesson XVR 460 Magnum travel at more than 2,000 feet per second, and are big enough to take out an Alaskan moose or a fully grown elephant, but the cylinder only holds five of them. Whereas Sten guns can pump out 500 rounds a minute.

However, as Chopper had had a wee pint or two, he accidentally killed five of his boys, while the equally well-oiled survivors took out eighty-five windows, thirteen pot plants, eleven cunningly concealed Sky dishes, thirty-three recycling bins, twelve bicycles, two Silver Cross Special Edition prams, thirty pigeons, a lot of car tyres and three cats. And the windscreen of the Zil-111. The racket could be heard for miles, but Trudi was still playing it cool.

'They're being a little bit noisy, aren't they, Daddi?'

Percy flung her over his shoulder and he and Viv ran for their lives. At dangerously closer range, Chancery, Fyok Yu and Hon Ki carried on cowering, while Arty-Crafty could but hope the Kremlin could point him in the direction of a replacement Zil-111 windscreen.

*

By the time the police finally got there, Sky News was already broadcasting live from the scene, which meant Trudi, Viv and Percy could follow developments from the safety of the flat. First came the wailing sirens and screeching tyres, then, leaping out of their motors and pointlessly pointing their machine guns in every direction, the black-clad goons. They looked scary and scared, but calmed down when the superintendent in charge of the operation bellowed: 'I see the birds have flown.'

Embarrassingly for the force, a constable was caught on camera grinning as he tripped over a small feathered corpse and saying: 'Dis one ain't gonna be doing much more of dat.' Lady Casement looked most put out. So did Fang when the same constable was seen picking up a dead cat by the tail and saying: 'Heads I win, tails you lose, moggy.'

In solidarity with her besties, Trudi copied what Daddy often did and flung something at the telly. Mummy thought that was a bit silly, though at least pink fluffy unicorns don't do as much damage as lead paperweights. Sky News got grief from the editors of *Your Cat* magazine and *Racing Pigeon Pictorial International*, but the hoo-ha died down eventually because there didn't appear to be any human casualties.

Chopper had got his luckier colleagues to grab what was left of the others and scarper, and the truth never did come out, as, before sneaking back to Belfast, they torched the corpses outside Pentonville Prison. Lady Casement would have thought it fitting, as Sir Roger was hanged there.

The second the bullets started to fly, Hank had also hobbled for his life, remembering this time not to shoot himself. He made a mental note to court-martial the others for cowardice when he caught up with them.

Trudi made a mental note of the faces of everyone involved. For some reason, she had a feeling she hadn't seen the last of them, but hoped she was wrong. Just this once. So did Percy and Viv, when her clear description told them exactly who they all were.

*

Next day, one of them was sitting at the usual table outside the Highgate Cemetery café drumming all ten of his fingers and gagging to tell Percy and Biff what he didn't know they already knew. In fact, because he hadn't dared poke his nose out from behind the Zil-111 until the shooting was safely over, they knew more than he did. Percy also had a hunch that many of the drunken layabouts had been laid out on a slab somewhere, or should have been.

'Green on green is such a cliché,' he murmured as he slipped into his seat. Spotting the reference to the Irish slaughtering so many of their own straight after they'd won the War of Independence, Biff glared at him. What came next didn't help.

'Just a pity McMurphy didn't shoot his entire army, then himself.'

Lady Casement tried to cheer her master up by shouting 'Brits out, Brits out, Brits out', but it didn't work. Biff was in such a rage that he just snarled at her to shut her shagging beak. She bit him in the ear, then did it again when they got back to Mayfair. He felt so sorry for himself that he actually stuck out his lower lip, which Trudi thought was ever so childish. But she was very interested in a plan Mummy seemed to be hatching, even though she couldn't at first make head nor tail of it.

'If they've got any brains under all that blubber, Erewego and Fealstite might have spotted the pressure could be ratcheted up on them any time,' she began. 'If so, they might be minded to ratchet up the pressure on our friend Tiddledick. Calls for counter-pressure. Agreed?'

When Percy and the others nodded and Viv reached for the computer, Trudi came over all loving and sat on her lap. That way, she'd be able to read what Mummy was, with difficulty, trying to write. Not that it made a lot of sense.

Girlie get-together, darling? My place or yours? Chequered path to Chequers?

Touched by how nice her daughter was being, Viv stroked her hair for the full twenty seconds it took Fanny to ping back her answer.

Check you out, darling! Ladies who lunch. At mine. Tomorrow.

Job done then, Viv thought, as she slipped into Fanny-speak. *Right-oh.*

Trudi got down again as the computer snapped shut and Viv looked meaningfully at Bakyt.

'Little jaunt tomorrow, dear? Just the two of us?'

Not everything had fallen into place, but Trudi got the idea. She wasn't old enough to know Oscar Wilde had written: *Nothing annoys people so much as not receiving invitations.* But her version was just as good: *Just you two? Just you wait.*

Counting down the hours before her big adventure was so painful that she turned to Lady Casement for help, whispering in the area where she decided the ear might be: 'Biff's so boring! Biff's so boring! Biff's so boring! Shagging eejit Biff!'

It's difficult to know whether, in her girlie-birdie way, Lady C has monthly mood swings, but she was in a funny mood, and definitely not minded to be nice to Biff. Which was why, when he responded to her repeating Trudi's words by ripping the plaster off his ear and throwing it at her, she deftly caught it in her beak and ate it. Percy sniggered.

'What was it Emperor Hirohito said when the Yanks took out Hiroshima and Nagasaki?' he asked, his face a picture of puzzled innocence. 'Oh yes, I remember now. "The war situation has developed not necessarily to Japan's advantage."'

'Just wondering how yours is shaping up, old chap.'

In for a penny, in for a pound, Percy risked irritating Viv as well, as he lit a ciggie to celebrate the moment. It was only a bit of fun, and he's by no means a cruel man, but the temptation to turn the knife in Biff's wound was irresistible.

'My dear, such femininity! Such multi-tasking! I'd no idea you could combine breathing my tobacco smoke with passive sulking.'

When Biff stuck his lower lip out, even further this time, Trudi gave Lady Casement a high five.**

** This is inadvisable in real life. Parrots tend to fall over.

*

Her plans carefully laid, Trudi wasn't the least bit surprised that everything turned out in the morning just as she'd planned.

Viv and Bakyt clambered into Simone-Sitrouenne, then out again, then headed for her bedroom to get her to start the wretched thing. They found her snoring unusually noisily on top of Fang, gently shook her and were pleasantly surprised at how quickly she woke up. Fang was pleased too, as she's not getting any lighter these days. It's a cat's life, he grumbled to himself.

At least this time she'd only stuffed him under her a few moments before the grown-ups moved in and got her to move on. It struck him as odd that before tripping out of the room, she popped both pillows under the duvet and arranged them so carefully that they could almost be taken for a sleeping child. But he padded after her and watched without any particular curiosity as she hammered the dashboard. What happened next did surprise him, however.

After slipping out of the car, Trudi stooped, untied Percy's shoelaces and flicked them around. Consequence inevitable, and all part of the plan. Fang did such a good job that Percy fell flat over backwards, Trudi called out she'd had a terrible night and must get back to bed, and seized her moment. While everyone was fussing over Daddy, she flitted round the car, slithered into the back and curled up into a little ball under the seat.

'Let the sweet little angel sleep on, she obviously needs to,' Viv called to Percy as she jammed the motor into gear before it had time to change its mind about going anywhere.

'Right-oh,' Percy answered, his mind already, clearly, on Fanny.

Only Fang, from his lower-than-everyone-else's viewpoint, clocked what Trudi was up to. He felt a bit miffed that she hadn't brought him along and had a good mind to dob her in it. But then, remembering that as a cat he'd struggle to make himself clear, he settled for trying to apologise to Percy for tripping him up. Clambering on his lap and purring loudly usually does the trick.

*

Simone-Sitrouenne farted along the A40 towards Ellesborough, a journey Viv did many times during Percy's spell as prime minister. Just over an hour, traffic permitting, in a government car, and just over two in hers. Absurdly impractical, but she was ridiculously fond of her little motor, same as her husband. In different ways, as she had to point out when he looked a bit sad.

Bakyt was a bit worried they wouldn't be able to get "mobilisation transportation vehicle" started when it was time to head back, but Viv wasn't.

'Oh ye of little faith,' she giggled. 'The beefcakes with the guns are hopelessly chauvinistic pigs. But they'll help all right, if only to get us off the premises.'

That won't be necessary, Trudi said to herself with a smile. If she could outsmart an ex-PM and her very much smarter mummy, the beefcakes would be a piece of cake, as well as a mixed metaphor. She couldn't wait to show them what's what.

Though there'd been churn among the security staff at

Chequers since Percy left, one of the old guard waved Viv through without too much phone fannying with Fanny. As Simone-Sitrouenne spluttered along the gravelled driveway, Viv noticed the once immaculately manicured lawns had also got churned up.

Peeping through the little gap under the bottom of the back door, Trudi was fascinated by the deeply gouged holes in the grass and masses of steamy brown blobby bits everywhere, but was scared by the thundering of fast-approaching hooves. She'd read something somewhere about the four horsemen of the apocalypse, and hoped this wasn't one of them.

Seconds later, Fanny proved it wasn't by galloping gloriously into view, her white silk scarf streaming behind her. Convinced she was about to leap off and break her neck, Bakyt screamed uncontrollably, but calmed down when Viv explained she was riding side saddle.

'Darlings!' she called out, 'so phantasmagorically fabbi-doos to see you! Welcome to my tacky little hovel! Nothing to do here all week but roger myself rigid on Roger here!

'He's eighteen hands! Transports of pleasure! But I still need my own hands to get me over the line!'

Viv and Bakyt got her drift. Trudi didn't. The head gardener, who'd heard it all before, leant despairingly on his rake, wishing it was a double-barrelled shotgun and he could give her both of them. He couldn't think why he bothered.

CHAPTER CHAPTER THIRTY

Trudi stealthily opened the car door and snuck into the house, keeping a safe distance behind the ladies. She'd once heard Daddy going on about all the world being a stage and people having their entrances and exits, and wondered when would be the best moment to make hers. Entrance, that is, she'd no plans to exit, now she'd got here.

She'd been spotted by one of the beefcakes. Only instead of cocking his machine gun, he fired off a furious text to her indoors.

Stop lacing soup with wacky weed, woman. Hallucinating. Kid in pink jim-jams entering Chequers? No can be. Bad trip. Repeat. Do not repeat.

His long-suffering wife decided he'd got pre-traumatic stress disorder and planned to show him what that meant when he got home. After drilling a small hole in the rolling pin, she carefully slipped a nail through it.

Trudi, meanwhile, had carefully slipped through the building's front door, where she was fascinated by the artwork and expensive-looking ornaments everywhere. Everything was so highly polished that it showed up Penislow Palace as definitely more shabby chic than Chequers chic. She made a mental note to raise the matter with Mummy later.

But for now her focus was on seeing but not being seen, from behind an elegant but large cream-coloured sofa, though it was annoying how little of the grown-ups' conversation made much sense. She gathered Daddy knew lots of things Horsey-Lady's husband ought to know, and needed to be told pee dee queue, whatever that meant. Also, she heard the woman say lots of odd things that she didn't understand but suspected Nanny might.

When Mummy gave Dobbin-Face a fat wad of documents and explained they contained a pole, poor Trudi was even more baffled. The only good thing that comes out of either pole is Father Christmas, and it was nowhere near that time of year. But maybe Mrs Clip-Clop was mad, as she seemed to think poles were for dancing on.

Trudi wondered if she was completely wasting her time when Mummy said not that sort of pole, but one that showed people really didn't want Chinese trains after all. For God's sake, only boys like trains, wherever they come from. She wondered whether mummies have to go through a phase of being boys before they become clever enough to turn into girls.

It got worse as Horsey-Haughty started muddling poles with proles, another word that didn't mean anything. She also said it was silly to take any notice of the silly people. Better to be like Azza-Pyjamas, or somewhere, where they just drown them like kittens, if that's not too good for them. Daddy had mentioned how Fang had once done wee-wees on this woman's frock. Suddenly Trudi could understand why.

Nag-Hag sounded almost lucid when she promised to onpass the pole pee dee queue, but then they all strayed off the point again, on to gunpowder, treason and plot. Guy Fawkes Day wasn't until November, so why were they going on about it now? Made no sense. And when Horsey-Horrid said she'd onpass that info pee dee dee dee queue it was the last straw. Trudi snuck back to her hiding place in the car to catch up on a bit of kip.

*

Two hours later, she awoke with a start when she heard her name mentioned, and clocked prospective profits.

'Damn it. Where's Trudi when we need her?'

Viv's irritation was understandable. Simone-Sitrouenne had cut such a dash when she arrived that staff members were hanging out of the windows gawping. But now she was really letting herself down. Bakyt tried her luck with the little hammer, in the end giving the dashboard a good thrashing, not that it made any difference. More rude words, more coins to shell out later. Trudi was having a lovely time. Mummy wasn't, when three of the beefcakes sauntered up.

'Need 'and, love?' It was the tone that got to Viv, the implication that only a silly woman would want to drive around in a glorified lawnmower with silly flowers all over the bodywork. The other two were just as bad, suggesting every bit as patronisingly that maybe a shove would help. Preferably over a cliff, ha ha.

Could be that Simone-Sitrouenne's little engine was as put out by the men's attitude as the ladies. Certainly, the more cutting the blokes' jokes got at the expense of women, the more point blankly she refused to start.

Though Trudi didn't quite follow the men's sneering, she got a sense of it, and decided now was the time to access her inner Emily Pankhurst. Seemed a nice idea anyway, as she was feeling horribly scrunched up under the seat. As she unfolded herself and clambered into the front, Viv and Bakyt looked as though they've just seen a giraffe in a tailcoat. The beefcakes did too as she reached for the little hammer, made the dashboard feel ever so much better and got the engine spluttering into life.

As the beefcakes wandered up for a closer look, Simone-Sitrouenne managed a smoky backfire, as though deliberately making a rude noise in their faces, before lurching up the drive. Trudi was very pleased. It was what she had in mind, but the double-tap technique didn't always work.

Bakyt cradled Trudi in her arms and told her she was a little big-screen cine-movie marvel. Dazzling Oscar trophy Wonder Woman. Viv just drove on, brows knitted, till Chequers was several miles behind them, before pulling over and snatching up her mobile.

Mission accomplished. And Trudi, dear heart? Have you checked? Still sleeping? The text was so spluttering with menace that Percy showed it to Biff before answering. In spite of his many drawbacks, the man had a sixth sense during their time together at Number Ten. And the expression on his face couldn't have been worse.

Trudi often sleeps on for hours, as she's given to writing stories in her little pink notebook till the wee small hours. The last one was particularly good, as well as richly imaginative, curiously spelt and possibly prophetic. It was titled: *When*

Trudi Rules the World. Or rather, to be specifically accurate: *Wen Trudi rools the werld.*

However, she had been unusually quiet for an unusually long time, and, thinking of the grief David Cameron jolly well deserved when all he did was leave his kid behind in complete safety in a pub for a few minutes, Percy started to panic. Lady Casement didn't help by adapting an old music hall song Biff had once taught her. *Has Anyone Here Seen Kelly?* became, disturbingly, *Has anyone here seen Trudi?*

Percy rushed into her room, tore back the bedcovers, had several heart attacks – at least, that was how it felt – and snatched up the phone, which had just started ringing. He'd never been one for getting down on his knees, but right now felt he owed God an apology when every prayer he'd ever not said was granted, courtesy of a cheery little voice.

'Hallo, Daddi, who's a sillibugga then?'

He was still crying when Vivienne took over the call. She'd take a while to forgive him, but he'd take a lot longer. Not that Trudi minded in the least. She was ruling the world already.

Seemed a bit strange when they got home that Daddy was making such a fuss of her. Telling her she was the most wonderful creature in the world and promising to buy her the best-ever Barbie doll to replace the one whose hair hadn't grown back after all. He was in such a state that he started rambling even more nonsensically than usual.

'D'you know what Oscar Wilde said to the lady who came to greet him when he was released from prison?' She didn't, obviously, so he blathered on.

'He said, "My dear, you are the only woman in London who knows, when meeting a friend who's been missing for some time, what hat to wear."'

Like father like daughter, Trudi was often fascinated by bits of random information, and promised herself she'd use that line one day, when the moment was right. Same as "bollocks to you". Meantime, she also vaguely clocked that he was terribly sorry about not noticing she'd gone for a ride with Mummy and Bakyt, and decided he needed consoling.

'Don't worry, Daddi, I was very pleased you didn't discover I'd gone. Actually, I'd have been very cross if you had.'

At this, Vivienne evaporated. Suddenly she could see the funny side. She and Percy had a good shared cry, and Trudi decided they were both bonkers.

*

Charlie Chancery also had a feeling he was losing the plot.

Back in his gay days, he'd happily hum that well-known naughty boys' anthem *So Many Men, So Little Time*. Lately, it'd been more so many masters, so little rhyme. Or reason. And home sweet home was the one thing home wasn't.

His morning had begun badly, with Spleeny first telling him the porridge he'd made her for breakfast in bed tasted too porridgy, then chucking it at him. After that, it was even further downhill, all the way. Not only did everyone think he was a halfwit, he thought they might be right. Not that he's against lying in theory, just that in practice he's not good at remembering what he's said and who he's said it to. Or whose side he's supposed to be on.

His first meeting of the morning, with Fyok Yu and Hon Ki, went badly when he referred to Chinese trains as "stinking rust buckets". Things got no better later, when he told the Yanks they were "bleedin' bargains, best in da bleedin' world". Though Hank managed to not plug him on the spot, he did decide he'd better run a couple of checks. Discreetly, as was his way.

'How's about you hand over the boom boom ballistics right now? We'll keep it safe for you. Sure will, buddy.'

Chancery's dodgy little heart sank. So far, the white stencilled label marked "huge nuclear bomb" had done the trick. But it wouldn't if they prised open the giant black ball and had a look inside. That was his problem. Hank's was that the slimy Limey might not, after all, be trying to trick him. Opening a huge nuclear bomb, or even quite a little one, was high risk. Definitely one for the boys, not for him.

After telling Shane, Wayne and Duane what they had to do, he hopped on a plane, irritated that hopping was the only way he could get on or off anything, but confident that Belfast was far enough away if it all went explosively wrong.

It didn't, obviously, and when Wayne took off his glasses and discovered that his cell phone was in his hand, he couldn't wait to pass on the bad news about the bomb being stuffed with nothing more deadly than fake grenades. In response, Hank gave him the good news about himself, that he'd been doing secret planning for the CIA. Not MIA then.

However, while playing safe, he couldn't resist playing away, and discovered hopping wasn't so bad, after all, if it was into bed with the right people. Though they generally weren't keen, they'd sometimes spot what he had in his hand and say: 'American Express? That'll do nicely, sir.'

It gave him an idea. Bored with his existing team, Hank

decided it was time for a recruitment drive. Though he'd never been big on equal opportunities, either regarding race or gender, he licked his lips as he set about giving chicks a chance.

CHAPTER THIRTY-ONE

While Chancery and Hank had, in their different ways, been doing a spot of reappraisal, so had Trudi. It was an overheard conversation between Mummy and Daddy that got her thinking.

'That child's got her feet on the ground, as well as her head in the clouds,' was Percy's take.

'Something of a stretch that, one way and another,' Viv answered with a smile, 'though you're probably right.'

For whatever reason, Trudi was so streaks ahead of all the other kids at school that she wasn't going to invite any of them to her fifth birthday party. It was under a hundred sleeps away already, and she liked to plan ahead. She just wished she could make head or tail of the weird talk in that big house on the day of her big adventure.

Percy was on a learning curve too when Viv filled him in. He decided Fanny Tiddledick wasn't as silly as he thought, judging by her reaction to the poll that was so at odds with everything the cabinet secretary, the permanent secretary at the Treasury and the chair of the Intelligence and Security Committee had to say about Chinese trains.

The promise to pass it on PDDQ might have meant an awful lot more to him than to Trudi, though as her parents chattered away, some of the pennies began to drop, along with several pound coins as Percy kept forgetting to mind his language. After a while, she decided they'd better not know how much she was getting to know, and pretended to have her head in a book. Eventually, she realised she'd got Daddy's copy of *Das Kapital* upside down and hoped no one noticed; it looked terribly boring anyway. Percy would have agreed with her there, up to a point.

He certainly agreed with Viv that Fanny had been quicker off the mark than either of them had expected when she finally realised a pole and a poll are different things. Because it was at this bit of the talk at Chequers that Trudi had lost the thread completely, she gave up and slipped out of the room to try and teach Fang the art of what she imagined could be pole dancing. Or poll dancing.

Annoyingly, every time she stacked up a load of Lego into a neat little tower and turned the music on, he dabbed the lot onto the floor. Lady Casement did obligingly jig about to the beat, but then less obligingly grabbed the bits scattered everywhere and fluttered off with them. In a fit of exasperation, Trudi made the other parts into a naughty step, but they both refused to sit on it. It was just too bad. She decided they were the two horridest monsters who ever lived and would definitely not be invited to her birthday.

It was a full ten minutes before she remembered that the way they'd bonded proved they were the loveliest creatures who ever lived and decided they'd be guests of honour at her party.

*

There'd been ups and downs in Primrose Hill as well. Fantasia was very much on top during her teenage trysts with Egeria, as she was so much taller. But, these days, the roles had reversed. And the more flustered the big fat woman got about the prime minister's dithering about those dratted Chinese trains, the more single-minded the little fat woman got about taking back control.

'Fact is, my dear,' she began stonily, 'I'm the one that does the serious talking to the prime minister and you aren't.

'But I have to admit the wretched man's been getting a bit above himself lately. Even suggesting he may need more evidence that Chinese trains are quite the ticket.

'As for reaching a compromise, with the help of compromising footage, you know all about that sort of thing, don't you, dear? He seems to have gone limp on the idea.

'Can't help but wonder if he's been leant on by someone,' she added, thoughtfully.

Although Egeria was concerned at the way things were going, the sight of her lover squirming was helping. She watched with a surly expression as Baubles and Squeaky nuzzled up to Fantasia. All little creatures looked the same to her, including moles.

'Moles!' she suddenly exclaimed. 'That's it, that idiot's changed his tune because he's been tipped off by someone from the inside.' Of course, she was right, but if someone had told her who the mole was, you could have knocked her over with a wet otter.

Listening in through the headphones in Kentish Town, Bakyt was rather struck too. Fanny very obviously had passed on the intel PDDQ, and, equally obviously, Ponsomby had sat up and taken notice. Viv would be very pleased to hear it.

*

Trudi was just pleased to see her favourite witch-lady, as she let her into the Mayfair flat. Had Fang come across *The Hound of the Baskervilles* – happily not, as it's hardly suitable reading for any cat – he'd have had Genghis down as even more scary. But as Bakyt had arrived with nothing more frightening than her husband, he brushed his body affectionately round her feet and purred contentedly. And as details were shared about Fantasia and Egeria's chatter, Trudi started feeling more in the picture about that strange conversation in the big house.

She still couldn't work out how pole dancing, or poll dancing, should make the prime minister change his mind about silly boys' toys, but it was clear he had, or at least started to. Looking back on how he bumped his head after she'd tied his shoelaces to Daddy's, Trudi decided it'd obviously made him cleverer. He'd been rather cross at the time, which just shows grown-ups don't know what's good for them.

Anyway, she'd heard enough. Putting down the book, which really was boring now that she'd had a proper look at it, she headed for her bedroom. It had been a bit bare when they'd first arrived, more shiny surfaces and pictures that toned with the walls, but the little tent she'd made out of spare bedding propped up on the backs of boringly elegant chairs were a great help.

The great big pink poster of Cinderella set it off nicely, especially now that the Barbie dolls sitting in neat little rows on Lego seats were looking so at home. Trudi enjoyed reading to them, as they seemed to pay more attention than Fang. Lady Casement was a bit better, sometimes repeating after her, 'oh bother,' just like Pooh Bear.

*

The previous Friday, Tiddledick had enjoyed a repeat performance of his own. Knocking off early before knocking up his lovely lady wife.

He wasn't disappointed. Fanny greeted him at the stately gothic front door to Chequers with her beguilingly mysterious smile. Mystery how she manages it, considering her uncanny resemblance to a horse. But there's a delicious ritual to these tender reunions, which begin before they've even started.

The limo's flagged down by the head gardener, who only withdraws his notice on the strict understanding that he will get a pay rise and the prime minister will assert his authority over his wife. Next, Tiddledick settles back in his seat and winks at his driver, hoping Fanny will give him as good a pounding as the lawns seem to get.

Because his expensive school was more into sport than classical literature, he has an unusual take on the line that Percy's fond of, the one about custom not staling some woman or other's infinite variety, and age not withering her. He's always thought Fanny has particularly tasty withers.

But Percy's right about her also having a brain, and though men strike her as generally pretty silly, women don't. Which was why, when Viv and Bakyt showed up earlier in the week, she was almost as attentive to them as she is to her dress code with Poncey around bedtime. Which can be any time from the moment he arrives.

One thing Fanny has in common with Egeria, and Trudi, is her built-in sense of how to potty train men. Let them think they're the ones pulling the strings/making the decisions/doing the thinking, and nappy days are gone forever. So, when conversation veered to boring stuff, like things troubling Tiddledick at work, she yawned her way through yet another pep talk about how he really must get on with buying those high-speed Chinese chuffers, then got the baby wipes out. Metaphorically speaking.

'Never quite sure whether you're trying to convince me or yourself, sweet Pickle-Ponce,' she drawled, in an abstracted tone.

Pickle-Ponce is the pet name she only usually uses when his petting's off target. Her way of advising him to pay more attention, and reminding him she knows best. Which, as any lady will testify, has to be the case. But he wondered whether that delicate hint could be made to fit other situations. Hence, his softly murmured question.

'Do you know something I don't?'

'Maybe I do. Maybe I don't.'

Two things in life Fanny likes. One is being clearly understood, and the other is keeping her mystery. The two are not as mutually exclusive as they sound, she's learned from sweet experience.

At this stage, having sown the seeds of doubt, her thoughts turned to other ways of sowing seeds. Or oats, more suitably, given her facial features.

CHAPTER THIRTY-TWO

Not much had happened in Mayfair for what felt to Trudi like most of her life. About three hours, in real time, but little girls know best.

Different in Cornwall, always something to do. Waiting till Fang had gone out for some shuteye then jumping out on him. Pepping up Nanny's hand cream with runny honey. Or, better still, persuading the poor young woman to give her delicious recipes a go. A bit of lower lip-wobbling and eye welling-up generally did the trick, even, once, getting her to try a special cake of mashed tomato and raw egg, topped with marzipan and grated chilli.

Seemed to go down a treat, till it came up again five minutes later. Not enough chilli, perhaps.

The flat's other drawback was that, it being so much smaller and tidier than Penislow Palace, Percy and Viv generally had a fair idea where everything was, including mobiles, computers and iPads. This made it more difficult for Trudi to check up on them.

Though she's always found the idea of old-fashioned millionaires rather romantic, she's a modern girl in the modern age. But she could see now that she was stuck with olden days' technology. A notepad and pen. At least pretending to be terribly busy writing a journal meant she could sit in on a lot more grown-up conversation without arousing suspicion. But before coming to any rash conclusions, she was sensible enough to consult her friends.

'It's killing two birds with one stone, pussy-wussy. Good plan, I'm sure you'll agree.' Fang agreed on principle, as in his judgement, the only good bird, with the exception of Lady Casement, of course, was a dead bird. Preferably within instant eating range.

Lady Casement did not agree, for equal and opposite reasons. But she was bound to be biased, and it was still two against one. Motion carried then, and without further ado, Trudi made herself comfy, cross-legged, on a cosy little deep red damask-covered armchair, and put on her enormous pink specs. They made no difference to either her reading or writing ability, as the lenses were clear glass. But she was satisfied that they proved she was a studious and intellectually accomplished young lady. The diamante-encrusted frames also confirmed that there was a best-selling novel screaming to get out of her. And absolutely did not make her look like Dame Edna Everage.

Viv and Percy, who'd wondered lately if the child was getting bored, were relieved she'd found a new way of amusing herself, and worried less about discussing the potential overthrow of the British Government in her presence. They stopped worrying altogether when she licked the end of her huge pink pencil and told them they mustn't interrupt because she was writing her memoirs.

Percy had the feeling they might not be all that long, given she'd not got many years' worth of memories to play with even if she added on the months before she was actually born, which seemed to be asking a lot, even for her. Lady Casement alone had a hunch about what was really going on. The little girl could read it in her face and was heartily relieved she'd never taught the beastly bird to say: *Trudi is a fibber-fox.*

*

Percy glanced briefly at his seated daughter, saw she was wrapped up in her own thoughts, and made a gloomy pronouncement.

'To use an expression favoured by a certain little person, Chancery is a fibber-fox.'

The ears of the little person in question pricked up, and she hastily covered them with her hair, as she didn't want them to show.

'Of course, he's a congenital liar,' Viv responded. 'So what's changed?'

'I suspect the bastard's holding back even further than usual,' Percy muttered. 'Got a feeling in my bones he knows something about that sodding bomb of his that he doesn't dare let on. And about the bloody tunnel.'

Trudi twitched involuntarily. On the one hand, that was a clear three pounds in the piggy bank, but on the other, she wasn't supposed to be listening. Gritting her teeth, she accessed her inner Greta Garbo and carried on writing.

Probably for the best, she thought, as what came next sounded worth knowing. As part of her work as a nuclear scientist, Bakyt had done a lot of research over the years about various types of weapon, including itsy-bitsy nukes. And for once, she dropped the Azerbaijan jargon that made the others laugh.

'Fact is,' she said softly, 'small-brain Americans once tried small-size big bang bombs. Maybe they still try.

'The W54 so tiny it fit in soldier's back back but still boom like ten tons of TNT. Just one take out half Whitehall and Houses of Parliament. I not joking. These jokers not funny if not joking.'

Trudi risked a lightning glance at Lady Casement, who, presumably just as worried, did a poo on Biff's shoulder. He pointed an angry finger at her, though to indicate she was sorry not sorry, she bit it.

For Trudi, this was a Katherine Hepburn, Ava Gardner and Marilyn Monroe moment, all rolled into one. If something's funny, you really do have to laugh out loud. But only if you saw what happened, and best-selling authors do not look up from their work. She followed Lady Casement's lead, and bit. In this case, her own tongue. It hurt, but did the trick. So did focusing on her literary endeavours.

Groan up showty place in dainja, she wrote. *Musst worn Pink-fayse. Marid to Hors-Fayse.*

Pee dee queue? she added, proud of her ability to soak up neologisms, even irritating ones.

Later, she'd Google Ten Downing Street and fire off a ferocious email warning of the clear and present danger, though she didn't plan to put it quite like that. Her way would be much more scary.

Sillibuggas got a big bomm, Gye Forks kumming bak. Wotch yaws.

She'd read another bit on the website, the bit that says:

Whilst all emails are read and carefully considered, I regret it is not possible to provide an individual response to all queries that are received.

To cover that point, she'd emphasise that if the bomb went off, the Government wouldn't find anything possible. In the short, medium or even, very likely, long term. Again, she'd keep it simple. *Doo ore dyy. Choyce is yoars, sillibuggas.*

*

As it happened, Viv and Bakyt had already sounded the alarm. Fanny had taken due note of what they'd told her, and though she had Westminster down as a nest of ugly, boring, rather stupid traitors, she felt that setting it to rights by blowing it to hell might be going a bit far. And Ponsomby demonstrated that he's cleverer than a retarded clam by getting on the blower to Mugwump, PDDDQ. Because he agreed with everyone else that POTUS had an unusually tiny brain, even by Yankee standards, it seemed best to keep it simple.

'Howdy, pardner, how's the golf? Got your handicap down? We Limeys love your handicap.'

A good opening gambit. Ignoring the usual rules, Mugwump gets his goons to form an enormous circle round him every time he tees off. He then turns away, going into the visionary-looking-into-the-distant-golden-future pose, and waits until whoever catches the ball pops it into the right place and bellows: 'Yet another hole in one, Mr President!' He then looks satisfied but not surprised.

However, he was very interested in another form of handicap, and was actively promoting a bill designed to ensure that any man, woman or child with any disability of any kind gets a lethal injection pronto. The bill's short title was: *Love the Bill. Get Handicap Down*. Which was how come he didn't quite get Poncey's drift.

But at the mention of the bomb plot, he puckered his little mouth, which some say looks like a mouse's poo-hole, and clenched his fists, which, it's noted, are no larger than a squirrel's. He worried for a nanosecond that some traitor in the White House had leaked his plan to nuke London if the Chinese train purchase went ahead, though he could always fire them all. Retrospectively, to prove he'd never harm anyone.

Meantime, he'd got this Limey creep to paint on a smile for.

'Hey, pardner, you little English are the cutest little motherhood and apple pie people in the world. Closest allies, always shoulder to shoulder. Especially in illegal wars.' He grinned conspiratorially, proving he and Poncey had always been best buddies.

'Our bond is unshakeable,' he added, more seriously. 'We go back millions of years. Okay, we didn't wanna let you Limeys roam free at first, didn't think you were ready. But we gave you independence in the end, with open hearts and free minds. God bless America.

'So your future's safe in our hands. Man, we ain't even nuked Mexico and all them goddam plotting paedophile Satanists.

'And you know something, buddy? Those same Satanists tried to take over the moon to harvest Mugwump-munching monsters. Only failed because it's made of green cheese and the guy who lives on it ate it.'

Mugwump flicked the switch on the video link, without first saying goodbye, in the finest American tradition, and heaved a sigh of relief that he'd thrown the Limey completely off the scent. And when Tiddledick realised this wasn't a glitch in the system but he'd been dismissed, he shook his head hard in the hope of resetting his brain, and turned to Fanny for help.

'Dearest darling dominatrix,' he began, coaxingly. 'Did we lose the American colonies in the reign of George the Third, or did we break free from them?'

'Oh dear little pea-brained Poncey,' she said, alluringly, 'freedom's nothing but the chance to be better.'

'Er, yes. Right.' Long pause. 'Who says so?'

'Albert Camus. French philosopher, author and journalist. Surely you knew that?'

'Er, yes. Right. Not exactly.' Tiddledick was astonished by what his wife had just said, by the look of wide-eyed innocence that went with it and by what came next.

'I did actually go to school, darling. And Daddy used to get funny about me bunking off lessons and never learning anything. How else d'you think I discovered whips work?'

'Er, yes. Right...' Tiddledick was feeling more light-headed than ever. 'Anything else you'd care to share?'

'*Mais bien sûr*. The most courageous act is still to think for yourself. Aloud.'

'Oh, for God's sake, what Froggy genius came up with that?'

'Coco Chanel, darling.'

Ever since she had first seduced Ponsomby on a professional-sized billiard table, practically in sight and certainly in earshot of large numbers of people, Fanny had given the impression of a woman who didn't overthink things. But here she was, suddenly coming over all clever. Knowing naughty stuff is charming. Knowing too much else can be, well, too much. Not that Tiddledick was stupid; he'd had time to read a fair few more books than Trudi. But a fair few fewer, it seemed, than Fanny.

'*Ay me!*' She smiled. '*For aught that I could ever read, could ever hear by tale or history, the course of true love never did run smooth.*'

Tiddledick tickled his you-know-whats. Discreetly. Inside his trousers. He is well bred, if not terribly well read. Like everyone else, he knows the last bit of that quote. Like not quite everyone else, he's got some idea which play it comes from. But all that stuff about reading, tales and history?

Never mind ay me, he thought. *Bugger me will do.*

CHAPTER THIRTY-THREE

Percy's often wondered, when Trudi does Viv's voice and says something clever, if she's got any idea what she's talking about. So does she sometimes, but enjoys keeping everyone guessing, including herself. But there's no room for doubt when Daddy does something particularly dumb, like throwing something so heavy at the telly that it actually breaks, and she says sharply: 'No need to be silly, now.'

But, generally, the feminine principle of hanging on to mystery makes perfect sense to her, as it has to Fanny Tiddledick, for a great deal longer. Surprise was ever her secret weapon. But there's OMG OMG and OMG WTF, which struck Ponsomby when, instead of pole dancing, she showed him a boring old poll.

'If it's competitive sport you're after, old sport, two can play at that game,' he said, producing the confidential memo Erewego had given him, with, it has to be admitted, a rather flaccid flourish.

Fanny glanced over it, threw back her head and positively

whinnied with laughter. Ponsomby looked at her irritably but didn't say *don't look a gift horse in the mouth*, settling instead for something safer.

'Care to share the joke, sweet Socratic sex-kitten?'

At this, she only roared all the louder, stabbed the paper with her fingertips and staring at him in something approaching disbelief. Eventually, he looked down at the paragraph she was pointing at, and did feel a bit silly. He couldn't believe he hadn't noticed what was titled on page one. *Anglo-Sino Solidarity Helpfully Offering Legitimate Expertise* had been shortened to the initials A.S.S.H.O.L.E. And couldn't help but wonder if he'd have got there if Fanny hadn't got there a bit sooner. Well, immediately, actually.

At least there was Verrigreen's info to fall back on, though his annoying wife was bound to tell him that was rubbish too. Tossing it in her direction, he came over all curmudgeonly.

'Well, what's wrong with this? Everything, I suppose.'

She didn't even have time to open it before her face turned scarlet and puckered alarmingly. Ponsomby's mood changed dramatically. Beloved, beautiful, seductive Fanny couldn't possibly be having a heart attack. Could she? She was young, strong, healthy. And not at all horsey. He knelt at her side and gripped her tenderly but ever so firmly. 'Look at me now,' he almost shouted. 'Right into my eyes.

'It'll be all right, sweet love, all will be well. Don't leave me now. I'll get the doctor. He'll sort you out in no time, love of my life, delight of my dreams.'

She continued looking like a woman possessed, still unable to speak. All she could do was slap her thighs, hard, and rock from side to side. But, happily, Ponsomby had misdiagnosed her condition. Her problem was the same as Trudi's when Lady Casement bit Biff.

*

So hard not to giggle when you really, really want to, at inappropriate moments. All you can do is take a deep breath, and another, and another, and another, and try to control yourself. It's ever so hard, but, bit by bit, Fanny did gradually start looking normal again. At least, as normal as she ever did. And, equally gradually, she worked out how to break it to dear, kindly, silly Poncey.

'Thing is, my hunk of a husband, Verrigreen is, shall we say, a complete and utter, well, I won't say the word, but it sort of rhymes with aunt.

'Not that his relatively healthy appetite is necessarily a bar on high office, darling,' Fanny murmured thoughtfully. 'Even though he does make a rampant rabbit look like a Franciscan friar.

'Tried it on with me once,' she added, then smiled at the look on his face.

'Don't worry, dear man. He ran away, tail between legs. Didn't seem to like having nine of them across his shoulder blades.

'Did you know, by the way, the colossal squid's eyes are as large as a football? Just saying.' Ponsomby tried to squint but still looked like a colossal squid.

'Anyway,' Fanny breezed on, 'I'm not one to cast aspersions. Quite sure he'd draw the line at having it off with a budgerigar. But he has been having to use his initiative since his wife barred him from the family shack, on the grounds you couldn't fit his sex drive into Buckingham Palace.

'Yet suddenly, miraculously even, he seems to have got hold of a tasty little flat in Pimlico. Wonder who gave him the money. And what he gave in return.'

As she said this, Fanny looked pointedly at Verrigreen's memo. Ponsomby did too, only in his case, sadly. *Bugger me*, he thought, for the second time that day.

'What the hell do I do about that? He's obviously being a... how did you put it? Let's shorten it down a bit, a CAUC. That's an acronym, isn't it?'

'Good... boy!'

Ponsomby clocked the inflexion. "Boy" pronounced several octaves higher and dripping with delighted fake astonishment. Same as a lady telling her dog how clever he is for doing what he's told for once.

'Fact is, though,' he continued in a voice that he hoped didn't sound too growly, 'the evidence is purely circumstantial. We've no actual proof.'

Fanny nodded thoughtfully, and answered mysteriously.

'Leave it with me, sweetie pudding-pie. I'll see what I can do.'

*

Guess what, darling! Poncey pooped his panties!

A classic one-liner. When Viv showed Fanny's email to Percy, his first thought was that she was almost as good with language as Trudi. And even better at spelling. But there was more.

CAUC cooked his goose? Take a gander! Proof's in the pudding!

Viv had a more knowing expression on her face than Percy's as she tapped out her answer.

Passport to Pimlico, darling? Tease out and tickle?

Percy was still baffled, though he knew there'd be an answer. Which didn't take long.

Prime proboscis, pronto! Smell the rat, darling!

Only one answer to that. Viv smiled as she wrote it.

Right-oh!

Pretending to be hard at work on volume two of her magnum opus, Trudi was loving the dumb show. She even risked taking off her glasses, easing Fang onto her lap and whispering: 'My, how Daddi's got his knickers in a twist!' Because she was better at stage whispers than the sort people can't hear, Percy looked at her sharply and felt fully justified in defying all womankind.

As Viv shut the silver laptop lid, he opened the silver cigarette case. Then, reaching for his antique Dunhill table lighter, he read aloud the inscription on its base. '*Ignorance is like a delicate exotic fruit; touch it and the bloom is gone.*' But as a concession to Viv's strongly held views, he opened the window before taking his first puff.

At that moment, a car that had been indicating left turned sharp right. The van that had been trying to pass crashed straight into it, and a couple of nearby cyclists went flying. It struck Percy as an omen.

'Definitely feels like something's about to happen,' he murmured. '*Never mind the bloom, please prune my ignorance.*'

'Hah! A little learning is a dangerous thing.' Viv smiled sweetly, took a typically ladylike sip from her pretty little Victorian coffee cup and completed the quote: '*Drink deep, or taste not the Pierian spring.*'

'Oh for God's sake, spit it out, love. Well, not literally, obviously,' he added hastily as she held the cup to her lips with a mischievous look on her face. 'But, please, tell me what is going on.'

Perched on her comfy little chair with Fang firmly gripped in her hands, Trudi wondered if he'd like to have his ears sellotaped together. He didn't. But though he sprang to the floor and fled, it didn't matter, as now was clearly the time to reach once again for the huge pink glasses, huge pink pencil and pink fluffy notepad.

CHAPTER THIRTY-FOUR

There are two versions of Percy and Viv's conversation. Trudi's is more fun, though the grown-ups' a shade more informative.

Viv fleshed out details of her and Bakyt's get-together with Fanny, mentioning how much more savvy she'd been than they'd expected, how she'd already got the goss about CAUC, and how she was going to set Ponsomby straight pronto. No surprise then that he'd been a bit taken aback, and she favoured a forage in Pimlico.

'And all that was in those emails she sent you?' As a journalist, Percy was rather disheartened, as he'd always thought he was the best in the business at keeping copy tight. Annoyingly, also, her suggestion was a good one. And, doubly annoyingly, she'd thought of it and he hadn't.

It was agreed that Monty and Biff should check out CAUC's new flat in the same way as Erewego's, and case the joint thoroughly for incriminating evidence. The conversation also covered the bomb plot, and Ponsomby's powers of perception. Though Percy was fond of the man, he thought he could be a bit of a tosspot sometimes.

Scribbling furiously, Trudi struggled to keep up, only risking the odd sideways glance at Lady Casement when she heard likely keywords. Joint, for instance, and case. And cork. And tosspot, though if they really must throw the crockery around, they shouldn't break too much of it. She likes to tell the story as it is. Or, rather, as she sees it.

Mummi and daddi gowing awai four sunndai dinner. Taisty joint. Paking caises? Ime cumming two. (Tho thay doant no it!!)

And norty half-wit stil tri-in to blo up parment. Musst tel toss-pot agen. Not lissenin. Silli toss-pot, not safe at table.

Must tel daddi to mynd his langwidge two. Neads to stik a cork in it, becos heez a cork two sumtymes.

Trudi closed the book, satisfied she'd covered all bases. Then remembered one more thing.

At leest hors woo-man not so silli as eye thort. Stil a hors, but a laidi hors.

*

Monty and Biff were as quick off the mark as, in her own way, was Trudi.

Usual drill. Nun's habits. Diversionary smokescreen. In and out in a jiff, but not before all light fittings had been fitted with bugs. The ceiling in the last room was particularly accessible, as all Monty had to do was perch on the conveniently placed large fibreglass object and reach up. Like Viv, but unlike Percy and Poncey at times, he's not a great one for swearing. Though he did allow himself a little lapse, just this once.

'Well, bugger me.'

Fair do's, you might say. It's not every day you find, instead of a bed in a bedroom, a speedboat.

Monty can never quite decide if he's got the softest spot for Holmes, Maigret, or Poirot, but he's always admired their powers of observation and deduction. And prided himself on being a quick thinker, same as them, though he skips the funny accents and weird dress code.

It occurred to him that the bedroom window did open to the river, and Battersea Heliport wasn't that far away. Then told himself not to be so silly. Then made up his mind to do a lot more looking. He'd got the locked cabinet in the study open in a trice, thanks to tricks of the trade he'd picked up during bygone days on the beat, from various old customers. Slippery ones, that is.

And, hey presto, in the back of a drawer was a bulky case. Again, locked. Again, no problem. Sifting through documents at the top, he found correspondence relating to the almost implausibly speedy purchase of the flat he was in. But no sooner had he stumbled on a mystery than a clue presented itself. Masses and masses of them, actually. Neatly bundled up in used fivers.

'Ello 'ello 'ello, he thought to himself. *What's all this then?* Just occasionally, he can't resist a bit of dated plod-speak, as he has a sneaky regard for his mum's favourite copper, *Dixon of Dock Green*. Which is why he allowed himself another quaint expression as he shut the case as deftly as he opened it.

'Starting to look like an open and shut case.'

*

Not often you catch Biff laughing, and when he does, it's more of a guttural growl. But as he and Monty were wandering back to the car, he was in such a state that his nun's habit nearly fell off. The intelligence that Verrigreen had taken such a big bribe took the biscuit, and his breath away. Same with Percy, though he went through an elaborate and, arguably, irritating ritual before sharing his conclusions.

Tilting back his black leather-faced executive swivel chair, he stared dreamily into the middle distance and placed his elegantly manicured fingertips together. And took such a long time that Lady Casement tucked up one leg, which she only does when she feels like she's tired and shagged out after a long squawk. Not that she approves of that expression, as we know.

'Elementary, my dear Watson.' Percy's way of finally breaking the silence struck Monty as utterly predictable and downright exasperating. Trudi, who'd been busy bringing Fang up to speed with the latest developments, having already impressed on Lady Casement the need not to call her a fibber-fox, just thought Daddy was being weird.

But at last he got on with it. Linking Monty's story with how he'd spotted Verrigreen greeting Fyok Yu and Hon Ki in the Commons, he announced it was an open and shut case. Monty snorted but managed not to throw anything at Percy. Fang thought about diving for cover, and Trudi snatched up the notebook.

Then it all calmed down. Percy was delighted that Monty had taken the precaution of photographing all the evidence, and Viv wondered if any other handy leg-ups for those wretched Chinese men might be included in the price.

'Anything's possible, including devastation if he does go

ahead with the purchase. The big bang's fine as a theory. In practice, it could leave a big hole where parliament used to be.'

Bakyt, who until then had been busy keeping Genghis and Fang as far apart as possible, suddenly broke into the conversation.

'We find out more. Now. About bomb. Explosives my bag. We bag bad men. Think they know everything? They not know us.'

'Us?' Viv raised a quizzical eyebrow.

'Yes. You and me. We infiltrate American gang. Before they cook London, we cook goose.'

Genghis placed his own interpretation on that, licked his lips and looked up at her expectantly. Afghans don't plead but do have a sense of entitlement. Monty wondered why on earth his wife had suddenly decided Fang was just going to have to get used to Genghis being around, but wasn't surprised at her crazy suggestion. Not that he was prepared to let her take that kind of risk.

'But, darling, lovely, loony lady, surely you don't think for a moment I'd stand by and leave you at the mercy of these violent criminals? Do you really imagine I would allow you to do that?'

'Yes.'

Bakyt was never one for wasting words. Monty tried again. 'You're really telling me you've no concept of the danger you'd be facing?'

'No.'

'But you'd do it anyway. Look, I'm sorry, but you're too precious to me. I simply can't permit it. End of story.'

Bakyt looked at her husband with an expression that was

hard to read. She'd never known him try the control freakery thing on her, and didn't take to it. Which is why she expanded her form of words fourfold.

'You try stop me.'

He looked despairingly to Percy for backing, and had one last go.

'For God's sake, watching clever women outsmart evil from a safe distance is very different from standing by idly as they place themselves at the mercy of trigger-happy hoodlums.'

However, as Monty suspected, the power balance in the Penislow household was well established.

'I'm just as terrified,' Percy purred, 'but may I suggest we let the ladies go into the field, with us behind, and Biff in front.' Viv's emotions were conflicted. She found Bakyt's idea exciting, thought Monty was right, and liked Percy's compromise, all at the same time.

Trudi, however, had no doubts. Daddy's plan was fine, but only if Mummy had foolproof protection. She slammed her journal tight shut, placed it firmly under her arm and marched out of the room, convinced the wrinklies would try and thwart her, if they dared read the latest entry.

Silli men thinc thay can protekt wimmin. Rong rong rong! Onli wun purson up too the job. Mee ov corse. Trudi rools ok!

Some might dispute that. Though she was certainly right about how her idea would play with the grown-ups.

CHAPTER THIRTY-FIVE

There are ways and ways of getting your own way. Trudi had it off pat by the time she was three. The wobbly lower lip and welling-up eyes always worked with Nanny, and with Daddy. Mummy could be a problem sometimes, but that was work in progress. Still is.

Egeria Erewego's always been just as fond of being obeyed at all times, but a great deal horrider if she isn't. On this day, she took it out on Baubles and Squeaky. The shock on their little faces as she tipped the tasty titbits laid out for them into the bin calmed her, as did Fantasia's response when she spotted the empty dishes.

'Dear, divine little creatures, eaten up every scwap mummy's cwossed London to get for you. Darling, darling ickle Baubles. And you, pwecious lovely Squeaky. No favourites in this house, sweet, perfect coochy coochy woochies.'

All this came out loud and clear a couple of miles away, in Kentish Town. Bakyt, who'd been listening in at her desk, ripped off her headphones, as she thought she might be sick. Ponsomby would have been pretty sick too, if he'd heard what Erewego had to say.

'Tiddledick can be such a tosspot.

'I make it perfectly plain he has to buy those wretched trains, and now he's less than a hundred per cent sure about them,' Erewego snorted. 'What do I hear? Some nonsense about a bit more research. Who the hell does he think he is?'

'Er, the prime minister…?' But Fantasia got no further. When Egeria's on one, there's no getting her off it.

'First, he gets all weedy about public opinion. As if that matters. Which it doesn't. And now he's got all pompous about wanting supporting data, when I've already shown him.

'I'll drag that Verrigreen creep to the top of the Elizabeth Tower and drop him into the chiming mechanism of Big Ben if he doesn't up his game.

'I'll knock down his door and squeeze his eyeballs till they pop if he fails to force the tosspot to believe those stinking Chinese trains smell of roses.

'Verrigreen's a CAUC, by the way? Did you know that? And what that acronym stands for? And where it comes from?'

It was too soon to open her mouth, and, of course, she'd got no answers, but Fantasia risked a look that implied she'd no idea.

'Well, I'll tell you then.' Erewego was still snapping, but slightly less like an alligator than she was. 'CAUC stands for Complete and Utter… well, I won't say the word, but it sounds like ladies' special bottoms, and where we keep them.'

At this, Fantasia genuinely did look puzzled.

'Think about it, stupid. The front.'

Fantasia got it. It rhymed fine either way.

'And the phrase CAUC was coined by kids in a novel by William Boyd. *Any Human Heart*. So now you know.'

Fanny Tiddledick knows that too, though she's never had the heart to tell her less literary husband. Percy and Viv have both read the book as well, and enjoyed it, as will Trudi, in time. Erewego just enjoys showing off how clever she is. Which is how come she was starting to think more like a competent administrator with a cool head than a megalomaniac demagogue with a filthy hangover.

This was lucky for Verrigreen, as instead of knocking down his door, she'd ring the bell. And instead of squeezing his eyeballs, she'd squeeze into his sweaty palm a wodge of dodgy dossiers to hand out to the like-minded Conservative MPs on that committee he'd set up. Because these guys would be told this material is confidential, they'd leak it far and wide.

In no time, they'd be huffing and puffing, appropriately for once, given it's trains they'd be on about. Not buying the Chinese ones, they'd argue, would be even worse than sending in food aid to undeserving third-world wallahs who should think themselves lucky we're not sending in gunboats.

'If that doesn't do the trick, nothing will,' Erewego announced, feeling rather pleased with herself.

Fantasia was wise enough to agree, if vaguely, as she was distracted by Baubles and Squeaky frantically juggling anything they could get hold of.

'That's odd,' she said. 'They only do that when they're really hungry. But they've just had all that lovely salmon paste I went all the way to Islington for. I don't understand it.'

Erewego did, and the thought of how miserable these

little monsters must be cheered her up no end, and she suddenly started being ever so nice. Fantasia didn't suspect a thing, Baubles and Squeaky went hungry and Bakyt went berserk.

'Stinky stinky cow,' she bellowed at her astonished husband. Though she couldn't see what Erewego had done, she could guess. She also guessed stinky stinky cow would waste no time in getting on CAUC's case. Monty was glad he'd got the Pimlico gaff safely wired up. What the, ahem, stinky stinky cow had in mind should make interesting listening.

*

Bakyt was right. Erewego was ever a no-sooner-the-word-than-the-blow kind of woman. Always had been. When her form tutor made the mistake once of suggesting she might try trying a little harder, the woman was on the scrapheap within a week. Amazing what anonymous letters alleging sexual impropriety can do for a teacher's career.

No surprise then that that very afternoon Monty was listening in on a most informative conversation. In theory, MPs can expect a little respect from civil servants. In practice, Verrigreen couldn't.

'Now see here, you contemptible love rat,' Erewego barked at the chair of the Commons Intelligence and Security Select Committee, 'you'll pass these on if you know what's good for you.'

More to the point, Sir Peregrine Verrigreen knew that the cabinet secretary knew lots about his past that he'd rather she didn't. He also knew that they were only standing in this flat thanks to the immense bribe he'd accepted from Fyok Yu and Hon Ki to pull the wool over Tiddledick's eyes. And that further services were likely to be included in the price.

He made a mental note to tell Fyok Yu and Hon Ki that the dodgy dossiers Erewego had handed him were his own handiwork. Many were the heavily disguised work of the Chinese Government, while the rest had been cobbled together by conspiracy theorists posing as investigative journalists. Every one was professionally laid out and coherently argued. He had to admit they were rather good.

'You can make a convincing case that the moon landings were fake,' Erewego smiled, venomously, 'so long as you miss out the fact the earth isn't flat.'

Verrigreen had no idea that anyone in the world was even more cynical than him. So maybe he could, after all, do business with this loathsome fat cow. Though he didn't put it quite like that.

'Oh, but, madame, you are wonderfully astute. As well as deeply beguiling, if I may say so.' He fluttered his eyelashes at her and paused to let his compliment sink in. Watching her expression soften a fraction, he decided he'd sooner try it with a rhinoceros than go anywhere near this overblown blob. But once again, he paraphrased.

'Truly, dear lady, we are natural bedfellows. I am seduced by your feminine wiles.'

It could be that this was over-egging it, and Erewego was suddenly smelling a rat. After all, he was a love rat, as she'd already mentioned. Or it could be to do with what she'd just noticed through the partially open door to the second bedroom. Something long, pointy and plastic.

Knowing the man was a slimy creep, she was okay with honeyed words laced with arsenic. She could also hardly fail to be a live-and-let-live kind of girl. Far from being an issue, then, a giant blow-up doll could have been just a bit of fun. But that fifteen-foot contraption? No accounting for taste, but bonking a boat? *Excuse moi!* Niceties over, she turned nasty.

'If otherwise intelligent people can be taken in by this kind of nonsense, a twerp like Tiddledick will be a doddle. Just do it, CAUC.'

Never having heard the expression, Verrigreen scratched his head. Back in Kentish Town, Monty didn't, but did feel a teeny bit sorry for that twerp Tiddledick.

*

Trudi has a special brand of TLC for when Percy's particularly put out. 'Never mind, Daddi, you'll feel better in the morning after a good night's sleep. Don't do any reading when it's tuck-up time for tinies.' She was ever a do-as-I-say-not-as-I-do kind of girl.

In his office in Number Ten, Ponsomby was also doing a lot of reading. Difference being, he wasn't liking it, as Erewego and Verrigreen's brusque encounter was briskly followed by a deluge of texts and emails indicating Tory backbenchers really were revolting. Some had always favoured hanging, flogging, fox hunting, bear baiting, witch-dunking, and the rack for unelected Brussels bureaucrats. But when he learned they wanted to put him on it too if he resisted the bargain of a lifetime, he skipped the convention about keeping civil servants out of internal party politics.

'For heaven's sake, Egeria, what's got into the swivel-eyed loons now?'

She tried not to look as pleased as she felt.

'But, Prime Minister, I've no idea to what you are referring. Would you care to enlighten me?' As hypocrisy goes, that was a corker. CAUC himself couldn't have done better.

'Everyone's telling me it's Beijing or bust. Can't think what's got into them.'

Erewego shielded her eyes, so he wouldn't see the glint in them.

'Must admit I've been a trifle confused, Prime Minister, by one or two things I've spotted on Twitter. Nothing to worry about, though, I'm sure.'

He recognised the signs, tried to look firm and decisive and told her to jolly well get on with it.

'Well, Prime Minister...' She cleared her throat, put on her little round glasses and peered down at her tablet. 'It says here... no, I don't think I should mention it.'

A technique Trudi had long since perfected. Pretending something had upset her terribly but she didn't think it fair to trouble Mummy and Daddy softened them up before she told them how desperately she needed a pony/frilly frock/special Barbie/Urban Bourbon ice cream or anything else that came to mind.

'Well, Prime Minister,' Erewego began, in the tone of a doctor who doesn't really want to mention the patient's cancer is terminal, 'it says here the prime minister's a tiddlebrain.

'Or will be if he doesn't buy Beijing. Of course, I'm sure the MP who wrote that would prefer to adopt a more nuanced position, but that's Twitter for you.

'Don't suppose it really matters too much, Prime Minister, but there seem to be hundreds of replies. Some of them, let's see now, no, all of them, apparently, in agreement.

'But, then, the devil does make work for idle hands. A matter of no importance. Sorry to waste your valuable time.'

The second she was gone, he buried his head in his hands, bitterly regretting that he'd always wanted to be prime minister, when what all he really needed was a bit of peace. He felt desperately jealous of Percy's lovely easy life, lolling around on the red benches.

CHAPTER THIRTY-SIX

At that precise moment, Percy was thinking what a lovely easy life he was not having. It was so clearly written all over his face that Trudi spared him the tuck– up-time-for-tinies routine, coming over all Florence Nightingale.

Clambering onto his lap, she gave him the wide-eyed loving look she usually saves for getting something out of him that Mummy's told her she can't have. But that was before she'd become Little Miss Lovely, who really cares about others.

'Tell Trudi-wudi all about it. You know you want to, and you'll feel so much better if you get it off your chest, won't you, Daddi-waddi?'

Daddi-waddi, aka Percy, wasn't too sure about that. Then again, he'd often confided in the past in Fang as a form of self-help, even though he was pretty sure the toe-tormenting psychopath wouldn't understand a word he was saying. Having no idea how closely Trudi was following developments, he thought he'd be pretty safe with her too.

Thanks to Monty's debrief after Erewego read the riot act to Verrigreen, and the Twitter feed about those wretched trains, he felt clued-up, up to a point. But still didn't know what on earth to do about it.

'Well, my dear,' he began, 'it's exasperating to know tosspot Tiddledick won't realise he's being had, and will start dropping hints he's definitely minded to buy that Chinese crap.'

Trudi coughed meaningfully, and Percy coughed up two quid.

'Of course, the stupid sod, yes, okay, here's another pound, the stupid, ahem, person will only be trying to buy time. In place of Tony Blair's education education education, he goes for vacillation vacillation vacillation. But the Yanks are likely to take it to mean the man means business. And won't be happy till he's bought it.

'Which he will, if he doesn't watch his sweet ass. These guys don't get British humour but do have the same response to a rubbish joke. Boom bloody boom.'

Trudi licked her lips in triumph, then remembered what a lovely little girl she'd turned into and decided just this once to let Daddy off with two for the price of one. Not as if she wasn't doing very nicely anyway. Percy paid up, dutifully, wondered if Fang might have been a better option after all, and reached for the silver cigarette case. The cat lifted one eyebrow – sneaky little monster – but settled down again when Percy poured him a bowl of brandy. Proof that politicians can buy silence, as well as time.

'Thing is,' he went on, carefully checking every word before he uttered it, 'I've said Mummy and Bakyt can check out the ordnance. We both know they're clever, same as you, dear, but they're not exactly gunslingers.

'Perhaps it's time for them to have another little word with that f… f… er, fu… nny Fanny lady.'

Though Percy said this almost to himself, Trudi was all ears. Much of what he'd said hadn't made any sense at all, but she had a feeling f… f… funny Fanny lady was the horse-faced woman she'd seen in the big house. Also, she didn't like the sound of boom-bloody-boom one bit. After giving Daddy a nice little kiss on the nose, she slid off his lap to make a few notes, and to empty the contents of her pockets into the piggy bank.

*

Percy puffed away thoughtfully until, sometime later, Viv came in to tell him she'd had a word with Fanny. Already. Despairingly, he read the emails.

Viv: *Guess what, darling, Erewego in cahoots with CAUC! Know who I mean?*

Fanny: *Smellygreen! Who else? Complete and utter vajayjay!*

Viv: *Fatty-go-go leading him up lady garden path! Porky alert! Poncey pounce-time!*

Fanny (obviously): *Right-oh!*

That was it. Once again, Percy marvelled at their way of squeezing a mountain of information into a molehill of words. One of which particularly intrigued him.

'What's this vajayjay thing, darling? Don't think I've come across one of those.'

'Oh yes, you have, dear ding-a-ling. Mine. Mmm.' Viv is living proof that appearances can be deceptive. For one who looks so demure, she can talk so dirty. Percy loved it, and went all pink.

The mood changed slightly when Viv spotted that Fang was sprawled out on his back, paws outstretched. Horrified, she got on her knees and peered at him closely. Closely enough to smell his breath. As she rose again to her feet, patting her short but shapely skirt flat against her short but shapely thighs, she noticed the ashtray and put two and two together.

'We might have fallen in love in a smoke-filled room, darling man,' she said wearily, 'but unlike cats, we've only got the one life. And I want to share mine with yours for as long as possible.'

Though Percy would sooner start knitting woolly hats or take up golf than kick the fags, he was touched by the affection in her voice, and wished he'd only had one or two instead of half the packet.

Caressing her cheeks delicately in his hands, he looked into her eyes and murmured softly: '*Da mihi castitatem et continentiam, sed nolo modo.*'

She looked back at him steadily and clocked something in his expression.

'Meaning? Dear heart?'

'Just a heartfelt prayer to God, from Saint Augustine. "*Give me chastity and continence, but not just yet.*"'

Viv snorted, tilted forward and bit his nose. Then licked it, the way Fang did sometimes after an attack, by way of apology.

'Beast,' she whispered.

Percy ran the backs of his hands across her breasts, and smiled. There was a faraway look on her face as she gave the softest of soft little gasps, and smiled back.

*

The mood changed again when, a few minutes later, there was a tap on the door and Bakyt appeared with Genghis. His expression was haughty. Fang's didn't change. Nor did he slink away, as he couldn't have done even if he'd wanted to. Trudi, however, made a point of marching back into the room, specs and pad at the ready.

Making herself comfortable in her favourite writing chair, she told the grown-ups they really mustn't interrupt her like last time, licked the end of her pink pencil and felt, if she did but know it, like the hacks who blew the whistle on Watergate. She got the gist of a planned meeting between the Yanks – whoever they were – and Mummy and Bakyt, but was puzzled to learn that Bakyt was a nuclear weapons expert as well as a witch, and so famous she never went anywhere without a minder.

The fact that Mummy was a crack shot and a karate expert was also news to Trudi. But what particularly interested her was the elaborate set of precautions planned for the ladies' protection.

Wearing a big floppy hat, a big floppy moustache and a French impressionist-style cape, Monty would take a nearby table at the Highgate cemetery café, his neat little police-issue Smith and Wesson safely tucked in his paint box. Biff would do the same, with his ancient Tommy gun lashed to his back under his coat. So what if he looked like a hunchback? He'd always had a bit of a stoop.

Percy would borrow Biff's nun's habit and prowl around, using a little girl as a cover. Though holy ladies, apart from the Virgin Mary, obviously, aren't supposed to have kids, they're surely allowed to take other people's out for a walk in the park, he reasoned. Trudi wondered who the little girl could possibly be and Viv started veering on Vivienne, but accepted one point in defence of the plan.

'Think about it, darling. She's the only one who knows how to start the car. Her in tow means a tow's the one thing we won't need when it's time to go.'

Now Trudi knew who the little girl was, she frowned ever so hard so no one would spot the triumphant gleam in her eyes, and committed her thoughts to paper.

Thanc god mummi and dadi beeing senzibl 4 wunce! Not saif without mee 2 loook arfta them!

Saivs mee having 2 doo pillo hiiding rooteen, sutch a bludi per4munce!

For a minute, she thought she'd have to activate Plan B, when Mummy pointed out that they could perfectly well go in Monty's car, so there was no need to expose a defenceless child to danger.

'Yes, but,' Percy countered, sensibly for once, 'there'll be no one to keep an eye on her. And, given her age and, ahem, temperament, leaving her on her own would mean the flat would be in danger.'

Viv gave up, unwillingly, and Trudi was so pleased with Daddy that she risked saying something nice to him. When she smiled and told him he didn't look a day over a hundred, he smiled back and told her she didn't seem a day under twenty-four.

She smiled at him again, this time sympathetically, wondering how come grown-ups always state the obvious.

*

When Simone-Sitrouenne spluttered up to Highgate the next

morning, Viv made a point of parking near the entrance to the old section of the cemetery, a safe distance from the café. It would have spoilt everything if the ladies and their crack protection team had been spotted all crammed into the same car.

Walking through the park, Percy pointed out Karl Marx's tomb on their right. He'd noticed Trudi's apparent interest in *Das Kapital* and thought she might be interested to know who'd written it. She was too nice to admit he looked as boring as the book, but was intrigued when they fanned out by two burly men with silly sunglasses at one of the café's tables. Last seen by her pretending to be dominos on Primrose Hill.

Percy, Monty and Biff were even more intrigued to see Hank and Shane, but no Wayne and Duane. In their place, two delicious-looking young women. Another astonishing thing was the look on Hank's face. No longer the bland blankness you'd expect on public buildings in somewhere like Basildon, but a grin. From ear to ear. And a twinkle in the man's eye. Not that they could see that, obviously.

On top of that, as Monty and Biff took their seats, neither could fail to notice these lovely ladies' accents. Definitely more Northern Irish than North American.

*

It'd all happened at lightning speed. Like Erewego, Hank is a no-sooner-the-word-than-the-blow kinda dude, and he'd actioned his Belfast plan as soon as he'd sorted two broads to replace those deadbeat losers Wayne and Duane. Their fate was easily sealed by a mock-up shot of them apparently writing a telephone number on a dollar bill, emailed to CIA

HQ in Virginia. They were on a transatlantic flight in hours. In cuffs.

One of Mugwump's more moderate policies, that. An executive order recommending the death sentence for anyone caught defacing the POTUS picture on a greenback. But, proof Hank is just as kind-hearted, he mailed his ex-guys pictures of their replacements in compromising poses. Guaranteed to get them sizzling all the way to the electric chair.

Isla and Ella were red-haired beauties both, with luscious figures and features to die for, and a lot of good reasons to be very grateful to Hank. The promise of blowing up parliament struck them as a lovely idea, if a little late. Also, his offer of 2,000 dollars a week was one up on their rubbish waitressing wages in a rubbish club in Belfast's rubbishest suburb.

The cash could be stashed away, to see them through their PhD theses. Isla's was snappily titled: *The lamentable history of the first 500 years of Irish oppression by perfidious Albion*. It neatly dovetailed with Ella's, headed: *The lamentable history of the second 500 years of Irish oppression by perfidious Albion*.

They'd tried asking Hank for a post-traumatic transatlantic perspective from Irish immigrants who'd fled the potato famine of the 1840s, and an American view of marauding Redcoats during their War of Independence. But they gave up when he told them doggone redskins sure as hell did have a lot to answer for, though Davy Crockett showed 'em, with that great big beautiful wall of his.

At least his nooky needs were easily met. Because he insisted on wearing his dark glasses even in bed, he never realised the Irish colleens he was sleeping with were made of plastic.

Isla and Ella toyed with getting a couple more, to keep Shane off their case. But after a couple of tokes of wacky baccy, he wouldn't have noticed if he'd gone to bed with a goldfish, so it seemed a waste of money.

CHAPTER THIRTY-SEVEN

For one reason and another, then, Isla and Ella were feeling pretty chilled in Highgate. Until they heard a shapeless-looking man a couple of tables away muttering something in a thick Belfast accent. Biff's biggest guilty pleasure is watching old black and white movies, like *The Hunchback of Notre Dame,* which is why, when the waitress placed in front of him his bottle of Perrier, he muttered to no one in particular, 'She gave me water.'

Given how much unpaid rent they'd left in Belfast, where everyone knows everyone but only trusts one another if they're of the right religious persuasion, Isla and Ella felt unsettled. Proddies, in their book, were born brutish and will die that way, as soon as possible. This proves they're nicely brought-up girls, with hearts of gold.

The best bit of the Catholic faith is reliving exciting moments in the confessional. Nice for the padre too, as being a celibate can be dull. His old heart would have been pounding at their reaction to the exotic, moody and sexy artist on the next-but-one table, though what they made of the explosives experts they were sitting opposite might have pushed him over the edge.

Viv was sexy, but Bakyt? Worth a Hail Mary or two. Or 200. Monty felt the focus, both on him and his wife. He was struggling as hard not to laugh as Fanny when Poncey was being a tiddlebrain, until he was distracted by an apparition thundering into view.

Trudi, who'd been enjoying the challenge of playing the invisible little woman, completely blew it, though her squeal, up there with the best of Hollywood bloopers, was understandable. Unlike Fanny Tiddledick, this really was one of the Four Horsemen of the Apocalypse. Clinging to Daddy so tightly that she almost pulled off his silly costume, she quivered at the sight of the rearing, snorting thoroughbred, only calming down when she spotted the horseman/woman/well, child actually, clinging on for dear life.

A gentle trot around Hampstead Heath had turned into a crazy gallop. Onto Highgate West Hill, right into the High Street, then swerving right again up the path to the café, apparently bent on rampaging round Waterlow Park, trampling over anyone in range. Including nuns and little girls, which didn't help Trudi get back into character. She felt grateful, after all, that Mummy and Daddy hadn't bought her that horse.

But that wasn't all. Though anyone with any sense knew Bakyt was a witch, Trudi hadn't realised she'd been brought up on her local equivalent to a Texan ranch. No one can accuse Kazakhstanis of being barbarians, because they're anything but. Which is why, faced with potentially lethal large beasts, they don't always reach for the AK-47s.

It's an open question as to whether they give traditional technology a whirl out of the kindness of their hearts, or because of the cost of bullets these days. But Trudi could only stare open-mouthed as Bakyt leapt to her feet, pulled from her bag a length of rope with a sort of knotted noose at one end, swirled it around, whipped it through the air and caught the beast by the neck.

He wasn't having any of it, until he heard a sound neither he nor Trudi had ever heard before. Not a shout or a shriek, or even a bellow of rage, but the kind of hideous hiss you'd expect from a large gathering of extremely angry snakes. The effect was instantaneous. The animal bowed his head, stood stock-still and stayed that way. At that point, strangely, the girl who'd kept herself bolted on as the horse bolted off, fell off.

Percy glanced down anxiously as Trudi started making a very funny noise, which sounded as though she was being sick or having a seizure. He wasn't to know that she was trying to imitate the strange sound, which could be so handy for discouraging Fang from attacking him. Or absent-mindedly trying to eat Lady Casement.

His perfectly reasonable and kindly question about whether Trudi was all right was met with a seriously scary stony stare. Again, he wasn't to know that she was copying the expression on Bakyt's face. Enough to get Joe Stalin emptying the gulag, it got the immobilised horse emptying his bowels. Trudi decided only to try it on Fang out of doors.

Because he still couldn't see what was going on, Percy settled for muttering 'gawd blimey.' Particularly inappropriate, given his disguise. He wasn't surprised at the language-daddy-language look, and promised to settle up when they got home. But for now, as Trudi could hear as well as see so much better than him, he asked her to fill him in on the table talk. She did, after another crack at The Look, to see if Daddy would disgrace himself in public like the horse definitely had and Fang probably would.

'Well, I'll be doggoned.' Hank's opening gambit wasn't up there with: '*One small step for a man, one giant leap for mankind.*' Though, in fairness, Neil Armstrong did have time to get it just right, as it's quite a long way to the moon.

But when Bakyt rejoined the party at the table, Hank made an effort to make sense.

'My pardner here says you're a goddamned weapons expert. I sure as hell believe him now, and could sure as hell use your help, lady.

'You better come round to our little old spread in this little old town of yours and gimme the lowdown on our little old box of fireworks.'

There was a sharp intake of breath at two nearby tables, and from some distance away, as Monty and Biff, and Percy too, thanks to Trudi, took in how much trickier the back-up operation would be away from a neutral public space. But now wasn't the time to discuss the matter.

*

Gagging to hear for himself exactly what was being said, Percy finally broke rule number one for nuns and gave into temptation. But, as he got closer, he let himself down in Trudi's eyes as well as God's by trying to sound as well as look the part. She decided Fang could have done a better job.

At least the people round the rather crowded table were

getting to the point. Viv and Bakyt agreed to show up in the morning at Hank's hidey-hole, the most expensive and vulgar hotel in London – no surprise there – and were disturbed at what he told them about the explosive device they needed to look at.

Partly truthfully, Hank said he'd tipped out a load of fake grenade from the metal spherical object marked "large nuclear bomb" and put in something his buddies at the Department of Defense had found. It ain't Hiroshima or Nagasaki, they admitted, but it'd do nicely, yes siree.

'Hell, if George Washington could never tell a lie, these guys ain't about to start now,' Hank declared, his grin so wide that his face looked as if it might break in half.

He went all dewy-eyed about past American triumphs, like Vietnam. Those goddamned commies, always eating their own young, crucifying grannies and tipping napalm over defenceless American children. Boy, they had it coming to them. Still, magnanimity in victory, he added thoughtfully. Out of the kindness of his heart, Uncle Sam liberated these little yellow men in the end, same as the yellow-bellied Limeys.

It was all from the gospel according to Saint Mugwump, who always gave credit where it was due. Okay, Hitler might have gone a little far, but he was doing his bit for mankind.

Shane lapped it up, Viv and Bakyt didn't, while the French impressionist and the hunchback harrumphed. The nun lifted her eyes in prayer that his little charge wouldn't chip in, possibly controversially. Isla and Ella too would have come down hard on Hank, if they hadn't been too busy longing to do the same, in another sense, on Bakyt. Also be rather nice if the artist cared to make up a foursome, at the risk of having to confess to a replacement padre the sin of having finished off the last one.

*

After a number of absurdly over-extended hugs and a ridiculous number of longing looks, Isla and Ella finally dragged themselves away from Bakyt. The young horsewoman trotted along with her idol to see the Ponies off, her steed now so chilled that he didn't bat an eyelid even when one of the Mustangs backfired in his face. As they roared off, the girl gave her most theatrical thumbs-up before allowing herself to be transported away, in transports of love. She couldn't wait to tell the girls in the dorm what a pash she'd got for the heavenly horse whisperer.

Percy, Biff and Monty couldn't wait to compare notes with Viv and Bakyt, while Trudi simply needed to get a few things straight. For a start, Mummy needed to know that Daddy needed to know how to do lady voices if he must go out again in that silly costume. Also, she needed to know how Bakyt did that clever trick with the rope.

These points were duly noted, before Monty outlined the only feasible strategy and Trudi got down from the table and looked really busy making a daisy chain. She cursed herself for not having notebook, pencil and glasses, as committing so much to memory is really hard.

Monty was going to use the Met Police warrant card he'd hung on to as well as his stash of guns, to secure the hotel manager's co-operation on the sting operation he was mounting with his Irish colleague. They'd need porters' uniforms, and pass keys to the suite of rooms occupied by two American gangsters on Interpol's most wanted list. Percy, who was gagging to come too, was sharply reminded by Viv that someone had to stay behind to look after Trudi. Can't be helped, she thought, not as if pillow under duvet wasn't a tried and tested strategy.

Shame about the trouble it'd get Daddy into, again. But what did he once say about people getting in the way in wars? Collapsing damage? Collateral rummage? Something like that.

CHAPTER THIRTY-EIGHT

Trudi was irritated that in her excitement she'd completely spoiled her daisy chain, and would have to start all over again. All Monty's fault, she decided, though maybe now was not the moment to point this out.

As the party finally headed off to where they'd discreetly parked Simone-Sitrouenne, she hid her spying operation behind a well-chosen question she was sure would put them off the scent, and probably interest Daddy.

'That Mr Washing-Line man, did he really never tell any ickle fibs?' she asked as she skipped innocently along. 'Sounds very boring to me.' Conveniently, they were approaching the Karl Marx tomb, so she pointed at it and said: 'Same as that ugly man, you know, Daddi, the one who wrote the boring book. Dus crappi? Crappi-something-or-other.'

For the millionth time, Percy was impressed at Trudi's memory, though Viv wasn't sure what to say. No one, including little girls, is supposed to tell fibs, but she did feel slightly compromised, having spent the last hour telling barefaced lies to those ghastly Americans. Percy too could see that disguising himself as a nun strayed as far from the straight and narrow as pretending to be looking after someone else's little girl. But he could at least answer the question.

'No, dear daughter mine, George Washing-Line, er, Washington, did not claim never to tell lies. A man who later wrote about him said he said that to deceive the American people into always doing what they were told.'

'So naughty Mr Washing-Line lied really. And the other man's nose grew too!' Trudi clapped her hands and squealed in delight. 'Silli bludi men, why didn't they just tell the truth? And admit they don't tell the truth?'

Percy's mind flashed back to Downing Street days. Whenever colleagues said, *I want to be quite clear about this*, they always meant, *I want to pull the wool over your eyes*. But Biff, unexpectedly, came to the rescue.

'Well, you see, wee colleen, there are big bad monster men prowling around, so they are. And for a thousand years, they tormented the truthful little people in a little country, so they did.

'All that time, the truthful little people pretended they didn't mind, not one little bit, but were actually making secret plans, so they were, to get good giants from a faraway land to help rid them of the big bad monster men who'd been so cruel for so long.

'And you know what? They won. The big bad monster men ran away. All because the truthful little people didn't tell them the truth about what they were doing.'

Percy looked at Biff admiringly. He'd never heard the history of Ireland, and how discreet lobbying and fundraising in the US by Éamon de Valera helped win its independence, told quite in that way.

Trudi was impressed too. It was the first time Biff had ever bothered to really talk to her at all, let alone say anything interesting.

By now, they'd reached the car; time for her magic starting trick. As she got out her little hammer, she looked at Biff mischievously and asked if he wanted to know how she did it. When he said yes, she told him it was all in the secret words she whispered so no one could hear.

'And what are they now? Bejasus, I so want to know, so I do.'

'If I told you, they wouldn't be secret anymore and the magic wouldn't work, would it? You silli man. Of course, I could make something up, but that wouldn't be true, and Mummy says I mustn't tell fibs.

'But I will say something that Daddi taught me.' Percy cringed and avoided Viv's eye as Trudi puffed up her little chest, cleared her little throat and gloated in anticipation.

'Bollocks to you.'

*

Six miles away, in Number Ten, Tiddledick was feeling just as outgunned by the gentler gender.

Egeria Erewego, in cahoots with everyone from the Treasury permanent secretary to half his parliamentary party, was trying to force him to sign up to the Chinese trains, while Fanny was fanning the flames in the opposite direction. Naturally, his attempt at reconciling the opposing views of these two powerful women got him nowhere.

'Look, Egeria, I have to take into account all factors and reach a balanced judgement based on all available information,' he began, not very hopefully.

'Of course, Prime Minister, you are absolutely right, as always.' Her words sounded respectful, though she meant exactly what Trudi had said to Biff.

'Every aspect must be weighed on its merits,' she continued, the edge in her voice becoming more serrated by the second. 'And, if I may make so bold as to paraphrase George Orwell, all facts are equal, but some are more equal than others.'

Tiddledick felt his brains starting to rotate. He reminded himself that he was the boss, not a whimpering kid being told off for wetting the bed, but didn't really believe it.

'Now see here, Erewego,' he continued, trying to ignore the woman's ever so slightly raised eyebrows, 'I have intelligence that some of the intelligence I have received may not have been as intelligent as it looks.'

There, he'd said it now. He felt like he'd told the Sunday school teacher to sit on a cowpat, and wished he had Fanny with him to push her down in it hard. While the cabinet secretary was short, fat and female, she was ten times deadlier than males like him. Her answer was more Molotov cocktail than cider with Rosie.

'Naturally, Prime Minister, your absolute ascendancy is beyond peradventure, and we civil servants mere humble slaves. If you care to select a new broom to sweep out the Augean stables, my resignation will be gladly given.'

Tiddledick could feel despair coming on, like a nasty dose of the flu. He knew he had to carry on, somehow, but more and more often, wished he could just jack it all in. Waving the woman out of the room, he called the chief whip. Not Fanny, alas, but the man who was supposed to put badly behaved backbenchers back in their box.

'I say, old chap,' he began, sounding like a polar bear clinging on to the last bit of ice floe that's melting under its very paws, 'what the hell's got into those fellows? Endlessly banging on at me to buy those confounded Chinese trains, now, when I need time to think.'

'Ah but time hath, my lord, a wallet at his back, wherein he puts alms for oblivion.'

Though Fanny would have instantly recognised that quote from Shakespeare's *Troilus and Cressida*, and probably finished off for him, it was a fat lot of good to poor Ponsomby.

'Oh, for God's sake, what the hell are you on about?'

The man wearily explained that Tiddledick may have seemed just about okay when he just about won the election. But that was then, this is now, and politicians are not sentimental. Ponsomby had always made a point of stressing the value of civility, even during times of stress. But, just this once, in sheer exasperation, he did not lead by example. Trudi would have loved it.

'Bollocks to you.'

*

Charlie Chancery was also feeling under the cosh. Simultaneously keeping Fyok Yu and Hon Ki off his back and buttering up Yanks had become even more confusing now that half of them had become Irish, and given to sniggering whenever Hank boasted about their high jiggy jinks. Besides, there was the awkward business of the bomb. Though he hadn't been invited to the Highgate meeting, Charlie had a hunch that Hank had a hunch he'd been double-crossed, even though he'd seen for himself construction of the Thames tunnel was coming along nicely.

Charlie's only consolation was that if these crazies really did put a mushroom cloud over Whitehall, the police might be too busy to notice him sneaking off to Thurso. Worth checking how Scotland was getting on politics-wise, as independence from England would make it bandit country again, meaning his needs and wants would meet neatly. Simply getting up in the morning, cheating a few elderly Scots out of their life savings and mowing down a few more in the speedboat would be just what the doctor ordered. Or the undertaker, in the swimmers' case.

At least Trudi wasn't having any problems with anything, as tomorrow's great adventure was falling wonderfully into place. Because the hotel rendezvous was scheduled for quite early, the grown-ups had decided to go in Monty's car, to be sure of getting there without having to rouse Mummy's little helper. Nobody could face it, for some reason that she couldn't understand.

Nanny usually uses a long stick with a fluffy end and tries not to hear all sorts of words she has a feeling aren't very nice, as they're Percy's favourites when he's not happy. Which he isn't, incidentally, if he's told it's down to him to wake Trudi.

Handy how he always tries to avoid her bedroom in the mornings, and getting into the car was looking easy too. Lady Casement would poo all over the front seat, and while the grown-ups were fussing around clearing up the mess, she'd sneak into the boot. Her solution to the problem of getting into Hank's hotel was also bird-inspired. She'd wing it. Her only mistake was confiding in the loveable creature, who immediately shouted, 'Trudi's a super-spy, Trudi's a super-spy.' Fortunately, she managed to get a towel over the vile brute's head before it had time to follow up with: 'Silly Mummi and Daddi! Tricked them agai-ain!'

Several minutes later, Trudi made up for being a little bit cross by digging out something really nice for Lady Casement's supper, which would also help the getting-into-the-car trick. Already in her pink jim-jams, in readiness for her nice early night in readiness for her unusually early morning, she smiled at her cleverness in choosing such special ingredients.

One small bar of ex-lax, ground up in two big bowls of prunes.

CHAPTER THIRTY-NINE

Next day dawned bright and clear, like Trudi's headspace after a good fourteen hours' sleep. Different situation altogether in Lady Casement's gut, though when it did finally get sorted, the relief put Mafeking in the shade.

In all respects, Trudi's plan worked like clockwork. She even managed to work the pink clockwork alarm clock that'd never been needed before.

The roar of the Wolseley's noisily modified exhaust announced Monty and Bakyt's arrival. As they stepped briefly into the flat before setting off for the hotel, Trudi leapt into action. Lady Casement hates messing up her own private space, so was very pleased to be let out of the cage and into the fresh air. But when Trudi pushed her through the driver's door and closed it behind her, she felt dumped right in it, so to speak, as she really couldn't hold on any longer.

The result was spectacular. Trudi made a mental note to try the recipe on Nanny if she ever made the mistake of waking her up before it was strictly necessary. Monty was taken aback, Biff had the grace for once to apologise and the resulting messing about gave Trudi all the time she needed for her next move.

She could have simply hopped in if had been just her, but it wasn't that simple. With no idea how long this adventure might last, she'd had to plan ahead. One little bag might have been manageable, but there were two, quite big ones.

Even travelling light involves a significant amount of equipment. Food and clothing, and recreational activities, in the event the stay, wherever it is, turns out to be a long one. Also, one has to be appropriately dressed whatever the occasion. So as well as several pairs of particularly pretty pink dungarees and carefully toning tops, she'd packed an admittedly slightly bulky rah-rah skirt with heavily sequinned flounces.

The other case was more practical. Besides the obvious half-dozen eyeshadow palettes that no sensible young woman would dream of travelling without, there were a couple of more digestible bars of chocolate than the type Lady Casement had just tried. Also, must-read *Winnie the Pooh* material. After careful consideration, Trudi had gone for the entire thirty-book box set, plus a dozen Barbie dolls in case she fancied giving her brain a rest.

Not that it was stretched by the job of getting herself and, in her judgement, minimal baggage in the boot, thanks to the grown-ups' endless toing and froing with buckets, soapy water and sponges. Percy helped too, by distracting everyone with a stream of those words that baffle Nanny but Trudi sometimes finds useful.

The short journey from Mayfair to Knightsbridge went without incident, but not without tension, as no one knew what to expect. Least of all the unannounced passenger in the boot. Like the Spanish Inquisition, no one expected that.[††]

After pulling into an underground car park a hundred yards from the hotel, the gentlemen headed for a side door, discreetly slipping into the building and the porters' uniforms the management had supplied. Then, on a given signal on their mobiles, the ladies went in via the front entrance. Two of them, that is. The third, dragging her heavy cases along with her, followed at a safe distance.

Given that Viv and Bakyt didn't seem to have any luggage at all, Trudi started to worry she might have overthought things. But, better safe than sorry, as Mummy was always saying to Daddy. Not that he often took much notice, from what she could make out.

*

The staggeringly vulgar-looking Hotel Yee-Haw is American-owned. Hank liked the staggeringly vulgar fixtures, fittings and décor, and the fact that the suite had its own passageway giving access to its five rooms. They all boasted staggeringly vulgar chandeliers and enormous prints of cowboys, squatting round campfires or gunning down Indians.

The fact that each of these rooms also opened to the hotel corridor suited Monty and Biff too. With the help of their pass keys, they moved swiftly in, leaving the door slightly ajar so they could move just as swiftly out. Extremely handy for Trudi, who snuck in when they disappeared into the internal passageway, fervently hoping her luck would hold.

[††] Author's note: This is an in-joke for the benefit of Monty Python fans. No one else can expect to understand it.

It did, for a while, though not as long as she'd have liked. Shame she's more an AA Milne than AC Doyle kind of girl, because Sir Arthur Conan's history of the Boer War would have given her the essential message of Mafeking. That any army holed up in a tight spot needs an exit strategy.

Hiding her luggage under a bed to give herself freedom of movement was smart. Sneaking into the very room Bakyt and Viv had been shown into, less so. She slipped behind a staggeringly vulgar sofa covered in clashing shades of gold and purple that was conveniently pressed against a wall by the door, and watched, fascinated, as Hank eased open a backpack. Bakyt tried not to seem shocked at what was in it; difficult, when it's a titchy nuke as powerful as a thousand tonnes of TNT. Hardly pack up your troubles in your old kit bag. More good-bye-ee good-bye-ee.

The guys back at the Defense Department were proud of their efforts, digging out a W54 warhead from the Cold War days. And pleased after all these years that this sexy little critter might be put to good use at last.

To an untrained eye, it might have looked like a piece of old junk. But Bakyt's nuclear physics course at uni had a module on secret weapons developed but never deployed, such as the Americans' Special Atomic Demolition Munition and its Soviet equivalent. Annoyingly, her lecturers never managed to get hold of a Yankee specimen, which meant disabling this one could all too easily mean good-bye-ee for her, and thousands of others.

She started to shudder and her eyes went weird. Trudi noticed only the whites were showing. But Viv managed her hand-on-arm technique in time to head off the Mongol war dance and blood-curdling howling that looked set to start any moment. When her twenty-first-century psyche kicked in again, Bakyt wanted to take the weapon away and have a good look at it. But Hank wanted answers. Pronto.

'So whaddaya think it is, lady? Do we have lift-off?' Viv could see the answer to that was yes, but didn't want this half-crazed halfwit to know it. She also felt it'd be safer if she did the talking.

'Hard to be sure at this stage,' she began. 'My colleague and I will need to conduct further research before reaching firm conclusions. Leave it with us.'

She meant leave not just the problem with her but the contents of the backpack as well, though that went straight over Hank's and Shane's heads. But Trudi got it, so did Monty and Biff, unlike Isla and Ella, who were lost in impure thoughts about Bakyt's performance. If she could get so worked up at the sight of one ordinary explosive device, her response to two sex bombs could be enough to wipe out the dinosaurs again, should they choose to reappear.

*

Minutes later, still clutching his bomb, Hank bade farewell to his guests, thanking them for their email addresses and looking forward to hearing from them real soon. Satisfied they'd heard enough through the hotel's paper-thin walls, Biff and Monty saw themselves out from the next room.

At this point, Trudi realised she might have overplayed her hand.

Not only would she never find her way back to Mayfair on her own, she'd no idea how to slip out unseen from behind the sofa. Easy when everyone was looking the other way, hard now the Yanks and Isla and Ella were actually sitting on it. Especially as, given his weight, Hank couldn't fail to notice a child-shaped lump pressing into his back.

'Well, I'll be doggoned' were his first words as he heaved himself up and spotted the problem. He'd have said the same if a spaceship landed in front of him and loads of little green men hopped out, but it seemed as good a way as any of breaking the ice.

Trudi thought it a rather silly thing to say. But for once decided to hear what the other person had on their mind before telling them what was on hers.

'Well, see here, lady, what in hell you looking for? Gold in them there hills?' Hank's clumsy idea of a joke. He naturally assumed the kid was lost, and would have been happy to shoo her out had Trudi not taken him the wrong way and gone for attack as the best defence.

'You're a big ugly man, but my dad's bigger than your dad. He's a lord, I'll have you know. Used to be prime minister. And he won't let you blow up his nice house. So there.'

Hank thought this was quite funny, apart from the bit about him being ugly, obviously. But Isla, more up to speed than him with the oppressor's politics, pointed out that there was only one British ex-PM in the upper house. And while Penislow was on Mugwump's side about the Chinese trains, he might not take too kindly to the bomb.

No one really wanted to hurt Trudi, but they couldn't risk letting her go either. Also be unwise to stay where they were, given there could be some connection between those weapons experts and this apparently rather well-connected child. If so, Isla added, they'd be back in no time and bring half the British army with them. Hank's objection, that he wasn't scared of a few Limey yellow-bellies, was quickly overruled, this time by Ella.

'There is a manpower shortage, so there is,' she murmured softly. 'But they've still got eighty thousand soldiers, so they have.'

This left Hank beyond doggoned, though the problem was solved surprisingly easily. Because the ladies didn't trust the men, they were permanently packed for a quick getaway, while the guys would only have to pick up their shooters and ammo. Away from their wives, they only ever wore clothes once then binned them and bought more. Washing machines? Irons? Hell, that was woman's work.

Minutes later, the party was ready to leave, with, at Trudi's insistence, her personal belongings. She was happy to see them placed in a large suitcase. Less so when they stuffed her in as well.

CHAPTER FORTY

Hearts back at Mayfair were not like singing birds. And that was before they'd even discovered the nest was empty.

Bakyt always has a touch of post-traumatic stress disorder when she's had one of her Mongol turns. Which was why she was doing the funny Kazakhstani funny talk, except it was less funny ha-ha than funny peculiar.

'Easy set timer and run like hell. Then leap in speedy transportation vehicle machine and drive like hell. Only way not die,' she explained sombrely.

'But what about deactivating the bloody thing?' Percy's question was hopeful, unlike the answer.

'Need time and big fat manual official how to fix book.'

Though the meeting was early and short, it was well past eleven, and Viv decided it was time to wake Trudi, which Percy thought was a pity, as he'd looked in on her several times and she'd seemed out for the count. Of course, he'd only seen an outline in a darkened room. And little girls never make any noise if they're somewhere else at the time.

In seconds, anguish turned to anger. Vivienne was beyond incandescent, and though she'd eventually forgive Percy, he'd carry guilt forever. It didn't occur to anyone that this was a repeat performance, till Lady Casement gave them a clue. Hard to tell whether she wanted to help or was just bored with being ignored. But the message was simple enough.

'Trudi is a super-spy. Trudi is a super-spy. Silly Mummi and Daddi! Tricked them agai-ain!'

At this point, despair turned to animation. During the dash to Knightsbridge, Monty even used the splendid original Winkworth bell attached to the Wolseley's front bumper. The distinctive ding-a-ling got applause out of a few pedestrians of a certain age but failed to get other cars respectfully swerving out of the way.

Fortunately, the traffic was light and in less than ten minutes they screeched to a halt on the kerb outside that bloody hotel. Seriously shifting, though even the most souped-up Wolseley in the world couldn't make time travel backwards. The lady on reception, who was clearly not American, thought the behaviour of the recently departed guests from the Yankee-Doodle suite highly suspicious.

'No question of waiting for me to draw up the bill, or to pop upstairs and check the mini bars, and no question of a card payment either.

'This frightful man just flung a great wad of nasty dollar bills on the desk, told me I could keep the change and go to hell, and staggered away. Staggeringly irregular.

'I'm certain he is a gangster. Like everyone else of his barbaric race.'

'Yes yes,' Percy replied, somewhat brusquely. 'Did he say where he was going?'

'To hell, I hope. I shall not be joining him.'

Hank and his gang, including its latest and least willing member, had headed for where the Chancerys were staying. They weren't struck on the place but chose the area because, like them, it was excessively suburban. Only just in Greater London, near a pretty little village, easily accessible via the A 21. With a pretty little village green and a pretty little name. If Pratt's Bottom floats your boat. Locals can be defensive about that. Pointing out that "bottom" is an olde worlde word for a valley, and the Pratts, who were gentry, thank you very much, once lived there.

An author called Sue Short has written a book about the place, called *Pratts Bottom: A Journey Through Life*. Which, as Percy would later decide, beats the title of a ballad that one of Shakespeare's characters had in mind about a dream he had. His name was Bottom too. And, with startling originality, he was going to call the song *Bottom's Dream*. However, finding Trudi remained one of Percy's dreams doomed not to come true for a while. Worse, Fyok Yu and Hon Ki would do better. Partly by luck, partly thanks to shrewd pre-planning.

*

Trudi was wishing she'd managed a bit more pre-planning. The journey from wherever she'd been to wherever she was going was so long that it would have got boring even sitting on Daddy's lap in Simone-Sitrouenne. Cooped up in this beastly suitcase was so much worse, though it gave her time to work on a strategy.

The Hansel and Gretel leave-a-trail solution might help later on, though it grieved her to think of having to tear out pages from any of her *Winnie the Pooh* books. She finally settled on *When We Were Very Young*, on the grounds that she wasn't very young anymore. She got a flashback to when she was extremely young, being lugged around in a sort of sling thing fixed to Daddy's chest. Then too she had no say whatever in where she was or where she was going, but at least Daddy was nice. Silly, but still nice.

A handy option, while stuck in the suitcase, would have been fishing out her little pink mobile and ringing Mummy. Except she was old enough to know that she wasn't considered old enough for anything grown-up and sensible. Shows how silly and not at all grown-up grown-ups are. What she did have was lovely; every key pressed played a different tune. Daddy had had it programmed to include *The Red Flag* and Cornwall's unofficial national anthem, *Trelawney,* both now firm favourites of Trudi's, as well as *Over the Rainbow* and *If I Only Had a Brain.*

But none of it matched up to a phone you could actually make calls on. She was sure Mummy would have bought her one ages ago, if she only had a brain.

Meantime, there was the question of how to handle the horrid man with the stupid sunglasses. Since he obviously wasn't clever enough to understand she deserved respect, there had to be a different approach. Butter him up now? Eat him up later? Not literally, given the care she always took with her diet, except in Palace of Westminster restaurants.

One thing she was not going to do was show her feelings. Though her best-defence-is-attack theory had not worked out, that was no reason to let the enemy see she was scared and upset. Especially as she was. Very, very much so. Missing Mummy lots and lots and lots. And Daddy. And Lady

Casement. And Fang. And no, she was not going to cry. Definitely, absolutely, out-of-the-questionly not.

She thought about the two pretty ladies in the room in that hotel in London. They may have wrecked her chances of being set free but wouldn't be allowed to spoil her survival technique. That was final.

As the suitcase was opened at long last and she crawled, blinking, onto the floor, she did not like where she was. Quite a large room, admittedly, but decorated in even worse taste than the last one. Disgustingly dated rose-patterned wallpaper and an old-fashioned eiderdown on the bed instead of a nice sensible duvet. Also, it smelt. Of nasty carpet cleaner and old bacon and eggs.

There was no sign of the big ugly man with the stupid voice, which was a pity, as she could have done with his sunglasses to give her eyes time to adjust to the light. Instead, the two ladies who she'd decided she might have a way of softening up.

Because they sounded a bit like Biff, she tried out on them his story about the truthful little people and their valiant struggle for freedom from the monster men across the water. At first, they thought she was being weird, hardly surprisingly, but when the connection was made, the effect was electric.

'Bejasus, you sound like a fascist bastard, so ye do, but ye think like us, so ye do,' Ella murmured, caressing her little face.

'But where did ye learn a wee story like that? That's what we'd like to know, so we would.'

Trudi toyed with telling them it came from grumpy Biff, but decided not to after mentioning Daddy to the big ugly man had played so badly. She'd had plenty of time to go through that conversation in her head and realised she'd really goofed there.

She wasn't to know that letting on to the ladies about Biff would have had exactly the reverse effect, as he was their MP and absolutely on their page politically. Which is why, had she come clean, they'd have made good and sure she got back safely, even if it meant borrowing Hank's gun to shoot him first. And Shane, if he objected.

As it was, they settled for cuddling and cooing over her and telling her how sorry they felt for her predicament. Turned out to be a bit of a day for reverse effects, as, far from being cheered up by their kindness, Trudi finally gave in to her feelings.

She sobbed. And she sobbed. And she sobbed.

But she did feel better afterwards, and not frightened anymore, as she could see the pretty ladies would protect her from the ugly men. What she wasn't to know, though, was that two more nasty men weren't far behind and would soon catch up.

*

Charlie Chancery, ever a shifty character, had got that much more so, thanks to the pressures of too much work for too many people, and Fyok Yu and Hon Ki had noticed. Which is how come they bugged his phone, and tracked him down.

There was a slight delay, as he kept moving about, but their breakthrough came thanks to a call he took while on one of his many trips to the internet café. Connectivity was dicky in the hotel, and he did have his business interests back home to keep an eye on. A good excuse to get away from Spleeny's screeching, though unfortunately she was always on the blower anyway. Once too often, as it turned out. In the hope that some of the – to use her expression – "sheep-shaggers" might go for specialist products, she needed the hotel's postcode so her supplier could send samples.

When Charlie told her, obligingly, on the phone, and reminded her that the place was not called Prattish Pratt's Horrible Hovel but Pratt's Bottom Luxury Hotel, Fyok Yu gave Hon Ki a high five. In no time, they cruised to a halt outside the building in their top-of-the-range black Mercedes complete with darkened windows.

They liked Spleeny's name for the place, and the familiar Mustang in the car park, but did not expect to see two more nuzzling puzzlingly alongside it. Not wanting to show their faces just yet, they waited till a local oik started gawping at the shiny motors. Sidling up to him, Fyok Yu explained in his best Oxford accent that he was just as fascinated but rather shy, and wondered if the young gentleman wouldn't mind awfully popping into reception and enquiring as to who owned these delightful vehicles.

The hairy yobbo told him he could naff off back where he came from, foreign slimebags coming over here and stealing our jobs, but changed his mind when Hon Ki waved a fifty-pound note under his nose. Minutes later, he came out, having learned that one of the cars belonged to an overweight English client and his rather rude wife who'd been there a while now, while the others had only arrived that day.

They were a Yank with a limp, another without, and two strange-sounding women with funny accents, who the lady on reception hoped were not terrorists. They'd told her that the very large suitcase they were dragging along contained nothing but books, though she wasn't too sure about that and wished times weren't so hard.

She also emphasised that Pratt's Bottom Luxury Hotel was a respectable house and don't you forget it, young man. Fyok Yu thanked him for his helpful information and slipped him another tenner. He said it was all right but they were still foreign slimebags who should slither off back where they came from, and then slithered off. Or would have done if one of the foreign slimebags hadn't leapt into the air and kicked him hard in both eyes. Looking down at the racist pig's sprawled form, they gave one another another high five, attached GPS trackers to all three Mustangs and proceeded to slither off back where they came from.

On the way back to the Boho Boutique Hotel in Notting Hill, they agreed there was something odd about the big heavy heavy suitcase the reception lady talked about and arranged with the embassy a twenty-four-hour stakeout at Prattish Pratt's Horrible Hovel, which definitely described it more accurately than Pratt's Bottom Luxury Hotel.

If the suitcase got put into one of the Mustangs, it'd be trailed, with the aid of the tracking device, then lifted and spirited back to Notting Hill. Whether whoever was in the car liked it or not.

CHAPTER FORTY-ONE

Trudi's journey back to London did not end where she'd have liked, and started sooner than she expected. All thanks to Hank.

His dark glasses have one advantage. They protect him from the sight of ugly things, of which there are many in Prattish Pratt's Horrible Hovel. In a stage direction to one of his plays, Oscar Wilde described a room as showing the influence of too many schools. He'd have written off this whole place as illiterate. Not that that would have troubled Hank all that much, even if he could have seen any of it. However, after lumbering into reception, knocking over several display cabinets stuffed with tasteless ornaments on the way, he did get a shock.

When he demanded to know where in hell was the ten-pin bowling alley, the lady told him she'd heard there was one in Sevenoaks, only a few miles away. She immediately learned that's a few miles too far, she could screw her horrible hovel and he was outta here. Which he was, along with Shane and the Irish ladies, the moment he'd got Charlie to entice Trudi back into her portable prison, on the strict understanding that this was for her convenience on the journey back to London.

A barefaced lie, of course, though thanks to Hank's instruction to follow on with the big case as soon as he'd located a hotel close by the bowling alley, Charlie was accidentally telling the truth. And the patience of the Chinese agents outside the horrible hovel was rewarded within the hour, when his Mustang roared out of the car park. As it screeched up outside the Hotel Sevenoaks-Seventy-Star, the Chinese agents, barely thirty seconds behind, informed him when he opened the boot that he'd better hand over heavy case or be crispy prawn cracker.

Spleeny informed them they'd better do one if they didn't want their eyeballs ripped out and fed to da rat, but relented at the sight of three Type 82 9-millimetre submachine guns pointed at her head. Only a Chinese rip-off of the Polish PM-63 RAK, but looked like they might do the job.

They did, to the tune of fifty rounds in the back of the Mustang, which quite put Spleeny off her stride. It's debatable whether this was to offer kindly reassurance she was right, or to discourage Charlie from following them. Always hard to read, the inscrutable Chinese mind. But one thing was certain. Trudi was now on her way back to London, as Hank had promised. Just a shame it was next stop Notting Hill, not Mayfair. Another indisputable fact was that Charlie had had enough.

His head as well as his car would be riddled with bullets if he admitted to Hank that the precious cargo had gone AWOL, or MIA, or whatever these foreign slobs called it.

Besides, if he owned up to Penislow that his precious brat was missing in action, or inaction, or anywhere else, he'd get it in the skull from Monty too.

Clambering back into the car, he told Spleeny to get in or get lost, and headed expensively off to the Kwik Fit he'd spotted a few miles back. By the time he got there, the wheels were as wrecked as the tyres, leaving him a grand light before starting his grand tour, but he felt light-headed at getting shot of them all before getting shot himself. The only downside was Spleeny apparently reverting to childhood, whining after just a few hundred yards how many more miles, Daddy?

According to Google Maps, between Sevenoaks and Thurso there are 700 of them.

*

It's only an hour or so, rarely more than three even when the traffic's impossible, to get from Sevenoaks to Holland Park. But long enough for Trudi to forget all about her memo to self about picking your battles, and get the right hump. So when Fyok Yu and Hon Ki finally let her out, she gave them a piece of her mind.

'You are very smelly people. If you don't take me to my mummy, and my daddy, my giant cat will fang you to death. And my huge flying monster will peck your heads off.'

She recognised both the nasty men from the Primrose Hill shoot-out, and that there was a slight exaggeration in what she'd just said. But they didn't need to know. Besides, there was more where that came from.

The killer line had to wait till she'd cleared her little throat several times and puffed up her little chest. She completed the build-up by looking them in the eye in the way Bakyt had stared at the horse before hurling the biggest verbal bomb in her arsenal.

'Bollocks to you.'

Fyok Yu and Hon Ki hid their faces. Rightly so, she decided, to cover their shame.

They were astonished at what high value their newly acquired commodity was. On Percy's Facebook page, there's a picture of him smiling and laughing with this very person. Never mind striking gold, this was a ton of platinum. But if they were to hold on to this hostage long enough to get Percy to switch his influential campaigning to full-throated support for the Chinese train deal, they'd need help.

Apart from posting armed guards outside the hotel, they assigned a round-the-clock rota of women inside it. Strong, capable women. Preferably mothers but, essentially, non-English speakers. Because if they understood a word Trudi said, they'd melt in no time and let her go. They weren't even sure they could trust themselves after her outburst in their direction, which struck them as so funny that they would in time tell their granddaughters about it.

However, business is business. First off, they managed to soothe their angry little guest a little by asking her to please read them a few verses from *Now We Are Six*, then they interested her by pointing out that Barbie dolls are not really American but mostly manufactured in China. The clincher came when they rang down to room service for a whole load of chocolate cakes.

Leaving her thinking the hell with the diet, and considering that at least this room wasn't as ugly as the last two she was stuck in, they turned to the computer to put together an email that'd make Percy's toes curl.

Dear Lord Penislow, it began, *we trust this finds you well, physically if not necessarily emotionally.*

The menace was there from the outset. Giving way in the next paragraph to explicit threat.

If you have any regard for the sanctity of your daughter's life you will not disregard this communication. Nor will you fail to comply in every respect with the instructions contained therein.

The child is safe and well looked after, at present. But that situation will only pertain in the future if you cease forthwith your vindictive campaign against the laudable objective of the British Government to act in the public interest regarding the purchase of trains for the High Speed Two project.

There can be no doubt the Chinese choice is the optimum and indeed only option open to it.

We have reason to believe your misguided efforts to persuade Ponsomby Tiddledick Esq that this is not the case may have a bearing on his continued failure to behave with due expedition in this regard.

For this reason, we are confident a reversal of the direction of your endeavours will have the effect we are seeking to expedite.

The moment the contract is signed, we shall of course be delighted to relinquish control of the aforementioned young person.

Regrettably, however, failure in this regard will result in a most undesirable outcome for all concerned. This is of course assuming you would not wish the child to predecease you.

We remain, sir, ever your obedient servants.

With that bit of English country solicitor's claptrap safely sorted, Fyok Yu and Hon Ki gave one another another high five. The only thing they couldn't agree on was which of them was the nastier piece of work. Because they were both trying so hard, neither could admit they'd so taken to Trudi that they wouldn't actually harm a pretty little blonde hair on her pretty little brainy head.

*

Percy was not to know that.

As far as he could tell, these were murdering monsters who wouldn't hesitate to take out his lovely little daughter. The carefully cropped picture attached to the email he picked up in his House of Lords inbox proved it. That image of her, sat on a neutrally beige carpet surrounded by the books missing from her room, was all the confirmation he needed.

Hon Ki had taken the photo just as Fyok Yu was telling her about the Barbie dolls, and so managed to capture the expression he was after. Shocked and rather put out.

She was looking a lot more cheerful a minute or so later, when he was on the blower to room service, but Percy didn't know that either.

He'd travelled to hell and back, or rather to hell and stayed there, since Trudi's disappearance. Angry Vivienne had turned into teary Viv since it became obvious when the escape took place. She blamed herself just as much as Percy for not wondering why Lady Casement should decide nothing short of a classic Wolseley would do as a loo.

Percy got so into slapping his forehead with the palm of his hand that it'd turned quite black and blue, which Fang found curious and rather disturbing. At least they now knew

Trudi hadn't run out into the street, got splatted by a passing car, scooped up and tipped in a skip somewhere, which was something.

It was also clear that Percy had it in his gift, hopefully, to get her freed. He was passionate about the potential threat to national security posed by yet more Chinese technology worming its way into the UK's digital infrastructure, but he cared a great deal more about the very real threat to his lovely child's life.

Problem was, none of it made any sense.

The initial prime suspects, the Americans, were threatening to blow up half of London if the Chinese train deal went ahead, and even they weren't so stupid as to demand he made sure it did. Nor would they, if they had Trudi in their clutches, pass her on to anyone else. Then there was the email itself. In a race between Hank coming up with that phraseology and a monkey trying to write a Shakespearean sonnet, it was obvious who wouldn't win.

Not that there seemed any Chinese inflexion in it. But Percy could hardly forget the devious way those men with the ridiculous names plotted to get uranium into the country, under his very nose, when he was prime minister. To some extent, he was still fighting the same war now, with the same couple of guys. And, not for the first time, he found himself paraphrasing a particularly well-worn literary cliché.

'To lose one battle may be regarded as a misfortune; to lose both looks like carelessness.' But here he was, at risk of losing his one and only child. As the full horror of the situation gripped him, he partially followed the example she'd set when the two pretty ladies were nice to her.

He wept uncontrollably. But did not feel better afterwards.

CHAPTER FORTY-TWO

Percy, Viv, Monty, Bakyt and Biff were all agreed. Going to the police would expose Trudi to even greater danger if they put out public appeals. Better to do their own sleuthing first.

Their only point of contact with these hateful Chinese brutes was Charlie Chancery. Indirect and unattractive, but a start. The problem being, he wasn't picking up. Or replying to any of their texts. As they thought they had him under the thumb, this seemed odd.

Would have struck them as less so if they'd known that for once the man was, more than one step, hundreds of miles in front of them. Fairly early in the journey northwards, he'd pulled into a service station to buy Blu Tack and stuffed loads of it in his ears to protect him from Spleeny's whining. And his stroke of genius came on the way out, when he stopped to stare at a beautifully restored open-topped E-Type Jaguar. So tasty that he started dribbling, embarrassingly, though the car would be practical as well as pretty. He'd no way of knowing if Monty or anyone else had spyware keeping tabs on him via GPS on either of his mobiles, one of which had gone missing. That solved one problem, while the other could go God knows where, in the back of the sexy motor.

The odds of the E-Type thundering up to Thurso had to be a million to one against, though if it did, he'd nick the thing just for the hell of it. Part of him half hoped somehow or other that it would, which proves that wants and needs aren't always the same thing. Not that Trudi had any problems earlier that day with gratifying her own needs, at least partly.

When Chancery was fussing about, turning around endlessly to scoop up all her essential possessions in readiness for the journey, she noticed the iPhones in his back pockets. The jeans being unpleasantly low-slung and the man's rear unpleasantly sticky-out, she tried not to look. Also, she tried, as she always does when she remembers she's a well brought-up girl, not to be greedy.

Which is why she only stole one of his phones.

*

But if Percy only knew what happened next, he'd have changed his mind about Trudi and Jane Austen, as she'd definitely found something to distress and vex her. Not trusting themselves, Fyok Yu and Hon Ki left her to the lady minders who didn't speak English, which made it hard to explain that she couldn't possibly do her wee-wees without absolute privacy. And when she did finally get it, she couldn't get Chancery's beastly phone to work.

Experience had taught her that flushing electrical things down the loo can make grown-ups cross, but she felt like doing it anyway, because she could only manage to make lights come on. The smelly thing didn't even play nice songs like her pretty little pink one, still less make the one call she had in mind. After that, the ugly little fat man could have it back, if he really wanted it. Or the silly Chinese ladies. Or anyone else, for that matter.

There was nothing wrong with Charlie's phone, and the code would have been easy to work out, as, out of blind fury at everyone, he'd gone for "Halfwit". Sadly, Trudi didn't know about passwords on mobiles, but happily this one was being traced by Mummy and Daddy.

Because Percy and Viv shared Fyok Yu and Hon Ki's profound mistrust of Charlie Chancery, they'd decided some time back to keep tabs on him. Confusingly, however, they now discovered he'd cut himself in two. One half halfway to Scotland, the other, more conveniently, in Holland Park. A little trip beckoned, up Park Lane and down the Bayswater Road.

The men got into the Wolseley, Simone-Sitrouenne out of action without Trudi to get her going, and Monty cocked and uncocked his handy little pistol. He didn't bother with the machine guns, as he didn't think Chancery would cut up that rough. But they'd donned the nuns' habits to make sure they saw him first, little knowing they'd have needed an astronomical telescope for that.

They were put out at finding no tell-tale Mustang outside the hotel, more so when a bunch of suspicious-looking Chinese guys with suspiciously large bulges under their jackets said they'd better go pray if they didn't go away. Though they were only pretending to be nuns, they actually did cross themselves. While Monty was handy with his handy little pistol, he was outgunned.

It seemed likely, however, that Chancery had accidentally led them to Fyok Yu and Hon Ki. And, as they rather wanted a word with them about where Trudi might happen to be, they decided on a return trip, with Stens.

Because of the risks involved, Monty was adamant that Bakyt must stay well away. No matter what she may say, it was absolutely out of the question. Percy had no more wish to see Viv splatted in a hail of gunfire but was that bit more realistic. Which was why, when he promised his full support, he crossed his fingers behind his back.

*

While all this was going on, Trudi had made an interesting discovery. One of her lady guards who didn't speak English did speak English, or at least had enough words to ask for a spot of tuition, and one or two other things besides. There was a lot more to Yu Yan than the beautiful smile her name suggested in Chinese. And a lot more than she wanted the authorities in Beijing to know.

For a start, if they knew more about her family background, or anything at all really, they'd have her down as the wrong sort of ethnic minority. Like the wrong sort of leaves on the track, only much, much worse. And if they'd realised what she studied at uni, and that she could speak a tiny bit of English, she'd have been spared what they lovingly call vocational education and training and treated instead to a bullet in the head. So it's little wonder she thought, to use her exact words, 他们是一群可恶的法西斯野蛮人.‡‡

‡‡ 他们是一群可恶的法西斯野蛮人 = They're a bunch of loathsome fascist brutes.

Trudi, by contrast, struck her as 一个完美的小天使, [§§]the seeds of beautiful friendship sown when Trudi sat on the floor and began reading aloud. She always loves an audience, settling even for one that doesn't understand a word she's saying. Yu Yan sitting down beside her and saying, 'Girl, read louder, please, be teacher' was a definite bonus.

Looking at her in some surprise, she cleared her throat in a rather theatrical way and wished she'd packed the large pink glasses to round off the effect. Though she'd no idea Charles Dickens had got there first, she planned one day to be a famous author going on national book promotion tours. Loving the thought of an enthralled and adoring public hanging on her every word, she cleared her throat again, more theatrically than ever, and gave *The House at Pooh Corner* real welly.

Yu Yan listened, learned, thought and smiled. No English person had taken the slightest notice of her before, yet this child wasn't just reading, but also, every couple of paragraphs, looking up from the book meaningfully, straight into her eyes. Actually, Trudi was just rehearsing for the huge venues where she'd be making sure her books were instant worldwide bestsellers, adapted as blockbuster movies. AA Milne managed a respectable following, but she'd do so much better.

Not that she's vain or anything, just realistic.

Having no idea she'd taken the performance rather too personally, Yu Yan decided to take the biggest risk of her life. Maybe to do with pent-up loneliness, as she couldn't tell her colleagues anything, or maybe she was so desperate to be

---

§§ 一个完美的小天使 = A perfect little angel.

heard that she'd confide in a rattlesnake if she thought it'd listen. Or maybe, just maybe, because this cute little kid had won her heart. That's probably it, she decided, as she took the plunge.

'I hate my country. Yours much better. Want live here!'

Trudi considered this from several angles. The nearest she'd got to China was the lovely chop suey takeaways Daddy sometimes brought home in Cornwall, which put paid to her diet as effectively as restaurants in parliament. Against that, those two horrid men who'd taken her prisoner had not made a favourable impression. The decider, however, was Yu Yan herself. So delicate, so pretty, so small. Like her Barbie dolls, only not that small, obviously.

And there was something else. She could almost taste this woman's fear, suffering and longing for liberation. Also, the love she so clearly wanted to share with her. All very well being nicer to Fang and feeling she'd discovered something, but this was so much bigger. Once again, she had a sense of not being very young but actually striding purposefully towards the grown-up world.

She knew no more of the beastly way the Home Office has of rarely granting political asylum than its dodgy way of letting people in through the back door if the right strings are pulled. But her feminine intuition always worked.

'My daddy might help,' she murmured. Her mind was racing as it scanned her new huge horizon. 'He is only a man, but a very important one. Shall we go together and ask him?' There, she'd said it now. The corner was turned.

Yu Yan could think of a million reasons why not, all ending up with that bullet through her head if she was caught. Against that, there was something in the look in this little person's eyes that made her feel brave, trusting and a little light-headed. She knew the hotel was only lightly guarded at nighttime and had noticed that the agent on the late shift seemed to have something on his mind. So the plan was laid, and at five to three in the morning, she gently shook the sleeping beauty and whispered in her ear: 'We go. Now.'

Trudi was so up for it that she was up in a jiffy. With no hint of those screaming habdabs that would've spoilt everything. Yu Yan softly turned the key and peered nervously up and down the corridor. No one to be seen as they tiptoed noiselessly down the thickly carpeted staircase and towards the entrance hall, and the hotel's tantalisingly close front door. In theory, both the receptionist and the Chinese guard would be awake and alert, poised at all times for action. But, as Albert Einstein liked to say: *In theory, theory and practice are the same. In practice, they are not.*

This was certainly the case here, as, far from poised for action, the receptionist was tucked up in the bed she had hidden behind the desk. And, proving Einstein right, so was the Chinese guard. In the same bed.

CHAPTER FORTY-THREE

The fresh night air smelt sweet to Trudi, and to Yu Yan, but they savoured rather a lot of it before they realised there really weren't a lot of taxis around at three in the morning.

So, hand in hand, they walked. And walked. And walked. Getting ever so close but not quite close enough to the Mayfair flat where, if they did but know it, Operation Rescue Trudi had been meticulously planned. When they finally stumbled on Green Park underground, they waited. And waited. And waited.

Eventually, they hopped on a train heading in the direction of the place Trudi told the nice man with the tattoo on his forehead she wanted to get to, the place where Daddy worked. The guy had his cap tilted back so everyone could read the words "down the tubes" just above his eyebrows. Because he'd been so helpful, Trudi told him it looked very nice. Even though she thought it looked rather silly, really.

As they stumbled drowsily out of the underground at Waterloo, the two new best friends enjoyed the early-morning sunshine. Still very early, actually, though luckily there was a nice little café nearby, perfect for a very early breakfast. Luckily also, Yu Yan had thought to bring her life savings with her. All ninety pounds of it. Which struck her as an awful lot, as she'd no idea what mean, loathsome fascist brutes the loathsome fascist brutes were.

She'd also no idea how you eat bacon and eggs without chopsticks. Or that you can eat them at all. Trudi considered her doubtful expression and realised that she'd be a busy little teacher in a lot of subjects. Propped up on the stools at the wide window ledge which served as their table, Trudi saw something surprising across the road and gave Yu Yan a crash course in something unexpected.

How to duck, extremely quickly.

Peering through the glass from below ledge level, she rubbed her big but very tired eyes in disbelief. There, stepping, or rather hobbling in Hank's case, out of a doorway, were two Americans she was particularly anxious not to bump into. Hank's sunglasses meant she'd have had to be as tall as Nelson's Column for him to spot her, but yet again, as Mummy always says, better safe than sorry.

As the two disappeared from view, Trudi's and Yu Yan's eyes slowly reappeared above the window ledge like four low-flying flying saucers. Straight into the equally wide-eyed eyeline of two Irish ladies Trudi was also nervous about. But Isla and Ella came bounding across the street, flung the café door open and their arms round her neck. She was relieved but bewildered that so many people seemed to have taken to her. Mummy was a soft touch and Daddy was a pushover, but even so…

Turned out her Irish friends were quite over Hank and

Shane. So stupid and so rude. The last straw being being told to stand guard over their stupid tunnel while they went and did important man things that girls needn't bother their pretty heads with. They went on to explain that these stupid men had put a bomb in their stupid tunnel, and told Trudi they'd show it to her if she didn't believe them, so they would.

Yu Yan struggled to understand anything they were saying. The Belfast accent can be a challenge to a Brit, so she didn't stand a hope in hell. Or anywhere else, including the Chinese provinces of Hebei, Hainan or Guangdong.

However, she did prick up her graceful little ears at the word "bomb", which not even Essex people can get all that wrong. The sight of her interested Isla and Ella very much indeed, which interested Trudi very much indeed, as it reminded her of how interested they'd seemed in Bakyt the day Daddy dressed up in lady clothes but was rubbish at lady talk.

Yet again, her feminine intuition was spot-on. The looks Isla and Ella were giving the beautiful young woman were like the looks Mummy and Daddy give one another when they're being all silly and sloppy. But though they fancied the pants off her, they did pick up on her steely alertness whenever they said bomb. She may have looked like a little doll, but was definitely one up on a Barbie.

*

Percy, Monty and Biff planned their assault with military precision. Or, rather, Bakyt did. Only Monty understood her logic, and that extremely unwillingly. He's no male chauvinist pig, far from it, but dearly loves his wife and fears her wild side could one day be even more self-destructive than Percy's.

She beat down his resistance by reminding him of the Kazakh proverb "*er karuy – bes karu*", which means "a warrior has five types of weapons", and by pointing out that they were traditionally part of a bride's dowry. He believed that, though wasn't convinced brides in the Middle Ages were also given machine guns to teach husbands their manners.

Nonetheless, he was beat, and Percy caved in too. Of course. Which was how come when the Wolseley cruised to a halt outside the hotel at a quarter past three, it contained three men and two women. Had it been twenty-five minutes earlier, the mission could well have been accomplished. But there it was; it wasn't.

Worse, the agent had just crept out of the receptionist's bed to have a pee, and, to prove he'd been awake and alert at all times, looked in on the little girl's by then empty bedroom. He'd then alerted his colleagues, who were charging up and down the corridors in their jim-jams in a right two and eight. So much for the stealthy deadliness of the pre-dawn raid, Einstein's theory about theory and practice and all that.

Bakyt's idea had been to take whatever bleary-eyed person was on guard in reception by surprise. First, discreetly lassoing him, then just as discreetly offering to slit his throat with her scary curvy dagger if he didn't immediately inform her, without raising his voice above a whisper, which room Trudi was in. As it was, he was very much awake and very much needed settling back to sleep. Just lassoing him wasn't going to do that, but Viv solved the problem by bopping him on the head with Bakyt's strange pointy helmet, hard enough to make him very dopey indeed for a very long time. His lady friend stayed in the bed, too terrified to move, which Viv was rather pleased about.

The men's less subtle approach involved charging up the stairs shooting at anything that moved. And, in Percy's case, as he'd never fired a gun in his life, a fair few things that would otherwise have stayed as and where they were. Within seconds, glass cases full of elegant little items of expensive silver jewellery were splattered all over the place. Likewise, thanks to Monty and Biff, five Chinese agents, with what looked like buckets of blood quite spoiling the carpets. As they charged past what was left of them, Percy fired a breathless question at Monty.

'What's the first casualty of war?'

'The truth, if you ask Aeschylus,' Monty replied, just as breathlessly.

'Wrong,' Percy snorted. 'It's the plan.'

That conundrum resolved, they put their shoulders into the job, starting with the door in front of them. Several rooms and several terrified but unconnected couples later, they crashed into a room containing nothing more responsive than two telltale suitcases. As he burst the first open, Percy burst into tears. The sight of his dear little daughter's dear little Barbies was too much for him. Biff opened the second, seconds later, and was astonished at what he found. He'd never seen a bulky rah-rah skirt, still less one with heavily sequinned flounces.

Though he thought Percy ought to man up a bit, he thought better of saying it. More helpfully, Monty offered his hanky, which was gratefully accepted. In time – felt like forever but was actually less than a minute – they noticed a chair placed by an open window. Because the room was only on the first floor and there was a tree close by, the child may well have simply safely skedaddled.

But where?

Possibly, but highly unlikely, she'd made off with stinky Chancery, who seemed to have squirrelled himself halfway to Scotland; no disrespect to squirrels, they're ever so much prettier and probably cleverer. Direct action was called for. A lot more local, and cutting out the middle men.

Very soon after they'd picked their way through the human and ornamental debris, climbed into the Wolseley and started up the road, Fyok Yu and Hon Ki sauntered up the pavement. Unlike Trudi on almost every day except this one, they're early risers, and enjoy taking the fresh morning air. Struck them as odd that the odd-looking car should be pulling away outside the hotel but thought no more of it. Until they got inside.

At that point, they wished they'd leapt into the top-of-the-range Mercedes and shouted at one another: 'Follow that Wolseley.'

But as they didn't, Percy didn't look anxiously in the rear-view mirror while the vehicle swerved wildly, crashing traffic lights and swooping death-defyingly the wrong way up one-way streets. Instead, he calmly got his mobile out, scrolled through his contacts and selected the highly confidential direct line number to someone who really needed to know what was going on. Someone he'd call in a few hours' time, at a less ungodly hour of the night. Someone he really should have spoken to some time back.

Ponsomby Tiddledick.

*

A few hours later, someone else had a really good idea about what to do with a phone. Though, in her case, it didn't produce the goods quite as quickly.

The full English breakfast didn't do it for the two Irish ladies, partly because it was English but mainly as they'd have sooner eaten Yu Yan. While they were all watching, fascinated, by her struggles to make sense of knife and fork technology, Trudi announced she needed to make a call.

She was horrified that both Isla and Ella, fed up with the ever-grumpier texts they were getting from Hank, had chucked their mobiles in the river. And not at all comforted by the suggestion she could always use a phone box, because to the best of her knowledge they only ever contained potted plants or second-hand books.

She'd already had a good look across the Thames and changed her mind about hunting for Daddy in the Palace of Westminster, as it clearly had an awful lot of rooms. But was confident that the flat wasn't more than fifteen minutes away anyway.

All they had to do was find it.

This was where the phone should have come in. Though Trudi had no more idea of the Mayfair number than its address, she'd called Cornwall many times. Usually on the way to the shops with Daddy to ask Mummy to remind him what he was supposed to be buying.

When Isla and Ella assured her that phone boxes in London actually had phones in them, and led her to one conveniently nearby, she still wasn't convinced, as it rang and rang without anything happening. But eventually her prayers seemed to be answered when she heard a familiar but extremely sleepy voice. Nanny had given in to temptation the previous evening, gone up to the attic and rather made a night of it. A bit vague at the best of times, she was away with the fairies.

'Oh, Trudi, lovely to hear from you, I've so missed you and your sweet little ways,' she sighed, not altogether sincerely.

'But Mummy and Daddy's address in London? Let me see now, it's Berkeley something-or-other. Close, I think. In, er, Maidenhead.'

Such were Nanny's appetites that as a kid she sometimes pressed unexpected parts of her dollies against unexpected parts of her body, with unexpected but delicious results. But her maidenhead was something she never got around to losing, in the more conventional sense. Which was why the poor dear rather had it on the brain.

Berkeley Close, Maidenhead, is a sort of poetic echo of Berkeley Square, Mayfair, but did put Trudi off the scent. She was puzzled when Ella went to an internet café, found the town on Google Maps and announced they needed to hop on the tube to Paddington then an overground train. At least Berkeley Close in Maidenhead is in an area called Pinkneys Green, which sounded rather nice.

Before they set off, Yu Yan put up her little hand and asked ever so politely if please if possible look at boom thing. Ella and Isla would have said yes if she'd asked them to strip off and do cartwheels all along Westminster Bridge. So the tunnel was a doddle. Its narrowness necessitated nuzzling up close to gorgeous little lady, which was much nicer than what they learned at journey's end. That she was less interested in them than the metal sphere marked "large nuclear bomb".

It may not have been large, they were told in hesitant but no uncertain terms, but it really was nuclear.

Yu Yan was a model student at her uni's fission and fusion faculty before the authorities took against her sort of ethnic minority and stopped her being any kind of student. This meant her PhD was no longer a passport to the post–doctoral studies she'd set her heart on, but didn't erase her knowledge of weapons like this. It's iconic, in its *Horrible Histories* kind of way, hence her sharp intake of breath and instant diagnosis.

'This big bang boom machine make big hole in ground. Parliament sink in river. In very small pieces.

'I know, I philosophy doctor. This my field. Field go to sky if bomb go bang.'

A bit late in the day, Isla and Ella registered that she was up there with Bakyt on this level, as well as so many others. They wondered if it was just coincidence, or whether all nuclear scientists were drop-dead gorgeous.

CHAPTER FORTY-FOUR

Around the time Trudi and her ladies got on the train to Maidenhead, Percy put in his call from Mayfair. Ponsomby Tiddledick is a bit quicker at picking up than Nanny on a bad day, but nearly as dopey when he's woken by the mobile he keeps by his bed in the flat above Number Ten.

He always hated having it there, but got the point the day he missed a call from the Australian prime minister telling him he was prepared to sign another UK/Oz trade deal, so long as he agreed to it pronto. Getting no reply from the UK prime minister, the man decided Tiddledick was a tiddlebrain, and went with the EU after all. Expensive missed call, that.

It so played on poor Ponsomby's mind that ever since he's answered early calls in a confusing way. This day being no exception.

'Why, hello there, cobber. You going a'waltzing Matilda today?'

'Er, sorry, old chum. Not quite top of my priority list. You feeling okay?' Percy had always had Ponsomby down as a bit odd, but not that weird.

'It's Percy here,' Percy pointed out. 'Percy Penislow,' he added, for clarification.

'Time for a pow-wow, Poncey. I'll be at yours in an hour. Should give you time to hose yourself down and alert the guards. I'll slip in via Whitehall entrance. Prying eyes and all that. You got that?'

By now, Tiddledick was on the way to remembering where and who he was. Though still slightly confused as to whether he was the prime minister or the prime minister's wife. Hence, his abrupt though somewhat falsetto way of saying he had indeed got that.

'Right-oh.'

As the iPhone was on speaker mode and Viv was with Percy when he made the call, she managed a wan smile, in spite of everything.

She then busied herself putting together all the evidence from all the various sources, pretty sure Tiddledick couldn't fail to grasp what the hell had been going on, dizzy though he was. Shame Fanny was at Chequers, but it couldn't be helped. That poll proving the Brits would sooner become French than allow Chinese trains anywhere near the HS2 project went into the folder. As did the Hansard record of the Lords debate which showed that peers agree. Even those whose ancestors came over with The Conqueror.¶¶

Then there was the nonsense Verrigreen had used to get Tory backbenchers backing Beijing. There were enough transcripts of enough phone conversations with Erewego on

¶¶ AKA *Le bâtard*. Historians disagree.

the subject to convince Tiddledick that they were up to no good. Especially as they included CAUC cackling about the dosh Fyok Yu and Hon Ki had paid him for the ASSHOLE memo. Plus, there was the photographic evidence from Monty's foraging in the Pimlico flat. All that cash crammed into a drawer had to have come from somewhere.

From the reverse perspective was the intelligence that he and Biff had picked up in the Belfast Europa piano bar, with its strong implication that the president of the United States would stop at nothing to prevent the Chinese train purchase. Suspicions, Tiddledick would read, borne out by a submission put together by Bakyt, which included a pic taken on her phone of the telltale markings on the side of the bomb.

Amazing how much had been happening right under Tiddledick's nose, and how little he'd done about it, Viv thought with a sigh. Present company excepted, British prime ministers struck her as stupider than gnats. Trudi could make a better fist of the job with both hands tied behind her back, she decided.

*

Has to be said, though, the little girl was not feeling terribly clever that morning. Far from ringing the bell at the flat, squealing 'surprise!' and dissolving into Mummy and Daddy's arms, she seemed to be further away from them than ever.

The area round Berkeley Close, Maidenhead turned out to be a lot leafier than Berkeley Square, Mayfair. And though she only knew how to find the flat by following one particular route, she could see the architecture looked different. Knocking on doors didn't help, as people just shooed her away. And, already cross with herself for wasting time in what was so obviously the wrong place, she gave the final nasty person a piece of her mind.

'My daddi used to be a very important man, I'll have you know.' The grumpy old git, who clearly did not know, spotted a way of getting rid of her when she stamped her foot and informed him just how important Daddy used to be.

'He knows the queen, I'll have you know. Used to go and see her every week. She liked him, by the way.'

'If dat's da case, why don't ya go and see de old bat and ask 'er yerself,' he snarled. 'She's gotta gaff just up da road, in Winsah.'

That weird way of talking reminded Trudi of her day out with Mummy and Daddy in Southend-on-Sea. A good call, as the old misery guts was indeed brought up there. Which confirms that you can take the man out of Essex but not Essex out of the man.

When Isla and Ella realised that by Winsah he meant Windsor, they really wanted to see the castle, so they did, because their infants' schoolteacher had told them it contained Queen Mary's dolls' house. Being a Proddie, the woman loved relics of the British Empire as much as they hated them. But they had a soft spot for dolls' houses and thought that if they showed this one to Yu Yan, she might let them touch her soft spot, so she might.

Besides, as they'd never crossed the Irish Sea, they were curious to learn what tickled their oppressors' fancy. Yu Yan was interested too, as all she'd seen of England so far was the insides of the Chinese Embassy and a boutique hotel in Notting Hill, the road from there to Green Park underground, a little bit of Waterloo and a few streets in Maidenhead.

Trudi's feelings were more complicated. Though she felt reasonably safe with her new lady friends, she really hadn't known them long, and urgently needed Mummy and Daddy. Though she so wanted to be strong, independent and adventurous, it struck her there might be more to life than that. Or, better still sometimes, less. Another call to Nanny beckoned. Tomorrow, but not before, as she was obviously on an off day today.

A trip to Windsor, or Winsah, would be a way of passing the time. Especially as, in her case at least, dolls' houses were more or less age appropriate. She'd grown up so much in the last few hours that they might be a bit childish, but now she'd discovered her inner little angel, it was hard not to be nice to the others.

Moral dilemma resolved, she was happy. So were Ella and Isla when they discovered that ringing for an Uber works just as well in Maidenhead as at Belfast Airport. Although the nuclear bomb they'd been lugging about was diddy by nuclear bomb standards, it was still a lump to hump around, so it was.

They'd decided to bring it along with them when Yu Yan explained what a big bang it would make. Though they were all in favour of punishing the Brits for being fascist pigs, there was an upcoming visit to parliament by the Irish president they didn't want to spoil. He planned to explain to MPs and peers in Westminster Hall that Irish unification was the only viable long-term solution to the problems created by Brexit. But his own viable prospects, long or short term, would be cut extremely short if Yu Yan was right.

Had Percy been with them, he'd have pointed to the parallel with the original gunpowder plot, foiled because someone couldn't bear the thought of a mate being reduced to a cinder. Viv would have raised her eyes skywards and said: *There he goes again.* And Trudi would very likely have put in her two-penn'orth too. More than once, if he'd been sitting down while sharing his thoughts, she'd pulled up a chair next to him, clambered onto it, patted him on the head and said: 'There there, Daddi, you do your best.'

Though she hadn't entirely followed the conversations about the bomb, she got the gist, and stood up once again for Daddy. Only this time taking his side, instead of the mickey.

'My daddi's in parliament too, sometimes. I'd cry and cry if he got blown up.' Also, because she'd rather picked up on Isla and Ella's take on the English, she set them straight.

'My daddi is not English, I'll have you know. He's Cornish. And his friend Biff is Irish, so there.'

'Biff? Biff!?! Not Biff McNasty? But he's our member of parliament, and our friend too, so he is.' Isla was gobsmacked. So was Ella.

'Well, bugga me,' said Trudi, enjoying the freedom to blurt out the sort of thing Daddy was always saying, without having to offer Mummy a refund from the swear box. 'I don't like him very much, but his parrot is my best friend.'

For the first time in a long time, the two Irish women stopped fixating on Yu Yan's naughty bits and gave a second's thought to their PhD theses. Trudi may be a bit of a Brit but she was loveable. And her dad didn't sound all bad either. A friend of Biff's, for a start.

So maybe when they did get on with writing the fecking things, they'd soften the anti-British tone, so they might. Only a bit, mind. Brits were still fascist pigs, and all pigs are equal. But, and it grieved them to admit it, some pigs are more piggy than others.

CHAPTER FORTY-FIVE

Back in central London, history of a more contemporary kind was being made.

A bittersweet moment for Percy, slinking into Downing Street via the side entrance in Whitehall rather than sweeping up to Number Ten in a flashy limo. Next to the black door, the back door never quite cut it. But he had an escort through the maze of passages, and an unexpected greeting from a crinkly bloke in the lobby.

'Pleased to see you back in the saddle, Prime Minister, sir. You were looking a bit peaky last time I saw you.'

That was half a decade ago, when Percy was being stretchered out after his bungled suicide attempt. As he came round after having his stomach pumped, he decided not even being able to top himself proved how useless he was. Today, less depressingly, he was struck by the old geezer's gift for understatement, as well as the clear evidence that he was bonkers.

Pausing on the stairs to glance at his own image alongside

those of so many other former prime ministers, Percy had to admit things could hardly have gone more horribly wrong. So many plots, so little time. Not that much of it was really his fault. As became clear when the full facts came out. Which is why, to this day, the likes of Ponsomby Tiddledick would always listen to him. Lucky, for all concerned, as Percy had a lot to get off his chest.

'You're in doodoo, dear, and so am I,' he began, the second he was sitting comfortably in one of the flat's cosier armchairs. 'Whose first? Your bad news or mine?'

Ever the gent, Poncey went for Percy's.

'My daughter's been kidnapped. A matter of some delicacy, which is why we need MI5, possibly MI6 and certainly Special Branch on the case.'

Tiddledick thought back to the Night of the Long Shoelaces and the God-awful headache he had for days after Trudi's little prank, and felt a pang of pity for her captors but didn't like to mention it. Nor did Percy mention yesterday's incident in Notting Hill that Sky and the Beeb had got so excited about. They couldn't decide whether the attack was a terrorist outrage or the result of a gangland feud, but agreed it was a bloody mess. Percy hoped Poncey wouldn't think to link that unfortunate episode and his own unfortunate circumstances.

Whether he did or didn't, Poncey was too polite to say, especially as what Percy told him about his own doodoo diverted his attention to (a) the fact he'd been well and truly had by his own top people and (b) if the bomb went off, there wouldn't be any top people left to worry about anything. That included himself, which he found dispiriting. At the same time, apropos nothing in particular, he glanced down at the red ministerial despatch box his visitor had placed on the floor when he came in. And remembered the hoo-ha when one just like it went missing around the time Percy disappeared off the scene.

Monty was no hoarder. But as well as the warrant card and various guns he hung on to when he left the Met, he did pick up a souvenir for his old boss. Percy read his host's thoughts accurately but decided – same as the shoot-out – that this subject was best left for another day. He did, however, hand over the contents of the box, and noted Poncey's eyes opening wider and wider as he skim-read what was in it.

Everything he'd just been told was there in black and white. With the exception of the kit-bag bomb pic, which was in full colour. W54 didn't mean anything to him, but Bakyt's bit about a thousand tonnes of TNT had a bad feeling about it. In the circumstances, he thought the hell with the flat's strict no-smoking rule, and let Percy light up. Though he'd given up twenty years ago, he jolly well had one too.

As the documents were copies, Percy left them with Poncey to consider at his leisure. But as he got to his feet, he was careful to hang on to what they'd been stuffed into. A quick wink, and the point was as well taken as the box, all those years back.

Ponsomby Tiddledick had never been one for swift and decisive action, but he was one up on the bloke in the lobby. First job then, ring the memsahib. Second, take in her every word. Third, act on them, pronto. And what she suggested left no room for misunderstanding.

'My dear, what did I tell you? Verrigreen's a CAUC. Time you Completely And Utterly C-C-Cut him. Orff with his head. Now's the time for Erewego-go-go too.

'And that frightful man from the colonies? Grieves me to think of doing anything he says. But lay back and think of England, like all us blushing brides.'

'Sorry, dear, lost me there.' Poncey was confused, as he was the one given to blushing in the bedroom. Procol Harum was before their time, but he'd often noticed as she got into her stride that she turned a whiter shade of pale.

'That sweet little poll, Viv, got you, darling. Who cares if the trains come from Tilbury or Timbuktu? If the dear little ordinary people don't want Chinese tonight, give them steak and kidney.

'So what if our trains are dearer? If the English want them, the English can pay for them. Won't come out of your wages, darling.

'By the way, forgot to mention, dear Great-aunty Flossie just popped her clogs. Left me a fortune. Aren't you the lucky one, being married to a lovely lady heiress like me?

'PLU really needn't worry, darling. So will you do as I say? PDQ?'

Poor Poncey, he'd always struggled with TMI. Even if Information's welcome, Too Much is still, well, too much. As for joining the ranks of People Like Us, lovely idea but would take getting used to. Who the hell was he then? Confusion confirmed by how he ended the conversation.

'Right-oh.'

*

Though the pace of events was hotting up in Westminster, it was slowing down in Windsor, because Trudi's day had been far too long for her liking. Getting up at three in the morning is four hours earlier than that unwelcome event on school days, and eight hours earlier than the happier beginning of all other days.

In short, she was done for.

Yu Yan was also finding that sunny smile of hers an effort to keep up. So the ever-compassionate Isla and Ella decided that their favourite doll's dolls' house could wait until tomorrow, and checked into a guesthouse. To save the lusciously tiny creature dipping into her lamentably tiny savings, they announced it was on them. They longed to be on her but could tell tonight wasn't the night. Not that Yu Yan spent the night alone, as Trudi gave her a big kiss and snuggled up with her. They were both, to borrow Enid Blyton's phrase, "tired but happy". In Trudi's case, ridiculously, excessively tired, but happy she'd soon be seeing Mummy and Daddy again. Though she still wasn't quite sure exactly when.

Yu Yan wasn't quite so horribly tired, as she'd got used to being forced to work all hours, but was happy she'd found friends who might help make her environment less hostile. She contentedly cuddled Trudi, fell fast asleep and dreamt of one day becoming a post-doctoral research student after all, in a not-at-all-hostile English university. She didn't know of Bakyt's existence, so wasn't in a position to dream of how one day they'd be colleagues.

After twenty hours' sleep, Trudi woke spectacularly gracefully. As her big blue eyes opened, slowly and entirely of their own free will, the first thing she saw was a fully paid-up member of her fan club offering her a nice cup of tea. Breakfast went well too, as Yu Yan mastered knife and fork technology and discovered bacon and eggs were perfectly edible after all. They checked out and soon made it to

Windsor Castle, where Trudi tugged the sleeve of the big man in the police uniform.

'Please, sir, is the queen home today?'

He considered this unusual punter's unusual query, tried not to laugh out loud and reached for his phone.

''Ere, Bill. Is 'Er Madge in residence this morning? Distinguished guest 'ere. Wants to know.'

'Do one, ya dumbo,' the sergeant replied, softly though, as he guessed what was going on. The constable glanced down at the small person in front of him, cleared his throat and stood to attention, as courtiers must when delivering a royal proclamation.

'Ever so sorry, madame,' he proclaimed. ''Er madge sends royal apologies, but says she's got a prior engagement at Buckingham Palace. With the President of Ireland.' Though the bloke only knew that because he'd read it on the Sky News website, Isla and Ella were so impressed that they barely registered what he said next.

'But she says to say one's frightfully welcome to go orff and 'ave a gander at 'er granny's dolls' 'ouse.'

Trudi was enthralled by the sight of miniature books by AA Milne, while the others were struck by the detail in this tiny world provided by Sir Edwin Lutyens. An hour later, another tug on the nice policeman's sleeve was followed by a polite request to thank the queen for the invitation to look at her granny's lovely things. He saluted respectfully and promised he would, but instead of giggling, found himself wishing his own kids were half as nice as this one.

'Anything else I can do for you, madame?' he asked, not expecting what came next.

'Yes, please, Mr Nice Policeman, can we please use your phone to make one little call? Of course we'll pay for it.'

Worried that it might only be in London where phone boxes didn't just have plants and books in them, Trudi had seized the initiative. Isla and Ella were dumbfounded, and so was the copper. But with someone like her, 'no' was not in his vocabulary. He perched her on a chair, handed her the handset, and as she slowly and clearly stated the number, keyed it in as carefully and obediently as if instructed by 'Er Madge herself.

'Hello? Oh hello, Nanny. You feeling better now?' Trudi thought it'd be unkind not to ask, even though she perfectly well knew the answer, and what would come next.

'Well, you see, Trudi dear, I'm ever so sorry, but I got a bit muddled about that address you asked for yesterday.' Nanny faltered. Trudi helped her out.

'I know, Nanni. Never mind. But would you mind getting it right this time?' Trudi was so good at doing Mummy's voice that you could hardly tell them apart sometimes, and Nanny, falteringly, did as she was told. Trudi repeated her words out loud to make sure there were no mistakes, and the enthralled policeman licked the end of his pencil and wrote it all down for her. He'd served long enough at West End Central nick to know off by heart the postcodes of swanky addresses like Berkeley Square, so was honoured to confirm the address was correct.

Trudi gracefully, if in some amazement, acknowledged his deep bow before she and the others headed off to Windsor station. And, when his shift ended, the copper headed off to the pub to boast about the royal princess/duchess/movie star he'd had the honour to serve.

CHAPTER FORTY-SIX

Back in London, there'd been a lot more heading off in a lot of surprising directions.

When Tiddledick curtly informed Erewego that the British Government would not be buying Chinese trains, and told her to be in his office, with Verrigreen, in two hours, she knew the game was up. So instead of preparing to defend the indefensible, she phoned Fantasia and Verrigreen, arranged to meet at his place pronto and discreetly got the hell out of there, via the Whitehall entrance.

By the time they got to Pimlico, Verrigreen had sorted the escape arrangements. Or, rather, had them sorted for him, by Fyok Yu and Hon Ki. Forget Battersea Heliport, they said, just whizz downstream and look out for a small submarine somewhere near Sheerness.

Easing his little speedboat into the river, he crossed his fingers that the two lumbering ladies wouldn't sink it. Fortunately, when they funnelled themselves out of the window and tumbled aboard, they balanced one another out, as in their long-suffering car. Verrigreen imagined their insights into the secret workings of the British Government would go down well in Beijing, but failed to factor in the negative impact of their personalities. For the senior embassy official who interrogated them in the small submarine, dispensing with them would be more than a duty. It'd be a pleasure.

As the three very important passengers/very despicable prisoners were transferred, in international waters, to a longer-range submarine, the captain was instructed to head for Pyongyang and dump them there. The ghastly little man with the vile hairstyle just might find the sight of people even fatter than him a comfort, and grant them a great and glorious future in the Democratic People's Republic. Or might not. The embassy official licked his lips.

*

Sitting in his office, Ponsomby Tiddledick drummed his fingers and made up his mind. Because he was Mr Nice Guy by nature, often referred to at the Carlton Club as a bit of a leftie but otherwise decent sort of cove, he hated having to play Mr Nasty.

Then again, bearing in mind what Fanny had told him, he could be Mister Huntin'-Shootin'-Fishin' for the rest of his life. Or, as he was more one for cooing over animals than summarily executing them, he could be Mr Loll-On-A-Lounger-With-A-Piña-Colada-In-Tropical-Sunshine instead. Might even make it to his sandy corner of heaven-on-earth in a private luxury yacht. Best to get ahead of himself, but when this horridness was over, his career definitely

319

would be too. End of. *Finito*. Past tense. Kaput. Funny thing, he thought, that rare ability to instantly sort things. Perfect asset for a good prime minister.

What the hell; it'd be someone else's turn now. The others were always spitting and scheming against him anyway, be a laugh watching them pushing so hard at an open door that they'd fall flat on their silly faces.

Tiddledick enjoyed suddenly not giving a tuppenny tiddle about how much more the high-speed train project would cost the nation. His only regret was how smug those beastly CIA men he'd been hearing about would be. On the other hand, Westminster wouldn't be blown to kingdom come after all, which was a Good Thing. It'd be a while before he discovered it wasn't him but Trudi who'd saved the day. And he'd probably never find out how smug the CIA guys would not be.

The second Mugwump learned of the British decision about the trains, he launched a twitterstorm followed by a two-hour video of himself reminding voters that his secret diplomacy put him up there with Abe Lincoln and George Washington. No, goddamn it, way ahead. A Nobel Prize for services to humanity would do for starters, but what he'd really earned was a sainthood. By the time he'd finished, he'd convinced himself he really did do all this single-handed. No help from anybody. And no one suggesting otherwise. No, siree!

Which is why, instead of being swept up to the Capitol for their Medals of Honor, Hank and Shane were shipped down to Guantanamo Bay for an indefinite stay.

*

Things didn't work out as planned for Fyok Yu and Hon Ki either. Just when they'd got their heads round a fitting song too. *Oh, What a Beautiful Mornin'*.

Unwisely, they'd been so sure of themselves that they'd already cashed in on their triumph. The lovely E-type Jaguar was a rare and wondrous find, certainly worth the trip to that nasty service station at Watford Gap, as well as the fifty-grand tab Beijing didn't know it was picking up. "Incidentals" are a wonderful column on anyone's expenses form.

After handing over the big fat wad of used fifty-quid notes to the shifty– looking geezer who didn't seem too particular about who they were, or too anxious to mention his own name, they headed for the cafeteria, crooning in unison about having beautiful feelings and everything going their way. An overweight family looked at them, puzzled, but after a Hon Ki managed a rather splendid descant a couple of underfed twenty-somethings gave them a round of applause. Probably music students, judging by their hairstyles.

Climbing into their trophy motor to set off back to Holland Park, they ran their usual quick check on Mugwump's twitter feed and abruptly changed both their planned direction of travel and tune. And the words. To *My Way*. Through gritted teeth they started bigging up the bit about having a few regrets, and got the blame game swinging along nastily.

The worst of it being, and they both knew this, that they were stuck with one another. More so than ever, now they'd got to make themselves scarce. A quick squiz through Google Maps, and they found the furthest they could get from civilisation while still in the English-speaking world, more or less, was a little place called Thurso.

Funny how things turn out.

The place is so little that in no time Chancery spotted the motor, but equally quickly changed his mind about the heist. Something to do with Fyok Yu and Hon Ki sitting in it. A normal punter would be extremely cross and report the matter to the police, who'd probably catch up with whoever nicked such a conspicuous vehicle in no time. These two, Charlie knew, would cut out the middle man by cutting out several of his vital organs.

So, instead, he jauntily approached them, announced he was going to open a hotel and asked if they'd like to work for him. Resigned to pretty much anything, they said what the hell, why not? Except he'd soon discover he was working for them, not the other way round. Spleeny, still out of sorts after so nearly being turned into a dollop of strawberry jam by those nasty Chinese agents, would become joint chief cook and bottle washer. Or, rather, leave bottle washing to Charlie while she became chief joint cooker. Roast hash in the homemade cookies should slip down a treat.

But first, they slipped down to Thurso station and chucked Charlie's remaining mobile into the coal stack of a heritage locomotive. Seemed fitting after all the fuss about what Penislow would not now be buying, to let a train take the strain.

*

Tiddledick, meanwhile, got so fed up with waiting for Erewego that he strode along the corridor and up to her desk, resolved to read the riot act then kick her out. He wasn't disappointed to find she wasn't at it, as it's easier being Mr Scary in the abstract than in the office. But he was surprised to find, in addition to all her personal stuff gone, a highly personal message neatly printed off and addressed to him.

Dear Hopefully-Soon-To-Be-Ex-Prime-Minister, it began, impolitely. *I have always found you a blithering, dithering tiddlebrain but have refrained from pointing this out.*

However, due to changed circumstances, I now feel free to offer dispassionate advice which I believe will be to the nation's advantage, as well as your own.

Resign.

Have done with it. It will, after all, be the first intelligent decision you will have made since taking office. As well as the last.

PS: You will find at my now vacated home in Primrose Hill two disgusting little animals. Feel free to feed them, either yourself or to your horsey wife's horses. We never forget you have a choice.

It occurred to Tiddledick that he'd never really taken to Erewego.

He hadn't really got any closer to finding Trudi either. Not a single sighting so far, in spite of the word being put out in all the relevant quarters. Probably didn't help that the spooks were on the lookout for an unhappy girl trussed up by very nasty men, not a cheerful girl hand in hand with very nice ladies, one of whom happened to be carrying a nuclear bomb.

Only one thing for it, Tiddledick decided… invite the Penislow party to Chequers tomorrow, to put their heads together. On the way there, he got his driver to swing by Primrose Hill, and discreetly let himself into Erewego's flat with the key she'd obligingly left him. At the sight of some of the fixtures and fittings, and the thought of what Fanny would make of them, his baby-like complexion deepened to shocking, or, rather, shocked, pink.

But he couldn't help but smile at the sight of two cute little furry creatures juggling as though their lives depended on it. Which it did, after such a long time without anyone giving them anything to eat. Of course Ponsomby pitied them, and of course he picked up the cage. There was always the risk Fanny would go for the second option on offer from Erewego. But one step at a time...

*

Next morning, very bright and early, the Wolseley screeched up outside the Mayfair flat. They were in such a rush that Viv even forgot her signature headwear. She found it a squeeze in the back with two men, Lady Casement and the cat cage, with the cat in it, obviously. In normal circumstances, in deference to Fanny's sensibilities, Percy would have arranged a sitter, but desperate times, desperate measures and all that. If Fang did another wee on the lady's frock, he'd just have to manage the situation as best he could.

But to everyone's amazement, it seemed Fanny had had some kind of Damascene conversion. As the motor shot up the drive to Chequers, she was standing in the doorway with her husband, and a dear little furry creature cradled in each arm.

No longer Baubles and Squeaky but Mills and Boon.

Though she at first favoured Oberon and Titania, she worried that silly semi-literate Poncey would get in a muddle and start calling them Oh-Bugger-Me and Titty-Titty-Bang-

Bang or something. And her new little friends milling about were such a boon.

As the party climbed out of the car, however, Lady Casement's wing-flapping manoeuvres suggested she didn't share Fanny's enthusiasm. Nor did Fang, judging by the way he arched his back and hissed horribly. Percy decided perhaps best not let him out of the cage just yet. But they were here to discuss Trudi, not an assortment of animals that didn't look likely to get on awfully well. Poncey opened the council of war.

'As requested, my dears, I have alerted all the security services and they've all drawn a blank. Anybody got any ideas?' Though he wasn't really a details man, he couldn't help but wonder if there was something vital, no matter how apparently trivial, that they'd all overlooked. But Percy had to admit the nearest they had to a lead was leading them nowhere.

'That chancer Chancery has divided himself into two, and spread out further than ever.

'Half of him could have been helpful, but not in Notting Hill. Ahem. The other half's halfway to Newcastle, bringing a load of coal for all I know.'

'Are we downhearted?' Poncey asked sympathetically.

'Yes, we fucking are.'

Poor Viv didn't say anything, just nodded in woeful agreement.

'I get hands on she-dog son Chancery, I slash hands from arms and give my dog to eat,' Bakyt cut in. Suddenly only the whites of her eyes were showing, and in spite of her distracted state, Viv gently stroked her arm before things got out of hand. Bakyt's, that is, not Charlie's, just to be clear.

'But everyone needs pay attention. Little girl missing, also nuclear bomb,' added Bakyt, back now in the twenty-first century, as well as the room. Fanny, sunny as ever in her view of the world, pointed out that now Chinese trains were off the menu, the child's Chinese captors might just as well hand her over and be done with it.

Every chance she'll just turn up, like the proverbial bad penny. Just a thought, but she had the good sense not to share it. At least not in so many words.

Poncey had by now spotted a possible connection between his guests' quest for Trudi and that unfortunate incident in Notting Hill that had left so many bits of so many Chinese men splattered all over the place. But, like his wife, he had a sixth sense about what not to say and when not to say it. The confidential Met Police report he'd been shown did mention bullets from machine guns of a certain vintage and type having been dug out of various holes in the Notting Hill hotel's walls, as well as in the Chinese victims' heads, shoulders and abdomens. Upper and lower, incidentally.

It struck him that if he bit his tongue any harder, he might need corrective surgery.

CHAPTER FORTY-SEVEN

Trudi was beside herself with excitement. The longed-for reunion was getting closer each second, and each yard. And Mummy and Daddy would be sure to love her lovely new friends, possibly even as much as Isla and Elsa seemed to love Yu Yan. Though she couldn't be sure of that.

Of course, she wasn't to know how her parents would take to two ladies who'd made it their life's work to progressively dismantle what was left of the British Empire. Or what they'd make of one of them carrying all that was needed to do the job in two seconds flat. However, the four of them made it to Waterloo without blowing anyone or anything up. And, likewise, tubed it to Bond Street with the population and street layout of London still just as it was. Trudi wondered why Isla and Ella were so particular about that heavy-looking bag they'd been lugging around, and why they seemed so anxious not to bump into anything.

'Is it a present for someone?' she asked. Her polite and tactful way of saying: *Is it a present for me?*

'Actually, it's a present for your mummy and daddy.' Isla was sorry to disappoint, but had a feeling a nuclear bomb wouldn't quite do it for Trudi, though if she fiddled around with it too much, it'd certainly do it for a lot of other people.

'But I'm sure Mummy and Daddy will have lots of lovely wee things for you, so they will,' Ella added, more consolingly than convincingly.

Yu Yan could see the disappointment in Trudi's face and gave her a cuddle, which helped, a little bit. Trudi cheered up lots, though, when the Uber dropped them at Berkeley Square and she could confidently lead them to the flat's front door. Even not being tall enough to reach the bell was only a minor irritant. Unlike the fact that nobody answered.

For only the second time since things started to go wrong when that horrid man found her behind that horrid sofa in that horrid hotel, Trudi's eyes welled up. No mummy to wrap her in her arms, no daddy to start crying like he always did when he was really happy. No Fang to look haughty and pretend he wasn't over the moon too. And no Lady Casement, who could well be so chuffed that she'd lay another egg.

A group hug helped. Briefly. But her lower lip was still quivering alarmingly when the building's concierge came out and wondered what was going on. Isla and Ella explained the situation and wondered if, by any chance, the good and kind lady, so she is, to be sure to be sure, had any idea where in the name of the blessed mother of Jesus and all the saints in heaven Percy and the others might have got to.

The good and kind lady would have preferred the question to have been shorter. Her English was better than Yu Yan's, but not much.

'They go in strange carriage. Old. Very old. Need big

bus. Many peoples, many animal. They go play game. I hear they say. Old game. We play my country too. Fine game. Chequers, we call.'

Yu Yan was baffled, Isla and Ella were confused, but Trudi was suddenly very happy. She took the lady by the sleeve and the bull by the horns.

'Please, lovely lady, let us into the garage. I'm going to play chequers too, with my mummi and daddi. My friends will drive me there, because they're the best drivers in the whole world.'

The concierge had her doubts, but she did recognise Trudi. And she thought Simone-Sitrouenne is worst carriage in world and not matter even if little girl's friends worst drivers in world and wrap round lamppost. As the garage door glided open, Trudi wondered who was going to drive. Isla drew the short straw, as a few years back she'd had three lessons. Doesn't sound a lot, but it was three more than Ella.

Wasn't going to matter anyway, as when she turned the ignition key nothing happened. No one could understand why Trudi's lower lip was still on a pretty even keel, until she climbed into the front passenger seat and got out her little hammer. As the engine spluttered into life, Trudi turned to Isla, who couldn't decide if she was more baffled than scared out of her wits or the other way round, and told her she'd got to push and pull the funny-looking lever by the steering wheel with her left hand to make it go. And if that didn't work, try twisting it.

Isla crossed herself several times, so did Ella. And Yu Yan was showing signs of going into a deep, meditative prepare-to-meet-one's-maker trance, when once again Trudi took them all by surprise. Explaining, briefly, that she was going to be the guide, she settled as comfortably as anyone can on the floor under the back seat of a Citroën 2CV, peered through the gap below the rear door and shouted her first command of the journey.

'Turn right!'

As the car lurched out of the garage, Isla was too busy gripping the wheel with both hands to cross herself again, but did utter a fair few Hail Marys. Then a fair few more as the terrifying contraption wobbled along the road. The sound of blasting horns died away as fellow motorists turned their attention to not dying.

The good and kind lady concierge hadn't got a lot of time for the mother of Jesus and her saints in heaven, but uttered a heartfelt incantation to Brahma, Devi, Shiva and Vishnu. Not forgetting Shakti and Ganesha. Maybe that's what made all the difference. Certainly, by the time they made it to Park Lane, Isla had started to enjoy twiddling the steering wheel and watching in the rear-view mirror other cars take extreme evasive action. She even found out between traffic lights on the Edgware Road where third gear is, which made for a much quieter ride.

It meant Trudi could make herself heard sufficiently to explain, between shouted left and right instructions, why she'd chosen such a relatively unconventional vantage point for pointing out the route. As they hit the relative – in this case extremely relative – safety of the Westway, she told of her one and only visit to Chequers.

'Mummi didn't know I was coming with her, so I hid here on the floor. Of course I remember the way, because I am a very clever person. Four and a half and a bit, I'll have you know.

'But if I don't look from down here, same as I did before, I can't be sure.'

'You are a very clever wee person, to be sure to be sure,' Ella told her. 'Everyone's agreed on that, so they are.'

'Not that ugly fat man with the silly hairstyle,' Trudi corrected her. 'Or those two nasty Chinese men.'

'Oh, but they did, so they did,' Ella smiled. 'They all thought you were a cute wee colleen, so they did.'

Trudi's big blue eyes went even more round and huge than they were normally. Not often she was stumped for words. But these things happen. Sometimes.

Yu Yan, who had by now decided that she and her maker weren't soon going to be on first-name terms after all, glanced down and said Ella was right. Taking in Trudi's peephole below the door, she spotted there was also a gap above it. Proof that the Citroën 2CV defied the laws of physics. One day, when Percy noticed this strange phenomenon, he asked the bloke in the garage if that was because the vehicle was usually parked with one side getting more sunlight than the other.

Was it the extra warmth, he wondered, that caused the door to shrink? Like the very hot wash the machine? As Percy had by then become prime minister, the Cornish mechanic decided that was a clue as to why the bleddy country was such a bleddy mess.

*

At that moment, ex-Prime Minister Percy was in a huddle with soon-to-be ex-Prime Minister Poncey and the others, struggling with how to find the – if they did but know it – now fast-approaching missing girl.

Mills and Boon, clearly less interested, were busily juggling away, not because they were hungry, Fanny had made sure of that, but because they liked showing off to Lady Casement. She was impressed in spite of herself, judging by the way she was bobbing up and down. Fang pretended he couldn't care less, but his rapid eye movement told a different story.

Our conquering heroine's rapid eye moment, meanwhile, was settling down nicely, now that Simone-Sitrouenne was finally bouncing along the little country road that led to the conspicuously unmarked entrance to Chequers. As the vehicle swerved, oddly, to a halt without managing to hit the sticky-up bits at the beginning of the driveway, Trudi did something little girls don't generally do when confronted by men with machine guns.

She clapped her hands in triumph.

Quite natural, as men with machine guns, who aren't always very nice men, are not in the habit of popping up all over the English countryside. But the sight of them here and now proved she really had remembered the way correctly. Not that there'd ever been any doubt about that. The big burly blokes recognised the car, and the little girl who had succeeded where they had failed to get the useless thing going. Having both been given a good talking-to and a bit more besides by their wives that evening, they now had a bit of respect. One of them also had a deep scar on his forehead.

Absolutely against the rules to just wave anyone through without ID, especially if one of those individuals was in possession of a nuclear bomb. They toyed with mocking up a pass using the picture of Trudi that'd been discreetly circulated to all security personnel, but reason prevailed.

They called the house and suggested everyone head for the front door.

To be safe, a couple of blokes would follow the vehicle on their bikes, if only to make sure it got there. Judging by the way it was – to use the term loosely – driven up the road, they couldn't understand how it had got anywhere. As Isla heaved the lever and the sickening crunch in the gearbox indicated the final meander was about to begin, a crowd gathered, like servants outside stately homes in period movies, awaiting the return from distant parts of Milord and Milady.

The sight of Simone-Sitrouenne got Percy's and Viv's hearts racing. The fact that the car was moving, under its own steam, could only mean one thing. But… but… but where was she? The colour drained from their faces as terror set in. Had something horrible happened to her? Was she laid out on the back seat? Perhaps unconscious? Maybe… even… dead.

Trudi's inherited passion for theatrics had got her ducking out of sight as the car drew near, to make her eventual appearance a break-a-leg moment. Not, mercifully, in the surgical sense. She sprang forth, scanned the sea of faces, was over the moon to see the essential ones bobbing around but was a little bit upset that Mummy was inappropriately dressed for the line she'd rehearsed.

It was what Daddy had told her about that writer who'd arrived from somewhere and knew just what to say to his friend: *My dear, you are the only woman in London who knows, when meeting a friend who's been missing for some time, what hat to wear.*

Bareheaded as Viv was, Trudi was forced to improvise, settling for something between a greeting and the sort of query to which the questioner already knows the answer.

'Surprised?'

Viv collapsed in a dead faint into Percy's arms. He caressed her head and sobbed all over it. Biff's eyes opened so wide that his glasses fell off and smashed, Poncey and Fanny gawped and Mills and Boon stopped juggling. Fang's whiskers and fur were so rigid that it looked like he'd stuck his paw in a lamp socket, and Lady Casement decided against saying Brits out or fecking eejit.

One way and another, regarding the enquiry, that'd be a yes then.

Still nobody said anything. Had Trudi been in her home comfort zone, she'd have done what she'd been dying to do for days. Cried as hard as Daddy and probably fainted like Mummy. But in front of all these others, there was only one thing for it. Brave face and a ball-breaker of an icebreaker. She cleared her throat, puffed up her chest, put a hand on each hip and readied herself for what could be misunderstood but could not be ignored.

In recent days, she'd got so much wiser about shades of meaning and emotion, other people's as well as hers. Which was why she knew how to deliver a familiar and normally offensive line with the kind of smile likely to keep everyone sweet. Guaranteed nonetheless to get a feisty little madame through life with flying colours.

'Bollocks to you.'